DATE DUE

FOLKTALES OF *Germany*

Folktales

OF THE WORLD

GENERAL EDITOR : RICHARD M. DORSON

FOLKTALES OF
Germany

EDITED BY
Kurt Ranke

TRANSLATED BY LOTTE BAUMANN

FOREWORD BY
Richard M. Dorson

THE UNIVERSITY OF CHICAGO PRESS

Library of Congress Catalog Card Number: 66–13884
The University of Chicago Press, Chicago 60637
Routledge & Kegan Paul, Ltd., London E.C.4
© 1966 by The University of Chicago. All rights reserved
Published 1966. Second Impression 1968
Printed in the United States of America

Foreword

In the Christmas season of 1812, when the shadow of Napoleon hung over Europe, booksellers in German provinces placed in their windows a volume destined for immortality, the *Kinder- und Hausmärchen* of the brothers Grimm. In English translations it became celebrated as *Grimm's Fairy Tales,* passing through hundreds of editions. Few books in the history of printing have enjoyed such commercial and intellectual success, delighting the tot in the nursery while engrossing the savant in the study. What was the enchantment cast over such unlike audiences by these peasant tales of magic and wonder and cruelty?

Although children avidly seized possession of the stories, it was an adult public for whom Jacob and Wilhelm Grimm designed their collection, and they later regretted including "Kinder" in the title. Intellectuals had known about Märchen ever since the publication in 1697 by Charles Perrault of *Contes de ma Mère l'Oye,* and indeed the Grimms took some of their tales from earlier German books. The novelty of their approach lay in the principle of obtaining tales directly from the lips of storytellers, and seeking in print other tales secured in a similar way. This new method led them and their emulators throughout Europe deep into a vast subterranean narrative lore of the unlettered peasant. At this moment in time, Christmas, 1812, an act of intellectual discovery had opened a window for the European educated classes into the submerged and despised culture of the peasantry, disclosing undreamt of riches in so outwardly barren an environment.

With this discovery the science of folklore was born, and the Grimms were heralded as its founders. They were not simply

presenting attractive stories, but undertaking an exploration of
the ancient mythology, romantic literature, and national soul of
the German people—all perceptible in the Märchen. The time
was ripe for the new science. Nationalism and romanticism
bloomed in the nineteenth century, and folklore was one of their
by-products. The way had been prepared by the preacher-poet-
philosopher of East Prussia, Johann Gottfried Herder, who
formulated theories of literary and linguistic nationalism, beginning with his first critical writing in 1764. Herder exhorted his
countrymen to collect folk poetry and himself edited a volume of
Volkslieder. From Britain the *Reliques* of Percy and the fabri-
cated *Ossian* of Macpherson excited his interest in provincial
songs as a vessel of the national spirit. This spirit was to be found
in purest form in the Middle Ages, before influences of the
Renaissance had overlaid the true Germanic tradition and
rendered German literature artificial. Through the ages, the
common people, uncultured and unspoiled, had voiced the inner
sentiments of the German race in folksongs. "Only who is there
who will collect them, who will trouble himself about them,
trouble himself about songs of the people, in the streets and alleys
and fishmarkets, in the unlearned glee-parties of the peasant-folk,
songs which often do not scan and which rhyme badly." [1]

Herder's call was answered. In *Des Knaben Wunderhorn*
(1805), Achim von Arnim and Clemens Brentano assembled a
garland of German country songs, repairing the faulty rhymes,
erratic meter, and uncouth phrasings of the original versions.
Among their friends were the University of Marburg students
Jacob and Wilhelm Grimm, who in turn began collecting tales
from their circle of acquaintances in Hesse and Hanau. The
daughter of an affluent apothecary, Dorothea Wild, sixteen in
1811, told the brothers such favorite tales as "Clever Elsie," "Frau
Holle," and "The Singing Bones" as they sat around the stove in
a summer house. Later Wilhelm married her, and Jacob, who
remained a bachelor, lived with them. Dorothea's mother and
sister also told Märchen to the brothers, as did their servant "Alte
Marie"—probably the source for the whole family. Even Arnim

[1] A. Gillies, *Herder* (Oxford: Basil Blackwell, 1945), p. 45, note.

furnished tales. The brothers did not at the outset, therefore, establish close contacts with peasant people, and it was not until their second volume in 1815 that they proffered the stories of their most remarkable narrator, Frau Katherina Dorothea Viehmann, a tailor's widow from Niederzwehren near Kassel.

In introducing the Märchen the brothers clearly stated their purposes. They prepared their storybook as a "great treasure of antiquity indispensable for research." [2] Particularly it would serve the causes of poetic criticism, mythology, and history. The Märchen and Sagen comprised a part of the national literature, the *Naturpoesie* of the German people, blending into the leaves, meadow grass, and bushes of the verdant countryside. So wrote Wilhelm in an introduction to the 1822 edition. During these years of the French invasion, when a Bonaparte was king of Westphalia and Jacob worked as his librarian, the minds of German intellectuals were strongly drawn to their Germanic heritage. The Märchen formed but one part of the broad researches of the brothers—Jacob leaning to the philological, Wilhelm to the literary side—as they pursued the murky medieval trails of Teutonic language and law, history, and religion.

Even in the field of folklore the brothers regarded the collecting of oral Märchen as one aspect of a larger endeavor. They coupled the Märchen with their *Deutsche Sagen* and *Deutsche Mythologie,* finding in legends and wonder tales the flotsam of heathen mythology. In 1828, Jacob published two volumes on German legal antiquities, *Deutsche Rechtsaltertümer.* The brothers buttressed the household tales with ample notes and informative essays which eventually, under the faithful care of two able editors, grew into a majestic five-volume work of reference. It is this full dimension of their work which won for them recognition as creators of a folklore science.

[2] T. F. Crane, "The External History of the Grimm Fairy Tales," *Modern Philology*, XIV (1917), 141. Crane's series of articles (XIV, 129–62; XV, 1–13, 99–127) is highly informative. Also valuable is Joseph Campbell, "The Work of the Brothers Grimm," in *Grimm's Fairy Tales* (New York: Pantheon Books, 1944), pp. 833–39. A full-scale study is Ernest Tonnelat's *Les frères Grimm, leur oeuvre de jeunesse* (Paris, 1912).

In curious contrast with the Märchen, the *Deutsche Sagen,* appearing in two volumes in 1816 and 1818, never received an English translation, and remain unknown to the English-speaking public. Yet on theoretical grounds they interested the brothers even more than the Märchen, which were told and accepted as entertaining fictions, because peasant audiences credited the Sagen as true accounts of supernatural events. The five hundred and eighty-five Sagen texts dealt with mountain spirits, the sorceress Frau Holle (who also appeared in a Märchen), dwarfs, nixes, mermen, kobolds, giants, dragons, spectral horsemen, the wild huntsman, werewolves, the ubiquitous devil, and human but legend-coated kings, kaisers, and counts. Jacob and Wilhelm gleaned the Sagen, like the Märchen, from both printed and narrated versions.

These collecting labors with Märchen and Sagen were not an end in themselves. Unlike the majority of subsequent collectors, who were content simply to record tales, the brothers sought the elusive oral texts as precious documents revealing the mind and soul of their Teutonic forebears. In 1835, Jacob Grimm published his *Deutsche Mythologie,* which promptly captivated the community of European scholars. Now the goal of folklore, as outlined by Jacob and rendered practical by Wilhelm, clearly was to reconstruct the ancient mythological pantheon preceding Christianity. Ogres and demons, heroes and princesses of household tales and village legends had descended from the heathen gods and goddesses. The meager philological evidence of hero-names and god-names surviving in the language from heathen times was being bountifully reinforced from the traditions of the peasantry.

> If these numerous written memorials have only left us sundry bones and joints, as it were, of our old mythology, its living breath still falls upon us from a vast number of Stories and Customs, handed down through lengthened periods from father to son. With what fidelity they propagate themselves, how exactly they seize and transmit to posterity the essential features of the fable, has never been noticed till now that people have become aware of their great value, and begun to set them down in collections simple and copious. Oral legend is to written records as the folk-song is to poetic

art, or the rulings recited by schöffen (sabini) to written codes.[3]

Specifically, Jacob Grimm wished to recapture the Germanic as distinct from the better-known Norse mythology. A philological mythologist, he sought clues to heathen deities through the evidence of names; but written records of the old German faith were singularly lean, owing to the disdain of the medieval Church—hence the value of popular tradition and custom. Now that regional collections were supplementing the brothers' Märchen and Sagen, knowledge of the ancient mythology was steadily increasing. Local traditions filled in information about the goddesses Holda, Perchta, and Fricka, the god Wodan whose traces survived in the aerial myth of the Wild Hunt, the legends of the sin-flood and destruction of the world. In the fairy tales were found such relics of heathenism as godfather Death, the three norns or prophetesses, speaking animals, metamorphized persons, hags of the night. Local rites and customs, legal antiquities, and festival plays all helped illuminate features of the old religion through their Easter bonfires, rain processions, sacred beasts, and dramatic enactment of the conflict between summer and winter.

Grimm indignantly rejected the imputation that nineteenth-century German magic and demonology derived from Greek and Roman sources rather than from the Germanic tribes. "I do not suppose," he wrote, "that the old German fancies about beasts crossing one's path, or about the virtues of herbs, were in themselves any poorer than the Roman." Jacob declared frankly that he wished to exalt the language, laws, and antiquities of his native land which had been unjustly neglected. What national pride could Germans take in remnants of heathen magic and superstition? Jacob's answer was to laud and admire the old gods and goddesses, heroes, and wise women who had become maimed and degraded by the medieval church. Although the legend of the Wild Host was now reduced to a "pack of horrid spectres," once it had honored the solemn march of aerial gods—and for

---

[3] Jacob Grimm, *Teutonic Mythology*, trans. from the 4th ed. with notes by James Stevens Stallybrass (4 vols.; London: George Bell and Son, 1880–88), III, xiii.

this degradation Christianity was to blame. The Devil and devilish spirits were unknown in heathen times, and only in the Christian era did they become attached to the heathen gods, spirits, and giants still remembered among the peasants. From the resulting mixture emerged the vicious medieval notions of witchcraft, black magic, and sorcery currently blamed on the ancient Teutons. Actually in antiquity the witches were venerated by men as "priestesses, physicians, fabulous night-wives." [4]

While Jacob investigated the mythological basis of the Märchen, Wilhelm addressed himself to their historical and comparative aspects. In the successive editions of the Household Tales he furnished valuable notes on the oral and printed variants of each tale, and in the 1850 and 1856 editions he appended a long treatise of more than a hundred pages examining and commenting on the story collections and story information available in Europe and other parts of the world. Wilhelm kept scrupulous track of the growing number of field collections appearing in the half century following the first volume of the *Kinder- und Hausmärchen.* He corresponded with collectors in other lands, searched diligently for obscurely printed volumes of tales, and ransacked the writings of the past for references to and examples of genuine traditions. The role he assumed was historian, shepherd, and presiding judge of *Märchensammlung.* In the 1856 edition of the Märchen, he presented "Various Testimonies to the Value of Fairy Tales," beginning with the *Lysistrata* of Aristophanes in which occurs the expression, "I will tell ye a story," through Strabo, Plutarch, Apuleius, Luther, Cervantes, Goethe, Scott, and lesser lights, who all recognized the appeal of oral stories. After this preamble, Wilhelm sketched the history of literary tale collections which had tapped tradition, identifying the celebrated storybooks which had preceded his own: the *Thirteen Delightful Nights* of Straparola (Venice, 1550); the *Pentamerone* of Basile (Venice, 1637); *Gesta Romanorum,* the fourteenth-century Latin collection of tales about the Roman emperors; and Charles Perrault's *Contes de ma Mère l'Oye* (Paris, 1697). William's critical judgments of these works testify to his capacity to separate tradition from invention, his sensitivity to style, and his

[4] *Ibid.,* xxix, 946, 1104.

scholarly zeal for identifying related plots and incidents. In appraising the *Pentamerone* he wrote:

> . . . this collection of stories was for a long time the best and richest that had been formed by any nation. Not only were the traditions at that time more complete in themselves, but the author had a special talent for collecting them, and besides that an intimate knowledge of the dialect . . . the manner of speaking, at least that of the Neapolitans, is perfectly caught, and this last constitutes one superiority over Straparola, who only strove for the customary educated method of narration, and did not understand how to strike a new cord. . . . Two-thirds of them [the fifty stories] are, so far as their principal incidents are concerned, to be found in Germany, and are current there at this very day. Basile has not allowed himself to make any alteration, scarcely even any addition of importance, and that gives his work a special value. . . . Basile has told his stories altogether in the spirit of a lively, witty, and facetious people, with continual allusions to manners and customs, and even to old stories and mythology. . . . This is the very reverse of the quiet and simple style of German stories.[5]

After thus considering his predecessors, Wilhelm turned to his contemporaries and the folktale scene in Britain and throughout the continent, with glances at Asia and Africa. In one aside he remarked that "a number of our jests are related in Asia." Always as he picked his way through the undergrowth of dubious fairy-tale titles he strove to winnow out the truly traditional stories. For Germany he was able to enumerate twenty-six Märchen books published between 1764 and 1822. Some clearly anticipated the brothers' work, for instance, *Kindermärchen aus mündlichen Erzählungen gesammelt* (Stories for Children, gathered from oral Tradition, Erfurt, 1787), but Wilhelm recognized that the unnamed collector had narrated them carelessly and largely spoiled their scientific value. The touchstone

---

[5] *Grimm's Household Tales with the Author's Notes,* trans. from the German and edited by Margaret Hunt (London: G. Bell and Sons, 1910), II, 482–83.

Wilhelm applied in the difficult task of identifying bona fide
peasant narratives was "the homeliness, which in conjunction
with wonders of all kinds, always manifests itself in genuine
stories." Again he defined the true Märchen as a "union of the
supernatural with the common events of daily life." Where the
past had not been torn asunder from the present, the Märchen
still bloomed, and Wilhelm reported close counterparts to the
German stories among the Dutch, English (a curious observa-
tion, for a substantial collection of Märchen never did emerge
from England), Scandinavians, the people of the Romance-
language nations, and Africans.

From these assembled bibliographic discoveries and from his
unpublished manuscripts, Wilhelm was able to cull out variants
to the printed Märchen and to discourse in his notes on their
resemblances and differences. For one tale, "Gambling Hansel"
(No. 82), Wilhelm furnished ten pages of notes, outlining
numerous variants of the story about the lucky gambler or smith
who trapped Death in a tree and plagued the devils in hell.
"Here is a very perfect instance of the wide circulation and living
diversity of a saga," he concluded, pleased to see evident marks of
antiquity. The smith with his hammer descended from the god
Thor, Death and the Devil from a monstrous giant. Reflecting
upon the dramatis personae of Märchen, Wilhelm mused on
"certain strongly-marked characters which reappear everywhere as
common property." He singled out the despised but ultimately
triumphant simpleton, the clownish giants, the wily dwarfs, the
Eulenspiegel trickster, the good-natured boaster, the skilful
master thief—all of whom in an earlier day must have constituted
a pantheon of Aryan deities.[6]

While conscious of the tentative efforts of various forerunners,
Wilhelm comprehended the historic role he and his brother were
playing in the development of folktale studies. "How unique
was our collection when it first appeared," Wilhelm wrote with
simple candor. He even hoped that Germans in America were
reading it with delight. The brothers' realization of their achieve-
ment induced not merely self-satisfaction but a sense of mission,

---

[6] The complete essay, entitled "Literature," appears in the Hunt
edition, II, 477–583.

and they enthusiastically encouraged the collectors of fairy tales, legends, and myths throughout Europe.

The influence of the brothers Grimm on nineteenth-century folklorists can be illustrated by Great Britain. In his national surveys Wilhelm devoted a dozen pages to England, Scotland, and Ireland, uncovering fugitive and elusive titles such as Benjamin Tabart's *Collection of Popular Stories for the Nursery* (four volumes, London, 1809). Although many of Tabart's selections were translated from French and Italian sources, he did include "three characteristic and genuine English stories" of Jack the Giant Killer, Tom Thumb, and Jack and the Beanstalk, which Wilhelm abstracted at length. Recognizing a kindred spirit in Sir Walter Scott, Wilhelm reprinted approvingly his statement in the notes to *The Lady of the Lake* (1810) beginning "A work of great interest might be compiled upon the origin of popular fiction and the transmission of similar tales from age to age and from country to country." Jacob entered into eager correspondence with the Waverly romancer in 1814 and 1815, seeking books and information about such antiquaries as Robert Jamieson, Joseph Ritson, and Francis Douce; Scott replied cordially and dispatched books on antiquities. The publication of the first field collection from Britain, T. Crofton Croker's *Fairy Legends and Traditions of the South of Ireland,* immediately excited the brothers, who translated the book within the year as *Irische Elfenmärchen* (1826), providing an elaborate introductory treatise on the fairy mythology of the British Isles. In the fairies, brownies, and pixies of Britain they believed they saw remnants of a Celtic mythology. To Scotland they devoted chief attention, relying upon a pioneer work that had escaped Croker, William Grant Stewart's *The Popular Superstitions and Festive Amusements of the Highlanders* (1823). Croker repaid the brothers' courtesy by translating their essay for the third volume of his *Fairy Legends* (1828) and enriched his notes with references they had sent him.

Meanwhile other English antiquaries were discovering and being discovered by the Grimms. Croker's associate in the antiquarian societies of England, Thomas Wright, wrote an extended essay, "On Dr. Grimm's German Mythology," upon its first

appearance, praising the work as one of the most admirable
books sent to England from Germany.[7] A third fellow-antiquary,
William John Thoms, in his celebrated letter to the *Athenaeum* in
1846 proposing the word "folk-lore," cited the second edition of
the *Deutsche Mythologie,* which had appeared two years earlier,
as one of the most remarkable books of the century. Throughout
the next three decades, when he was editing *Notes and Queries*
and amassing data on British folk traditions, Thoms continually
invoked the *Deutsche Mythologie,* along with the *Märchen* and
the *Sagen,* as the bible of folklore. He hoped that some folklorist
would resurrect for Britain the old heathen mythology in the
manner Jacob had done for Germany and so illuminate the pre-
historic meaning of domestic rites and customs surviving in every
English village. So illustrious did the great work become that
Thoms and the members of the new Folk-Lore Society founded
in 1878 were able to obtain a handsome four-volume translation,
Grimm's *Teutonic Mythology* (1880–1888), making available to
all English folklorists and amateur antiquaries the erudite ety-
mologies and mythic speculations of the formidable opus. The
translator, James S. Stallybrass, stoutly declared, "There is no
one to whom Folk-lore is more indebted than to Grimm." [8]

As with Britain, so with the countries on the continent. The
brothers corresponded with, encouraged, stimulated, admired, and
were admired by collectors from France to Russia and from
Norway to Hungary. Their links with the giants who followed
them are direct and clear. They exchanged letters with Asbjörnsen
and Moe in Norway, with Emmanuel Cosquin in France, with
Vuk Karadzić in Serbia, with Elias Lönnrot in Finland—all
hallowed figures performing Grimm-like services for their countries. Aleksandr Nikolaevic Afanas'ev, called the "Wilhelm
Grimm of Russia," lavishly praised the *Volksmärchen* of the
brothers as a model for presenting the folk literature of his own
country. As a result of the Grimms' prodigious and timely influence, scholars in one country after another utilized folklore as

[7] Thomas Wright, *Essays on Subjects Connected with the Literature,
Popular Superstitions, and History of England in the Middle Ages*
(London, 1846), I, 237.
[8] *Teutonic Mythology,* I, vi.

a vehicle to promote a national language, literature, history, and mythology.[9]

Wilhelm's notes and essays to the Märchen formed the basis for a separate work remarkable and indispensable in its own right. This was the *Anmerkungen zu den Kinder- und Hausmärchen der Brüder Grimm,* prepared by Johannes Bolte, a well-known German folklore scholar, and the Czech Georg Polívka, a Slavic specialist. Wilhelm's son, Professor Herman Grimm, entrusted the unpublished papers of his father and uncle to Bolte as a basis for the *Anmerkungen,* which was issued in five volumes between 1913 and 1932. Bolte in his 1914 preface to Volume II compared his situation to that of the Grimms issuing the Märchen at the time of Napoleon's invasion of Russia and uttered the plea, "Gott schütze unser teures Vaterland!" The first three volumes presented a meticulous coverage of the known variants to two hundred and twenty-five household tales. Volumes IV and V, "Zur Geschichte der Märchen" (1930, 1932), by various collaborators, expanded the historical survey of *Märchenliteratur* written by Wilhelm Grimm in 1856. The fourth volume considered the literary appearances of wonder tales from classical times up to and including the Grimms' own work, and the fifth examined the collections published in the wake of the Grimms throughout Europe, Asia, Africa, and the Americas. Not surprisingly, twice as much space was needed to describe the books of magic tales, folk legends, jests, lying tales, historical stories, and local beliefs issued in Germany as in the lands of the Celts and the Czechs, Germany's closest competitors.

Another ingenious reference work growing out of the Märchen was the *Handwörterbuch des Deutschen Märchens* (1933–1940), which unfortunately expired after two volumes. Lutz Mackensen was the general editor, and Bolte shared the title page of the first volume. This encyclopedia-dictionary of the folktale was designed to offer informative articles by specialists on the themes, characters, incidents, and forms of Märchen, as well as accounts

[9] These influences and relationships are well documented in *Brüder Grimm Gedenken 1963* (Marburg, 1963) and "Jacob Grimm zur 100. Wiederkehr seines Todestages," *Deutsches Jahrbuch für Volkskunde,* Vol. IX (Berlin, 1963).

of leading tale collectors and interpreters. Subjects included
Goethe and the German folktale; Frau Holle in myths, legends,
and Märchen; the modern geographic-historic method of studying
the dissemination of tales; the *Bauer* (peasant) as a leading folktale figure. A provocative article by Walter A. Berendsohn dealt
with *Einfache Formen,* the primary forms of folklore as outlined
in a noteworthy book of that title written in 1929 by André
Jolles. Jacob Grimm had recognized only the Märchen as a basic
form, while Jolles saw the *Legende, Sage, Mythe, Rätsel, Spruch,
Kasus, Memorabile,* and *Witz* as also constituting elemental
materials for the storyteller's art. The abortive *Handwörterbuch*
indicated tendencies to revise the principles of the brothers
Grimm.

The first period of German folktale collection and study was
one long eulogy for the Grimms. The second period, following
their deaths (Wilhelm, 1859; Jacob, 1863) has seen an increasingly
severe criticism of their method and theory.

Once so enticing, the mythological theory of Jacob has long
since been elbowed aside by more persuasive systems. His country-
man Max Müller, who emigrated to England and became one
of the world's leading Sanscrit scholars, introduced a new hy-
pothesis of the Vedic origin of Aryan gods, linking European
myths and fairy tales to an ancient Indian mythology. In the
Grimms' opening tale, "The Frog-King," Müller identified the
frog squatting in the pond as the sun sinking into the water.
Müller referred to a Sanscrit story about a beautiful girl named
Bhêki (Sanscrit for frog) wooed by a king whom she wed only
on condition he never show her water; when he did, she died—
that is, the sun set.[10] Andrew Lang took an entirely different tack
in his celebrated introduction to *Grimm's Household Tales* as
translated by Margaret Hunt, and interpreted the Märchen in the
light of the anthropological doctrine of survivals.[11] These peasant

[10] Max Müller, *Chips from a German Workshop* (New York, 1872), II,
244–46.

[11] Andrew Lang, "Introduction," *Grimm's Household Tales* (London:
G. Bell and Sons, 1910), I, xxxvii, lvii.

tales contained the remnants of savage beliefs in cannibalism, totemism, and metamorphosis which had flourished in the misty dawn of history. Hence the idea of a frog wooing a girl, as in "The Frog-King," exemplified the savage belief in kinship between humans and animals. To reinforce his point Lang presented a table of analogous ideas found in Aryan Märchen and in savage tales collected in the nineteenth century from Zulus, Hottentots, and Eskimos. Evolutionary theory in turn receded before the new fashion of psychoanalytic interpretation. Freudians recognized the frog as the penis, repellent to the unconscious in moments of distrust, and read the tale's moral as the gradual overcoming by the maiden of aversion to the sex act.[12] Jungians regarded the frog as a miniature dragon-serpent, loathsome in appearance but representing the "unconscious deep" filled with hidden treasures. The frog is the herald summoning forth the child from her infantile world to the land of adventure, independence, maturity, self-discovery, and at the same time filling her with anxiety at the thought of separation from her mother.[13]

Other theories have held and still command attention. One of the most respected of all was advanced by the German folklorist Theodor Benfey and his disciple Reinhold Köhler, who argued that the great master-tales had originated in ancient India and made their way by trade routes through central Asia and the Middle East into the countries of Europe. Such are the modern propositions: dissemination through traders and travelers, origins in dream fancies and the racial unconscious, and if they in turn have their critics and qualifiers, no one in the present century bothers to consider the Grimms' long obsolete theory of Teutonic mythology as the source for German peasant tales.

In their methods too the luster of the brothers has dimmed. Through the successive editions of the Märchen, Wilhelm steadily veered from the concept of fidelity to the spoken text toward an ideal synthetic tale, adapted from the available variants and re-

[12] Ernest Jones, "Psycho-Analysis and Folklore," in *Essays in Folklore, Anthroplogy and Religion* (London, 1951), p. 16.

[13] Joseph Campbell, *The Hero with a Thousand Faces* (New York, 1949), pp. 49–53.

fined with his editorial hand.[14] Consequently, he abandoned the *Volksmärchen* or true folktale collected exactly from the lips of the storyteller for the *Buchmärchen* or literary version shaped by the editor. To perfect stories, he did not scruple to add dialogue, nicknames, homely phrases, whole episodes. This practice robbed the tales of their true narrators, of the *"Hausherr"* to whom each Märchen variant belonged, and substituted the style, the values, and the perspective of the intellectuals for those of the folk.[15] Nor did the brothers rest content with producing composite texts; they selected stories from literary sources lacking a proper foundation in folk tradition, and so misrepresented the repertoire of German Märchen. Some of the best-known and most frequently reprinted of the Grimm tales, like "Little Red Riding Hood" and "Snow White and the Seven Dwarfs," are *Buchmärchen* rather than *Volksmärchen*.

In selecting and refining their household stories, the Grimms were able to emphasize some attitudes as particularly Germanic, and so convey the impression that their edition reflected praiseworthy national traits of the German people. These traits, as Louis L. Snyder has indicated, exalt authoritarianism, militarism, violence toward the outsider, the strict enforcement of discipline. As the tales centered on the king's court and the lord's castle, with the peasant village set at the foot of the hill and the mysterious forest placed beyond, so did the social classes fall into a corresponding scale of values. The king, the count, the leader, the hero are glorified, and the lower class, the servants and peasants dependent upon them and obediently executing their commands, is praised. In contrast stand the avaricious, mendacious middle class of merchants and quack doctors and scheming Jews —outsiders who intrude through the dark forest into the orderly system of manor and village. Hence the loathing for the stepmother (actually changed by the Grimms from the mother in "Snow White" to make the villainess an outsider to the family circle). A tale such as "The Jew in the Hawthorn Hedge" (No.

[14] Alfred David and Mary Elisabeth David, "A Literary Approach to the Brothers Grimm," *Journal of the Folklore Institute,* I (1964), 72–88.
[15] Max Lüthi, *Das europäische Volksmärchen, Form und Wesen* (2d ed.; Bern and München, 1960), p. 100.

110) not only pictures the Jew as a miser and skinflint but finds amusement in having him dance on thorns and be strung on the gallows.

In the wake of the Grimms, late nineteenth-century nationalists extolled the brothers and their Märchen for helping acquaint Germans with a sense of folk unity and an historical past. Under the Nazis the original edition of the tales with their bloodletting and violence was reintroduced. As Snyder has written:

> All the cruel pieces of the fairy tales, which had been eliminated under the Weimar Republic, were restored in Hitler's Germany, and the study of folklore was raised to a special place of honor. . . . In Nazi Germany the unexpurgated fairy tales were read by children and a large part of Nazi literature designed for children was merely a modernized version of the Grimms' tales, with emphasis upon the idealization of fighting, glorification of power, reckless courage, theft, brigandage, and militarism reinforced with mysticism.[16]

Apart from the distortion by the Nazis, modern German folktale scholarship has largely disavowed the premises and methods of the Grimms. The powerful interest they generated in *Märchensammlung* and *Märchenforschung* has maintained its momentum up to the present time, but with altered directions and revised emphases. Seven research approaches may be distinguished.

(1) *The philological.* This method closely examines Märchen features on the basis of the original classic collection. Scores of doctoral dissertations have been written at German universities on such topics as "The Forest in the *Kinder- und Hausmärchen.*" These studies pay no attention to the folktale as a living entity but concentrate on the printed canon of texts established by the Grimms. Of these text inspections, citing each authorized tale by chapter and verse, the best known is Lutz Röhrich's *Märchen und Wirklichkeit* (1956; revised edition, 1964). Röhrich deals with the commonplaces of the Märchen, their references to food and drink and costume, and with their interior ideas of magic and metamorphosis. The elements of wonder no longer correspond to

---

[16] Louis L. Snyder, "Nationalistic Aspects of the Grimm Brothers' Fairy Tales," *Journal of Social Psychology,* XXIII (1959), 219–21.

peasant folk belief and so are seen to belong to an earlier period
of thought.

(2) *Regional and ethnic collecting.* As the sources for Märchen-
telling dried up under the conditions of modern industrial society,
collecting opportunities diminished. A handful of creative collectors, scouring the borders and outlying districts, succeeded in
salvaging invaluable materials. The renowned Richard Wossidlo
gathered all kinds of Mecklenburg oral narratives, many of which
are only now beginning to be published.[17] Ulrich Jahn in 1891
published a basic collection from Pomerania and the Baltic island
of Rügen.[18] Reinhold Bünker brought out in 1906 a gathering
from the Hungarian border, based on the repertoire of an illiter-
ate street cleaner.[19] Wilhelm Wisser in eastern Holstein, Hertha
Grudde in East Prussia, since become part of Poland, and
Angelica Merkelbach-Pinck along the French border each performed notable field excursions.[20] But central Germany, the
Marburg to Göttingen area associated with the Grimms, produces
no more Frau Viehmanns. There the Märchen has yielded to the
jest, anecdote, experience, witticism.

(3) *Märchenbiologie.* Due attention to the personality, biog-
raphy, and artistry of the folk narrator and to the continuous
process of rebirth undergone by the Märchen in their passage
through the folk mouth was first cultivated by Julius Schwie-
tering, a classics professor at Frankfurt-am-Main. His student
Otto Brinkmann sat in on actual sessions of peasant tale-tellers and
wrote a dissertation on storytelling in a village community

---

[17] E.g., *Mecklenburger Erzählen . . . aus der Sammlung Richard Wossidlos,* edited by Gottfried Henssen (Berlin, 1958); *Herr und Knecht . . .
aus der Sammlung Richard Wossidlos,* edited by Gisela Schneidewind
(Berlin, 1960); *Volksschwänke aus Mecklenburg, aus der Sammlung Richard Wossidlos,* edited by Siegfried Neumann (Berlin, 1964).

[18] Ulrich Jahn, *Volksmärchen aus Pommern und Rügen* (Norden and
Leipzig, 1891).

[19] Reinhold Bünker, *Schwänke, Sagen und Märchen heanzischer
Mundart* (Leipzig, 1906).

[20] Wilhelm Wisser, *Plattdeutsche Volksmärchen* (Jena, 1922); Hertha
Grudde, *Plattdeutsche Märchen aus Ostpreussen* (Königsberg, 1931);
Angelica Merkelbach-Pinck, *Lothringer Volksmärchen* (Kassel, 1940).

(1933).[21] The Austrian collector Karl Haiding described the role
of gestures and mimicry in the narrative art of the Märchen-
teller.[22] Gottfried Henssen published a detailed life history and a
complete repertoire of an accomplished narrator and folksinger,
Egbert Gerrits, a sometime farmhand, peddler, and house painter
from Münster in Westphalia. This work, *Überlieferung und
Persönlichkeit. Die Erzählungen und Lieder des Egbert Gerrits*
(1951), giving recognition to Gerrits on the title page, marked
the full swing away from the collector-editor—as in *Kinder- und
Hausmärchen der Brüder Grimm*—to the teller as the possessor
of the tale.[23] The hitherto faceless narrator was now well
photographed and interviewed in the storybook.

(4) *The psychological.* A generation acquainted with Freud
could be expected to find connections between folklore and
dreams. As early as 1889 Ludwig Laistner, in *Das Rätsel der
Sphinx,* elaborated a theory of dream origins for ghoulish legends.
The nightmare with its physical constriction of the chest gave
rise to horrendous accounts of hags and demons astraddle suffering mortals. On the other side of the coin, some dreams might
be sweet wish-fulfillment fantasies, as Friedrich von der Leyen
contended in his oft-reprinted *Das Märchen.*[24] The reputation of
von der Leyen, who conceived and edited the international series
Die Märchen der Weltliteratur, enhanced his theory of the
Wunschtraum. Turning from the individual to the collective
unconscious, followers of Carl Jung found a satisfying feast of
archetypal symbols in Märchen set forth in the three-volume
treatise of Hedwig von Beit, *Symbolik des Märchens* (Bern,

[21] Otto Brinkmann, *Das Erzählen in einer Dorfgemeinschaft* (Münster,
i.W., 1931).

[22] Karl Haiding, *Österreichs Märchenschatz* (Vienna, 1953) and "Träger
der Volkserzählungen in unseren Tagen," *Österreichische Zeitschrift für
Volkskunde* (1953), 24–36; *Von der Gebärdensprache der Märchen-
erzähler,* Folklore Fellows Communications 155 (Helsinki, 1955).

[23] Henssen founded the Zentralarchivs der deutschen Volkserzählung
at the University of Marburg from which many of the present tales are
drawn.

[24] Friedrich von der Leyen, *Das Märchen: Ein Versuch* (4th ed.;
Heidelberg, 1958), chap. 2, "Die Ursprünge des Märchens," esp. 63ff.

1952–1957). Another recent Jungian exegesis, *Enter These Enchanted Woods,* by Aarland Ussher and Carl von Metzredt, offers readings more wondrous and magical than the adventures in the tales. In "Rumpelstiltskin" the authors perceive a "farcical parable of the Subconscious,—that 'Guardian Angel' of a Collective Potential which so easily becomes a Demon, taking away the life it gave. . . ." [25] In what they and others call the greatest fairy tale, "The Juniper," Ussher and von Metzredt recognize the tree of Juno, the great goddess, linked with the generative rhythms of woman.

(5) *The ethnological-comparative.* A few investigators patiently assembled and compared tale variants collected in adjacent countries or regions and thereby sought to isolate distinctive national traits in tales. Löwis of Menar contrasted the hero in Russian and German folktales, finding key differences in mood, style, motivation, and moralization; Elisabeth Koechlin examined German and French versions of the tale of Cupid and Psyche; K. H. Langstroff analyzed the interethnic folk narratives on the Franco-German border, following up Merkelbach-Pinck's field studies. [26] These studies of overlapping ethnic cultures made use of border areas as field laboratories. Kurt Ranke has undertaken a monumental work of this kind in the North German provinces of Schleswig and Holstein, once owned by Denmark. Three volumes of *Schleswig-Holsteinische Volksmärchen* have appeared to date (Kiel, 1955–1962), presenting a panorama of the entire known repertoire of international tales in the district. In place of the Grimms' artificial *Buchmärchen,* Ranke set down the multiple variants of each tale recorded in local dialects by earlier collectors, providing information on the narrators and surveying

---

[25] *Enter These Enchanted Woods: an Interpretation of Grimm's Fairy Tales* (Dublin, 1957), p. 51.

[26] August Löwis of Menar, *Der Held im deutschen und russischen Märchen* (Jena, 1912); Elisabeth Koechlin, *Wesenzüge des deutschen und des französischen Volksmärchens. Eine vergleichende Studie zum Märchentypus "Amor und Psyche" und zum "Tierbräutigam"* (Basel, 1945); K. H. Langstroff, *Lothringer Volksart. Untersuchung zur deutsch-lothringischen Volkserzählung an Hand der Sammlungen von Angelika Merkelbach-Pinck* (Marburg, 1953).

the distribution of the tale type in meaty headnotes. These are truly household stories in all their variation and homeliness.

(6) *The literary-historical*. From yet another perspective, folklorists view the Märchen as a genre of literature, aesthetic in itself, and influential upon dramatists, poets, and novelists. A controversial theorist of the past generation, Albert Wesselski, who criticized the Grimms for not having published true Märchen, regarded literary sources as a primary influence in preserving and disseminating Märchen. Hence the folktale scholar must thoroughly explore classical and medieval literatures. Wesselski himself undertook such a study in *Märchen des Mittelalters* (1925). Lutz Röhrich published a major work of literary history tracing the influence of oral tales on literature from medieval to modern times.[27] The Swiss folklorist Max Lüthi has dealt with folktales and folksongs as a substratum for narrative poetry and artistic narrative.[28] Elfriede Moser-Rath has excavated all kinds of folk narratives from Jesuit sermon literature of the Middle Ages.[29]

(7) *German developments of the Finnish method*. In the present century, folklore studies have largely followed the so-called Finnish historical-geographical method, which seeks to reconstruct the life history and *Urform* of a tale through the exhaustive assembling of its oral variants. One revisionist of this method is the Baltic German folklorist Walter Anderson (1885–1963), an enormously learned and personally courageous scholar who spent his final years at the University of Kiel in Germany as a colleague and co-worker of his former pupil Kurt Ranke. Anderson postulated a *Normalform* which in the course of time has replaced the *Urform*. This normal or typical form is the result of new and attractive elements entering the variants and becoming accepted by new generations of storytellers. Anderson explained

---

[27] Lutz Röhrich, *Erzählungen des späten Mittelalters und ihr Weiterleben in Literatur und Volksdichtung bis zur Gegenwart* (2 vols.; Bern, 1962–1965).

[28] *Volksmärchen und Volkssagen: zwei Grundformen erzählender Dichtung* (Bern and München, 1961).

[29] Elfriede Moser-Rath, "Erzähler auf der Kanzel," *Fabula*, II (1958), 1–26.

the long stability of oral tales through a law of self-correction;
tellers hear a tale often enough so that their own personal whims
are restrained, while the audience, which has also heard the tales,
further checks novelties.[30] Ranke followed the theories of Anderson in his own historical-geographical monograph on *Die zwei
Brüder* (*The Twins or Blood-Brothers,* Type 303, and *The
Dragon-Slayer,* Type 300), in which he examined over a thousand variants of these widely disseminated, interwoven stories.
He concluded that the normal form probably emerged in western
Europe, most likely in France.[31]

Kurt Ranke is the outstanding folktale scholar in Germany
today, sharing the enthusiasm of the Grimms for Märchen and
Sagen, but critical of their Märchen-polishing and excessive
chauvinism. In a paper of 1951 he pointed out the literary
character of many of the Grimms' tales.[32] In contrast to their
prideful nationalism, Ranke has taken the initiative in organizing
folktale studies on an international basis. While professor of
Volkskunde at the University of Kiel he planned and presided
over the first international congress devoted exclusively to the
folktale, held at Kiel and Copenhagen in 1959.[33] From this
congress developed the International Society for Folk Narrative
Research, with Ranke as president, and the journal *Fabula,* a
medium for international papers on the folktale, with Ranke as
editor. At his present chair of Volkskunde in the University of
Göttingen, Ranke and his associates are preparing vast reference

[30] Walter Anderson, *Kaiser und Abt* (Helsinki, 1923); Emma Emily
Kiefer, *Albert Wesselski and Recent Folktale Theories* (Bloomington, Ind.,
1947), pp. 29–33.
[31] Kurt Ranke, *Die zwei Brüder: eine Studie zur vergleichenden
Märchenforschung* (Helsinki, 1934), discussed by Stith Thompson in *The
Folktale* (New York, 1946), pp. 23–32.
[32] Ranke, "Der Einfluss der Grimmschen Kinder- und Hausmärchen auf
das volkstümliche deutsche Erzählgut," *Papers of the International
Congress of European and Western Ethnology, Stockholm 1951* (Stockholm, 1955), pp. 126–33.
[33] The papers were published in *Internationaler Kongress der Volkser-
zählungsforscher in Kiel und Kopenhagen,* edited by Kurt Ranke
(Berlin, 1961).

archives of printed examples of international folktales according to the Aarne-Thompson system.

The present volume represents the first major collection of German folktales to appear in English since the translation of the Grimms' *Kinder- und Hausmärchen*. Offering genuine *Volksmärchen*, it will serve as a healthy corrective to the *Buchmärchen* of that celebrated but misguided enterprise.[34]

RICHARD M. DORSON

[34] An excellent survey of recent folktale scholarship by Linda Dégh is "Überlick über die Ergebnisse der bisherigen Märchenforschung," in her *Märchen, Erzähler und Erzählgemeinschaft* (Berlin, 1962), pp. 47-65.

Introduction

The contribution supplied by Germany in this volume consists of tales collected in the last hundred years. This edition contains examples of all kinds of folk narratives: Sage, Märchen, legend, anecdote, animal tale, etc. The texts have been taken from the stock of the "Zentralarchiv für deutsche Volkserzählungen" in Marburg/Lahn and have, with the exception of a few examples, never been published before. I wish to express my most cordial thanks to the present Director of this Institute, Professor Dr. Gerhard Heilfurth, who has so generously placed at my disposal this material. The Marburg Archives, now part of the "Institut für mitteleuropäische Volksforschung," are the greatest regional archives in Germany. Others are in Munich, Tübingen, Bonn, Münster, Göttingen, Kiel, and above all, in Rostock. The texts published in this volume represent only a small selection from the very extensive store of manuscripts.

With the exception of Switzerland, which will be represented by a separate volume, we have tried to consider all the German-speaking territories. This volume therefore contains tales from provinces that no longer belong to Germany: Silesia, Posnania, East and West Prussia, and Pomerania. The narrative repertory from the former German linguistic enclaves is also represented. Special attention has been given to Austria and to German-speaking Lorraine.

As is true everywhere, the different kinds of tales have not had the same intensity of life. Some provinces are downright poor in Märchen, for instance Bavaria, Swabia, Lower and Upper Saxony, whereas others are rich, as for instance Schleswig-Holstein, Mecklenburg, East and West Prussia, Westphalia, Hesse, etc. This divergence may have its causes in the special talents of the different groups of the population. But there is no doubt that the degree of collecting, varying from province to province, as well as the specific interest of the collectors, have played an important part in this respect. Wilhelm Wisser, the great collector of folktales in Schleswig-Holstein, has given his preference above all to Märchen. Richard Wossidlo, the equally great collector from Mecklenburg, was more interested in Sagen. The difference of religions must not be overlooked either. The Catholic South of Germany is naturally more interested in legends than the Protestant North. Anecdotes and jests, however, being decidedly rational categories, appear in the same vitality everywhere right up to the present.

The narrative quality of the single texts differs greatly. Beside stories related at great length and with gusto there are others related in a short and concise manner. Rich combinations of motives are found beside others that may have lost part of their original substance. But the tales all belong to the tradition and are worth receiving our objective consideration.

The translation has presented some difficulties. Most of the tales were originally told in dialect. The dialect contributes essentially to their specific character and, of course, is lost when translated. An attempt has nevertheless been made to maintain in the best possible way the regional and individual styles of narration in the English version. My collaborator, Mrs. Lotte Baumann, has undertaken this difficult task with great devotion and, to my mind, with success. She has thus been of great help in the completion of this volume and I wish to express my special thanks to her.

KURT RANKE

Contents

XIII   TALES OF LYING

Part I
Animal Tales

·1· *The Fox and the Hare in Winter*

• The hare is able to support himself even in the coldest winter. He is satisfied with the buds he finds in hedges and shrubs.

One cold winter, the hare met the fox. Surprised, the fox asked the hare, "How fine and well fed you look! What are you living on these days? I am so hungry and I cannot find anything to eat."

The hare replied, "I have been living on eggs of late."

"On eggs! How on earth do you get them?" the fox wondered.

The hare answered, "This is what I do. There are women coming along here with basketfuls of eggs that they are taking to market. When I see a woman coming, I let myself fall flat on the ground before her, as if I were wounded by a shot. Then the woman puts her basket down in order to catch me and to take me to the market. Just as she thinks she has caught me, I stagger on for about ten steps and let myself fall to the ground again. I repeat this several times, until I am far away from the basket. Then I hurry back to the basket and carry it into the wood, and there I have enough food for a whole week."

The fox replied, "I like that. Wouldn't you help me get some eggs, too, in these hard times?"

"With great pleasure," replied the hare, "if you will be kind enough to let me have my share."

As agreed, they took their positions behind a bush on the road. The fox got a basketful of eggs in the described manner, and he hurried into the wood with it. The hare followed him in order to get his share. When he reached him, the fox had divided up the eggs into several little piles. The hare asked him with astonishment, "Why so many shares?"

Pointing to the different piles, the fox replied, "This one is for my father; this one for my mother; the other one is for my brother and my sister; and the last one is mine."

"And where is my share?" asked the hare in surprise.

"There is nothing left for you," was the answer. Too weak to punish the fox, the hare left angrily. But he decided to watch for a chance to pay back the fox.

After some time, the hare and the fox met again. It was very cold, and the earth was covered with snow. Again the fox wondered at the hare's prosperous look, since he himself was suffering terribly from hunger. Thus he asked, "What are you living on now?"

"On fish," the hare replied.

"Please," said the fox, "couldn't you let me have some as well to appease my hunger?"

The hare answered, "I shall help you once more. Not far from here, by the castle, there is a fishpond. The inhabitants have made a hole in the ice in order to catch fish. In the evening I go there; I stand on the ice and put my little tail into the hole, and after some time, I draw it out and there are plenty of fish hanging on it."

"Well," replied the fox, "this sounds all right to me. With my long tail, I should be able to catch a lot."

The hare said, "You will find me at the fishpond tonight."

At night they met at the appointed place, and the hare said, "Sit down by the hole, put your tail into the water, and remain like this until I come back. I shall go over to the garden to eat some cabbage."

The hare went away, and the fox remained there patiently, happily thinking of appeasing his gnawing hunger. After a while he tried pulling and found that his tail was getting heavy. But he continued to sit there, just as the hare had told him to do.

It was a long time before the hare came back and asked, "How are things going?"

The fox replied, "You have been away for a very long time. I have tried once, but my tail is so heavy that you will have to help me get it out."

The hare said, "Pull hard!"

But the fox could not get it out. He pulled as hard as he could, but the tail was frozen fast in the ice.

Now the hare approached with a stick, hit him over the head, crying, "This one is for my father; this one is for my mother; this one is for my brother and my sister; and the last one is for me!" He knocked him on the head from the right side and from the left, until the fox fell down dead.

· 2 · *The Fox and the Wolf*

· THE FOX and the wolf once divided the produce of their common work in a field. But the fox cheated the wolf when sifting the chaff from the corn: he kept the corn for himself and left the chaff for the wolf. The wolf was satisfied with this distribution, because his heap was bigger than that of the fox. Then they both went grinding. When the corn was being ground, the millstones noisily said, "cricks cracks," but when the chaff was being ground, they only said very softly, "climm clamm," so that the sound could barely be heard.

The wolf listened to this with astonishment. He could not explain it, and asked, "How is it that before the millstones said 'cricks cracks,' whereas now they only whisper 'climm clamm?'"

The sly fox gave him the advice, "Throw small stones and sand among it; then you can hear the grinding better!"

This is what the stupid wolf did. And hark! What a noise the millstones made now. They grated so loudly that one had to shut one's ears. The wolf jumped for joy when he heard the millstones making more noise when grinding the chaff than when grinding the corn.

· 3 · *The Little Hen and the Little Cock*

· A LITTLE HEN and a little cock lived together in a big poultry yard.

One day in autumn the little cock said, "I wonder if the nuts are ripe. Let's go and see and gather nuts tomorrow."

The next morning they set out to gather nuts on the mountain.

When they had been gathering for quite a while, the little cock suddenly shouted, "Come and see what I have found!"

He did not have to call twice. The little hen came over in a great hurry, and look what he had found—a little pot of butter. So they stopped gathering nuts, took the pot, and went home.

In the evening they put the little pot in a place where they were sure that nobody would find it and then they went to sleep. They had hardly closed their eyes when there was a rumbling noise. The little cock roused the little hen, and she went to see what it was. When she came to the butter pot, there was no one there; but since she was there, she thought she might as well have a beakful of butter. Then she went back and told the little cock that it must have been the wind, for she had seen nothing. After a while, the little cock called her again. The little hen flew willingly down from the perch to have a look, and again there was nothing. This time she pecked a little longer and told the little cock that she had seen nothing and that he must have been mistaken. When she noticed that he was fast asleep, she went back to the little pot, for it had tasted very good, and pecked until it was almost empty. But now she was getting afraid; she took sand and filled the little pot with it. Then she went to sleep.

In the morning when the little cock awoke, he thought he might as well taste the butter. It must taste fine early in the morning. But, oh Lord! As he went pecking down, there was only sand! This was too much! Angrily, he ran to the little hen, who was asleep, and shook her and put her in the water butt. But when he drew his little hen all wet and ruffled out again, he felt very sorry and put her on the fence to dry in the sun; however, when the hawk saw her, he took the little hen with him to hawkland.

The little cock was desperate. But after having thought things over for a long while, he made himself a cart out of two shoe soles and two eggshells and went to hawkland in order to fetch his little hen. On his way he met an old house dog, whom his master had driven away. He had served him for many years, and now that he was old and worn out and had lost all his teeth, he had to go.

The little cock told him, "I have made a cart out of two shoe soles and two eggshells. I am going to hawkland to rescue my little hen, whom the hawk has stolen, and if you want, you may go with me."

The dog gladly went with him. After a while, they met a cat.

"Where are you going?" asked the cat. "I have served my master for many years, and now that I am old and lame, the naughty boys beat me with their sticks; therefore, I must go away. Please take me with you."

So the little cock told her, "I am going to hawkland. The hawk has stolen my wife, and I want to fetch her. The dog has been driven away, because he is old, and I have made myself a cart out of two shoe soles, etc., and if you wish, you may go with us." The cat gladly went with them. They went on, and after a while, they met a rotten egg.

"Hey, where are you going? Take me with you! They have put me aside because I am rotten, and now I don't know where to go."

"All right," said the little cock. "The dog is old, and his master has driven him away. The cat has been beaten lame. We are going to hawkland. The hawk has stolen my little hen, and I am going to fetch her. I have made a cart out of two shoe soles and two eggshells, and if you want, you may go with us.

The egg gladly joined them, and everyone told a story about his life. Suddenly they heard a fine voice asking if it might join them. It was a pin that somebody had lost.

"All right," said the little cock. "The dog is old, and his master has driven him away. The cat has been beaten lame. The egg has been put aside because it is rotten. We are going to get my little hen, who has been taken to hawkland by the hawk. I have made a cart out of two shoe soles and two eggshells, and if you wish, you may come with us."

Soon they would be in hawkland. Suddenly an old cock was standing before them. He wanted to join them, for in his poultry yard they did not suffer him any longer because there were a lot of young cocks.

"All right," said the little cock. "Our dog is old. His master has driven him away. Our cat has been beaten lame by the boys. The egg has been put aside because it is rotten. The pin has been carelessly lost by a girl, and I am going to hawkland to rescue my little hen, for the hawk stole her when she sat in the sun to dry. I have made a cart out of two shoe soles and two eggshells, and if you wish, you may go with us." The cock went with them, too, and very soon they got to hawkland.

When they arrived in hawkland, the hawk had just gone out.

So the little cock said to the cat, "Come. Lie down on the hearth!" He said to the dog, "Lie down on the dunghill!" He said to the egg, "Lie down in the ash." The pin went into the towel, and the old cock sat on the roof.

When the hawk came home, he wanted to prepare something to eat. He saw two red-hot coals and wanted to light the fire, but when he came to the hearth the cat scratched him badly. Well, he thought, what was this? He stirred the ashes, and the rotten egg flew into his face. "Fie," he cried, reaching for the towel and scratching his whole face with the pin. Terrified, he ran out.

In the darkness he went near the dunghill, and that was no good either, for the dog bit him badly in the leg. Now he was very scared; he left the farm; and, oh Lord! At this moment the cock crowed insolently, "If you wish, you can have some more!"

But he ran to his companions and told them what had happened to him.

"Just imagine," he said, "I come home, and there I see two red-hot coals. I try to light the fire with them, but it scratches me terribly. After this, the fire comes whizzing out of the ashes. I go to the towel, but the scratcher is in there, and my face is all bleeding. I think I am bewitched or dreaming, and I run out to the yard. I get near the dunghill, but there is the blacksmith, who scratches my legs with a pair of sharp tongs until I can hardly move. And on top of the roof there sits the joker laughing at me."

Meanwhile, the little cock had rescued his little hen, and they went home happily. They never quarreled again, but then they have not found another pot of butter either.

·4· *The Struggle between the Wolf and the Fox*

· THE WOLF was ravenously hungry. In the forest there was nothing left for him to catch, and so he had to attack the villages in order to appease his hunger.

Getting near the village, he met the fox and said to him, "Tell

me, fox, how can I get something to eat? I am starving.
You know this place. If you don't tell me, I will tear you to
pieces."

The fox replied, "Be quiet. I shall get enough food for you.
There is a beekeeper who has four big pots full of honey in the
cellar. As soon as he goes to bed we can go there." After a while,
the fox said, "Now we can start. Follow me. He has gone to
sleep." They went along the hedge to the house of the beekeeper,
and the fox said, "Here is the vent of the cellar. There is nobody
around. You need not be afraid." The fox crept inside, and the
wolf followed.

In the cellar, the fox said, "Here are four pots. The first one is
for me—I have already had half of it. The second one is for you."
The wolf fell to his pot, and the fox went to his. When the fox
had enough, he went to the vent to see if he could still squeeze
through. He could, and so he went back to eat. Then he tried a
second time.

The wolf said, "Where are you going all the time?"

The fox replied, "I just go to see whether the road is clear. You
just go on eating."

That seemed all right to the wolf. The fox went for the third
time. But the beekeeper was not sleeping any longer. The fox
went to tell him that the wolf was in the cellar eating the honey.
He advised him to take a club in order to kill the wolf. The
beekeeper got a stick, went to the cellar, and fell upon the wolf.
The wolf tried to get out through the vent, but he was too fat and
could not get through. He managed to get his head and front
legs out, but not his body. The beekeeper gave him a sound
beating. In his great distress, the wolf finally freed himself.

The fox waited behind the hedge in order to find out if the
wolf would come back.

"Now I am going to tear you to pieces!" the wolf shouted.
"You have betrayed me. It is your fault that I was beaten."

The fox justified himself as well as he could by saying, "I had
to run myself. I had no time to warn you."

But the wolf was very cross. "You are a liar, and I am going to
kill you."

Now the fox was in a corner and said, "You can, of course,

kill me, for you are stronger than I; but I am innocent. If you kill me, you will have to be ashamed in the presence of the other animals."

The wolf saw his point and said, "I will give you a chance. I declare war against you. You take three animals of your choice, and I will take three of my choice. Within three days at noon you will have to be at the border of the forest, where the big oak stands. If you don't come, and if I find you later, then I will tear you to pieces."

The fox said, "You can rely on me. I will be there."

On the third day the wolf was still looking for animals. He met a bear. The wolf said, "Tell me. Would you help me to make war?"

The bear asked, "Against whom?"

"Against the fox," said the wolf.

"When?"

"Today at twelve o'clock," said the wolf.

"Where?" asked the bear.

"On the border of the forest, where the big oak stands, near the village."

The bear didn't need to think it over for a long time and said, "I will go with you."

After a moment there came a wild boar. Stop, thought the wolf, you better take him with you. "Tell me, would you help me to make war?" he said to the boar.

"Against whom?" asked the boar.

"Against the fox," said the wolf.

"When?" asked the boar.

"Today at twelve o'clock on the border of the forest where the big oak stands."

The boar went with them, and the wolf thought, now I have two of the biggest animals in the wood with me. I need not ask a third one. Whatever the fox will do, we will get the better of him.

They went to the oak in the forest, but there was no one to be seen or heard. The bear said, "The fox certainly is not coming. It's past twelve o'clock. He only said that in order to get rid of you."

The wolf said, "He is bound to come. If he doesn't come now, I will tear him to pieces later."

The bear said, "All right. I will climb up the tree in order to see if he is coming."

The bear climbed to the first twigs, but he could see nothing. He looked around once more and said, "I must go even higher up." He climbed high enough to see as far as the village, but it was no use. He still could not hear or see anything.

However, the fox did come, and we are now going to see what kind of animals he brought with him. The fox was on good terms with all the animals of the village. They believed him to be the most gentle and honest creature. First of all he met a cat, but it was rather a big one.

The fox said, "Cat, would you help me to make war?"

"Against whom?" asked the cat.

"Against the wolf," said the fox.

"When?" asked the cat.

"Today at noon on the border of the forest where the big oak stands."

The cat thought it over for a moment. If it doesn't turn out well, he thought, then I'll climb up the oak and the wolf cannot do me any harm. "I will go with you."

There was also a cock strutting about. Stop, thought the fox, you better take him with you as well. He went and asked, "Cock, would you help me to make war?"

"Against whom?" asked the cock.

"Against the wolf."

"When and where?"

"Today at noon on the border of the forest where the big oak stands."

The cock did not think it over for a long time either. He thought, if it doesn't turn out well, I'll fly up in the oak and there the wolf cannot do me any harm.

They went on and met a billy goat, but he was rather a big one. The fox thought that he might take him along as well and asked him, "Billy goat, will you help me to make war against the wolf? These two animals are coming, too."

The billy goat, who was not stupid either, thought, the wolf cannot do you any harm. You are in the village in one leap. You can jump over digs and shrubs, which the wolf cannot. Thus he said, "I will go with you."

They went on and saw a grazing ass. He was a rather big one, too. The fox thought, stop, you better take him, too. He asked, "Ass, would you help me to make war?"

"Against whom?"

"Against the wolf. These three animals are going with me."

The ass did not think it over for long. He was not afraid of the strongest animals; he kicked them in the mouth with his hind legs until their teeth fell into their throats. He said, "I will go with you."

They went on, and they came across another cat. He had been fighting with a fellow cat and was limping.

Stop, thought the fox, you'd better take him with you as well. He went to the cat and asked, "Cat, would you help me to make war?"

"Against whom?"

"Against the wolf," said the fox.

"When?" asked the cat.

"Today at noon."

The cat asked, "Where?"

"Near the woods, where the big oak stands. These animals are going with me."

The cat thought, the ass is walking ahead of you, and if things do not go well, you can soon be in the village.

The fox said, "Now line up!" He marched in front, and they went toward the woods in a long line.

Halfway between the woods and the village there was a sharp corner, and the bear, who was still sitting in the tree, said, "As soon as they get around the corner, I can see them." After an instant he said, "There is the fox coming around the corner." Then he said, "Another one is coming behind the fox. As soon as he is around the corner I shall recognize him." When he had gotten around the corner, the bear said, "It is a fellow with a lance." (It was the cat. He had his tail sticking in the air, and the bear took it for a lance.) Then he said, "There is another one coming around the corner." When he could see him well enough, he said, "It is a warrior who has got spurs on his boots and is blood red around the face with rage." After one more moment he said, "There is another one coming around the corner. He has a long white beard hanging down his chest." As soon as the goat was completely around the corner, the bear said, "One has got a hayfork with long pointed ends on his shoulders." (It was the he-goat. The bear took the horns for a hayfork.) After a short while he said, "There is another one coming around the corner. Oh, but he is a tall fellow! He is much taller and stronger than I am, and I shouldn't like to fight him." When he could see him completely, he said, "He also has a bar on his back." (It was the ass's black chine that the bear took for a bar.) Then he said, "There is another one coming around the corner with a lance, and he is also picking up stones." (It was the cat who came limping behind. As the cat was bending down, the bear thought that he was picking up stones.) Now this was too much for the bear and he said, "You didn't tell me all this; otherwise, I should not have come with you. I am going to stay up here in this dark tree where they cannot see me. You can fight alone."

The boar was frightened, too, and said, "You did not tell me either; otherwise I should not have come with you." There was a shrub with lots of leaves standing nearby, and the boar said, "I am going to hide under these leaves, so that they will not see me."

Now the wolf was standing there all alone and thought, if I run away, I shall have to be ashamed in front of all these animals. The fox has only got to come up to the oak. This is what we have agreed upon. He will certainly be glad to make peace with me. Doing so, I shall even acquit myself creditably.

Alas, he was mistaken. As the fox saw the wolf standing there all alone, he was full of joy and thought, he hasn't got one animal with him. They don't like him. Now we shall get the better of him. The fox advanced. Then the wolf was afraid to be encircled and he therefore went backward in order to keep his back free. The other animals followed, the ass stamping the ground with his legs and clattering with his irons.

Then the boar was frightened. He had never heard anything like this before. When boars get frightened, they move their tails. At this moment the cat happened to be near the shrub and heard the rustling of the leaves. He believed a mouse to be there. Now a cat never lets a mouse live. Whatever happens, he first of all catches the mouse. So looking at the wagging tail behind the leaves, the cat thought it was a mouse. With one leap, the cat reached the tail, grasped it with his claws and teeth until the blood ran out. The boar, not knowing what was happening, ran screaming into the woods and disappeared. When the cat noticed what a big animal it was, he was frightened. He therefore ran toward the tree and started climbing. The bear heard the boar's screams, and, looking down, he saw the cat coming up.

He thought, there is the one with the lance. This is your last hour. The boar has already been slain. If you climb up the tree and he climbs better than you, he will stab you. You had better rush down through the twigs. And while the one with the lance is getting to where you are now, you go down and run into the woods and there he won't get you. Thus he rushed down through the twigs.

The ass, who was standing underneath, heard the rustling of the twigs, looked up, and saw a bear coming down. The ass, who was not afraid of the strongest animal, did not run away but took his position. As soon as the bear had reached the ground, the ass kicked him in the ribs with his hind legs, so that he spinned around three times and then fell into a ditch. But he pulled himself together, got out of the ditch, and ran into the woods. At this sight the wolf started running off and disappeared in the woods, too.

Now the enemy was put to flight. The fox and his allies had gained a splendid victory. They met under the oak and enjoyed their triumph. It was no use following the enemy. They said, "Let's go back to the village together." However, only the cat and the ass had had a chance to fight; so the other animals said, "We have come in vain. The cat and the ass had a chance to fight, whereas we had not."

But the fox, who always knew what to do, said, "I know where the wolf is hiding in the woods. He has made a house and nobody knows it. If anyone is after him, he hides there and no one can catch him. But I have found it. It is in a thicket where nobody can get through. I know where to get in. If you wish, we can all go there and then you will all be able to fight." This plan was adopted unanimously. They lined up, one after another with the fox at the head, and thus they went into the woods.

After a while, the fox said, "Here we are. There is the thicket. Come on!" The fox worked himself through, and the others followed. He waited for them and then he said, "There is his house. Let's approach. We will force the door open, rush forward, and attack him." Thus they all tried to break the door down. But it was a strong oak door and did not move. They kicked at the shutters, but the wolf had closed them, too, and they could not open them.

They did not know what to do and said, "We have come in vain. If we had an ax with us, we could knock the door to pieces. We might as well go home."

But the ass said, "Let me try. Perhaps I can knock the door to pieces." He placed himself at the door and kicked with his hind legs until the house was trembling. There was one sharp blow after another, but it was a new oak door and resisted. The ass said, "Let's go home; it is no use."

But the fox was cunning. He said, "I have an idea. The ass must place himself under the roof; the cat must leap on his back, then onto the roof, go to the chimney, peer down, climb down, and open the door. Then we can rush inside."

This plan was accepted unanimously. The cat jumped on the ass's back, from there onto the roof, and to the chimney. From there he looked down.

Inside, everything was dark; nothing was to be heard, and the cat thought, if I go down and open the door, and if the wolf hears the lock squeak, he will fall on me and tear me to pieces and the other animals cannot help me either. But the cat was a crafty animal as well and said, "Let's see if the wolf does not open the door for me himself!" The cat climbed down and looked around. Inside it was pitch black, but the cat could see in the dark. Therefore the cat saw the wolf cowering in a corner. Foot after foot, he silently went toward the wolf, hit him with his two claws over the eyes—one stroke after the other—so that the wolf thought fire was coming from his eyes. Not knowing what had happened to him, he jumped up and pulled the door open in order to get out. This was what the cat was waiting for.

As soon as the wolf came out, the ass kicked him in the ribs with his hind legs, so that he toppled over three times and rolled to the goat. The billy goat believed the wolf to be very heavy and kicked him with all his might in a round curve over the cock. There was a pond with water and the wolf fell into it with a splash. The cock flew onto the roof in order to see where the wolf was. He saw him falling into the water and thought that he was drowned. He therefore started crowing on the roof.

However, the wolf was not drowned; he worked himself out of the ditch and ran into the woods as fast as he could.

The bear and the boar were standing together. The boar said to the bear, "What was that? My tail is bleeding. I have no idea what happened to me."

The bear reported what had happened to him as well and said to the boar, "The one with the lance came up the tree; so I rushed down on the side through the twigs, and when I got down, the one with the bar tossed me so hard that I toppled over three times and fell into the ditch. Then I got up and ran into the woods as fast as I could."

At this moment the bear and the boar saw the wolf coming. They went toward him, and the bear said, "What is the matter with you? You are soaked to the skin and all muddy and dirty, and you are bleeding under your eyes. What happened? Your face is bleeding, and blood is running out of your nose, too."

The wolf said, "I was hiding in my house, but the fox found out all about it. I had the doors and shutters closed, so that it was dark; but suddenly there were three bangs at the door, so that I thought the door was smashed to pieces. When I thought they had left, I got slapped in the face, so that I thought fire was coming out of my eyes. I jumped up, flung the door open to get out, and there was the big one with the bar standing there and he hit me in the ribs, so that I toppled three times over and came near the one with the hayfork, who took me with his hayfork and whirled me over the warrior's head, and I fell into a pond. At this moment the warrior jumped on the roof—never in my life have I seen such a leap—and there he cried, 'Bring the scoundrel up here!' If he had gotten me, he would have killed me. My side hurts terribly. The one with the bar must have broken three ribs."

The bear said, "I have also been hit with the bar. I have such a pain that I am sure to have three broken ribs, too."

Having told each other their woes, the boar and the bear said to the wolf, "Now you better go and try to make friends with the fox again. We have been on good terms with him up to now. Try to get on with him as well."

·5· *The Mountain Hen and the Fox*

· THE MOUNTAIN HEN was in the woods with her chicks. Suddenly the fox came, and she fled to the top of a tree. The fox told her that unless she threw one of her chicks down, he would come up and eat her and all her chicks.

When the mountain cock came home, she told him all about it. "You silly one," he said, "if he comes again, you tell him to come up and get them. He is not able to climb a tree."

The next day the fox came again and said that unless she threw two chicks down, he would come up and eat her and all of her chicks.

But she told him, "Then you come up and get them!"

He left in great anger.

The following Sunday he came again, and the mountain cock, the mountain hen, and the chicks were in the forest glade. The mountain hen and the chicks could just manage to reach the tree, but the cock could not make it.

The fox said, "Now I am going to eat you to the last morsel."

"All right," said the mountain cock, "but today is Sunday. You must first let me say the Lord's Prayer."

So the fox sat down and waited for him to pray, but the mountain cock flew to the top of the tree.

The fox cried, "All meat gone. All meat gone!"

.6. The Tale of the Little Sausage and the Little Mouse

• ONCE UPON A TIME there was a little sausage and a little mouse who lived together.

One day the little mouse asked, "Little sausage, whenever you cook, the meal tastes much better. Tell me why."

"Well," said the little sausage, "I always run once across the soup!"

The next time the little mouse was cooking, it wanted to run across the pot as well, but, alas, it was scalded and drowned. The little sausage came home, and seeing what had happened, sat down on the sill and cried.

A dog came by. "Little sausage, why are you crying like this?"

"Little mouse has been drowned running through the cabbage, and therefore I must cry."

"Well then, I will howl with you."

The cat heard the noise. He thought, you must see why the dog is howling like this. "What has happened to you two?" he asked.

"Well," said the dog, "little mouse has drowned in the cabbage pot. Little sausage is crying about it, and therefore I must howl with it."

"Well then, I will mew with you. Mew. Mew."

Well, thought the fence, what's going on here? "What's going on here?" it called.

"Mew. Mew."

"Bow-wow."

"Alas. Alas. Little mouse drowned in the cabbage pot." Little sausage was sitting on the sill crying. The dog was howling. The cat was mewing. Crash! The fence fell down.

Then came a cow. "Fence, why have you fallen down?"

"Mew. Mew."

"Bow-wow."

"Alas. Alas! Little mouse has drowned in the cabbage pot. Little sausage is sitting on the sill crying. The dog is howling. The cat is mewing, and so I fell down."

"Then I will moo, moo," said the cow.

Now came the calf, the sheep, the cock, the hen, etc.

"Mew. Mew."

"Bow-wow."

"Alas. Alas."

"Baa-baa."

"Cock-a-doodle-doo."

"Cluck-cluck." Etc.

Finally the master came and asked, "What's going on here?" So the dog told him what had happened. "Well," he replied, "is it that bad if a mouse dies? You go back to your places—all of you. And you, little sausage, let it be a warning to you. Cook your soup alone and do not tell anybody why it tastes so good."

·7· *Bear, Fox, and Man*

• ONCE THE BEAR came to the fox and said, "You are a clever fellow. Tell me who is the most intelligent creature in the world."

"Well, I certainly can tell you. It is man, the human animal, who is the most intelligent and the strongest being in the world."

"All right," said the bear, "I should like to fight him. If only I knew where to meet him."

"You go down to the road," the fox replied, "and there you sit down, and if somebody passes by, you ask him who he is."

First of all, there came a little boy on his way to school.

The bear asked him, "Who are you?"

"I am a boy," he said.

"All right, go on. You are not a man."

After a while, there came an old man along the road.

The bear asked him, "Who are you?"

"I am an old man."

"All right, go on," he said.

Then there came a smart hunter, his hunting knife on his side, his gun on his shoulder.

"Who are you?" asked the bear.

"I am a man," the other one said.

"All right," he replied. "If you are a man, let's scuffle. I have heard that man is the strongest and the most intelligent creature in the world."

"Yes, this is true," said the hunter.

"Well then, let's scuffle."

The hunter said, "First of all we shall throw stones."

The bear took a huge stone and wanted to throw it at the hunter. The hunter, however, took his gun, shot, and hit the bear's head.

The bear cried, "Stop."

"This is nothing," said the hunter.

"Now we shall scuffle," said the bear, and then he uprooted a tree and attacked the hunter.

The hunter took his hunting knife and thrust it firmly at the bear. Now the bear went to the devil—that is to say—to the fox.

The fox had been watching the whole thing. The bear told him that they had been throwing stones and that he had been hit with the first stone.

"Then we were scuffling, and now he took out a rib," he said, "and with this rib he knocked and thrashed me so much that I had to run away."

"There you can see what a boaster you are!" said the fox.

But the bear said, "Let's fight together tomorrow. I'll bring the lion and the wolf, and you bring two animals as well."

The fox considered, "Whom could I take with me? Well, I shall take the neighbor's cat and the neighbor's dog."

The bear stood on top of the hill with the lion and the wolf, waiting for the fox to come with his two companions. The cat held his tail in the air and the dog went all bent.

At this sight, the bear cried, "Let's run away! One of them has his bayonet fixed and the other one is already gathering stones!"

And thus they went to the devil, and the fox remained triumphant.

.8. *Why the Dogs Sniff at Each Other*

• RATHER A LONG TIME AGO all the dogs met together. They wanted to complain about getting only the bones without any meat. They had to work for people all the time, especially for the hunter—as the hound said—and for the farmer—as the chain dog, who had to run in the old treadwheel all day long, said. The greyhound and the bowlegged badger dog and all the dogs from the smallest to the biggest were discontented. However, it was no use to complain to people, for in the long run the dogs would only get gnawed-off bones with not one little bit of meat left. It could not go on like this! Yet if they would not work any more, they would not even get nibbled-off bones, but only the dog whip. In order to change things, they decided to address their complaint to St. Peter, and to prevent him from forgetting, they would inform him by letter. The letter was written, and now one of them was to bring it to Peter. But how? They could not take the letter in their mouths, for with all their panting, the letter might easily get lost or slobbered. That would not do. At last they decided to hang it under the tail, so that people would not see what they carried. The greyhound was to deliver the letter. He rushed away. But he had to cross a river. The bridge was merely a tree trunk.

Marching along this trunk, the greyhound suddenly saw that underneath there was another dog running who also had a letter under his tail and who was going the same way.

Now only one letter had been written, and he was to bring it to Peter, and therefore this looked foul to him. (Of course it was his reflection, for the water was smooth as a mirror.) He jumped into the water in order to take away the other one's letter. But at this moment the other dog disappeared, and he searched and searched, until his letter was all wet and got lost.

Each dog believes that every other dog has the false letter, and therefore he sniffs at every other dog to this very day, for the letter might still be under the other dog's tail.

.9. *The Skinned Goat*

• THERE ONCE LIVED a father and his son, and they had a goat. The boy had to drive her to the pasture every day. But this goat was an old hag. In the evening the father used to ask her, if she had had enough to eat and to drink. But she always answered, "How can I have had enough to eat and to drink, if I have not even seen one stalk of grass and one drop of water?" Then the son always got a sound beating.

One day the father decided to find out for himself. He saw that after having eaten off three meadows and drunk up three ponds, she still pretended to be hungry. Now the old man decided to slaughter the goat.

He had already stuck and halfway skinned her, when he noticed his knife was getting blunt. He went into the house to sharpen it. No sooner had he gone than the goat got up and ran into the woods, where she hid in a foxhole.

When the fox came home and wanted to get into his hole, he was terribly frightened, for out of his hole there came a voice saying; "Halfway skinned and halfway killed, I am a piece of mutton. Come on in and I'll eat you up!"

The fox was afraid and went right away to his brother-in-law, the bear, and told him about his grief. The bear went with him to the spot, got into the hole, but turned around immediately, when he heard the horrible words.

"I can't do anything in this matter," he said and ran away.

In his distress the fox went to the panther, then to the tiger, and finally to the lion. But none of them could help him, and they all took to their heels.

At last the fox met the bumblebee, to whom he poured out his complaints. The bumblebee said, "I will help you."

"Bigger ones have tried in vain to help me, and you think you can do it?" replied the fox. But he obediently led the bumblebee to the hole. It flew buzzing inside, sat down on one of the skinned parts, and started stinging vigorously. The goat soon felt the pain and ran bleating out of the hole, where she fell again into the

hands of her master, who had been looking for her, and so she
was killed completely.

· 10 ·   *The Hedgehog and the Hare*

· ONE DAY THE HEDGEHOG and the hare sat together, praising
themselves to the skies. Finally the hare laughed at the hedgehog
and called him a tortoise, because he had practically no legs. But
the hedgehog replied, "Why are you boasting like this, longlegs?
I bet I can run down this field and back again faster than you."

"Agreed! What will you bet?" called the hare, pricking up his
ears.

"A life-and-death footrace," replied the hedgehog, "but before
we start I have to count the steps from here to the other ridge. I'll
soon be back, and then we'll start."

When the hedgehog was back, the hare said, "Holla," clicked
his tongue, and set off swiftly like the wind. He did not look
back, but when he got to the other ridge, the hedgehog was
prancing before him. Taken aback, the hare stood up on his hind
legs, and returned at full speed. When he got back, after running
twice as fast as before, the hedgehog was again prancing before
him.

"Confound it!" the hare cursed. "What's this? I am running
my legs off. You seem not to budge an inch, and yet you reach
the goal before me!"

"Come on!" replied the hedgehog. "We will race one another
until one of us is dead."

Thus the hare ran himself to death, because he did not get the
point: he did not notice that on either ridge there was a hedgehog
that looked exactly like the other one.

· ONCE UPON A TIME there was a cock who did not want to live on the farm any more. On a fine summer morning he left. Not far from the farm there was a big forest. This is where the cock went. He had not got very far when he saw a fox sitting before his kennel.

"Where are you going, cock?" he asked.

"I go traveling!"

"Take me with you!"

"Why not? Squeeze in behind and you'll come with me." The fox did so, and the cock proudly went on.

After a short while there was a bird of prey, a kite, sitting on a stone. "Where are you going, cock?" he asked.

"I go traveling!"

"Take me with you!"

"Why not? Squeeze in behind, and you'll come with me." The kite did so, and the cock proudly went on.

After a while a wolf came running along. "Where are you going, cock?"

"I go traveling!"

"Take me with you!"

"Why not? Squeeze in behind, and you'll come with me." The wolf did so, and the cock proudly went on.

The cock soon got tired of traveling. He turned around and went home. From the fence he called in a loud voice over the whole farm:

> Cock-a-doodle-doo!
> Dear master, pray
> Look here! I say,
> You'll never guess,
> What is in me! [1]

---

[1] Kikeriki!
   Gnädiger Herr, hört her,
   ich bitt' Euch sehr!
   Was in mir ist,
   Ihr ratet's nicht.

It was after lunch, and the master was taking a nap. But the
servants and maids went to him and told him that the old cock
was back and that suddenly he could talk like a human being.
When the master came out of the house, the cock craned his
neck and crowed in a loud voice over the whole farm:

> Cock-a-doodle-doo!
> Dear master, pray
> Look here! I say,
> You'll never guess,
> What is in me!

His master could not believe his ears. At last he ordered his
maids, "Catch this brawler and put him with the hens. There he
will be quiet."

In the hen house the cock walked proudly up and down. When
the maids left, he called, "Fox, come out and eat to your heart's
content!" The fox came out at once and ate one hen after the other.
Then he went back into the forest. The cock stood in the middle
of the hen house and crowed in a loud voice over the whole
farm:

> Cock-a-doodle-doo!
> Dear master, pray
> Look here! I say,
> You'll never guess,
> What is in me!

His master was furious. "Throw this brawler into the fountain
and let him get drowned!"

The cock clung to the wall of the fountain and said softly,
"Kite, come out! There is water enough for you. Drink as much
as you want!"

The kite, who is always thirsty, came out at once. He drank
and drank until there was not one drop of water left in the
fountain. Then the kite went back to the forest. But the cock
flew to the edge of the fountain and crowed in a loud voice over
the whole farm:

> Cock-a-doodle-doo!
> Dear master, pray
> Look here! I say,

> You'll never guess,
> What is in me!

The master was raving mad. "Shut the brawler into the cattle shed and let him be trampled down by the cattle!" he ordered his servants.

But the cock was cautious. He did not go near the cattle. As soon as the door was locked, he said, "Wolf, come out and eat to your heart's content!" The wolf came out at once and ate one cow after the other. When the wolf had crept back to the forest, the cock flew onto a crib and crowed in a loud voice over the whole farm:

> Cock-a-doodle-doo!
> Dear master, pray
> Look here! I say,
> You'll never guess,
> What is in me!

Now the master was at his wit's end. He thought it over and over again, but he did not know what to do. At last one of the maids said, "Master, let's kill the cock. Then he will stop brawling!"

He agreed, "All right, kill him; I will eat him for supper."

Thus the poor cock died, and he was served for supper all brown and crisp. The master ate him up completely. There was nothing left. After the big meal and after all the excitement, he was sitting there quite happily. But his happiness did not last long. For in his belly something started stirring, and before he realized what had happened, a loud voice was calling through rooms and kitchen:

> Cock-a-doodle-doo!
> Dear master, pray
> Look here! I say,
> You'll never guess,
> What is in me!

The master leaped about as if he had bees in his trousers. In his fright he told one of the maids to come with the knife and to cut off the cock's head with the wicked beak. But, alas, the knife wounded the master badly. He died.

The cock, however, flew away. He lived happily, and if he has not been eaten in the meantime, then he is still living happily to this very day.

•*12*• *Straw, Bean, and Coal*

• THE STRAW, BEAN, AND COAL went for a walk and came to a river that they could not cross. The bean jumped into the water and swam until it got to the other side. But the coal had no idea how to get over the river. The straw, however, could swim, too. So it said to the coal, "Come on. Sit on my back. I'll take you over with me." So the coal sat on the straw. They swam to the middle of the river, but by that time, the straw was burned through, and the coal drowned. Now the bean, on the other side, laughed so much, that it burst asunder. But there came a tailor, who sewed it together, and it has a seam to this very day. I heard this tale when I was a child.

Part II
Spirits, Ghosts, and Giants

·13· The House Damsel

· DURING HOLY TIMES in the house of the farmer Lederer in Tirschenreuth there used to appear a tiny being on the stove whom they called "house damsel." Once they had a new maid-servant; when she saw the house damsel for the first time, she was afraid and told her mistress. The mistress entreated her by no means to do the house damsel any harm and not even to talk to her.

Whatever was removed from the table was placed on the stove, and very often the leftovers were completely eaten up, and the dishes and plates were cleaned and placed in the platerack. One Saturday, when the servants were very tired from hard work, the mistress told them that they might leave the washing and sweeping for the following day. But early in the morning everything was clean and neatly polished. The house damsel had performed this kind act for the tired servants.

Once the servants forgot to place the leftovers on the stove. Thereupon the house damsel left and never came back.

·14· The Household Spirit in Rötenbach

· THE OLD HEATHENS believed that there were not only gods that were hostile to human beings, but also gods that were not hostile, and these could be relied upon. And thus popular belief knows not only bad, but also good spirits. Long ago in a house at Rötenbach there lived a household spirit in the shape of a tiny man. He did a lot of useful work in the house; above all he liked to rock the small children. In the evening he used to sit on the top bench of the stove; this was his place, and no one else was allowed to sit there. Once the farmer had a pert servant who usurped the household spirit's seat. But he did not enjoy it, for the household spirit gave him a smack, and he whirled from his throne down into the room.

Otherwise the household spirit never did any harm to anybody.

Later on, a Capuchin put him in a small box, took him (in the shape of a beetle) into the forest, and laid him underneath a tall beech.

· 15 ·   Household Spirit Brings Food

· ON A FARM in Dannefeld there was a woman who had a household spirit. He did everything in the house for her. He also brought the food, so that she needed to do no cooking. She only had to put the dishes on the table and to say what they had to be filled with. The stableboy had long ago noticed that the woman never did any cooking and that nevertheless food was ready in time.

One morning he hid in a big barrel and looked through the bunghole. Thus he saw the woman placing dishes on the table. When the household spirit came, she said, "Here you shit roast in and here you shit dumplings!"

Now the household spirit said, "He is looking!"

She: Put his eyes out!

He: He is crossing himself!

She: Oh, come on!

He tried to do what she asked him to do, but he could not put the boy's eyes out because wooden sticks were nailed crosswise on top of the barrel.

At lunch they all enjoyed their meal. Only the boy did not want to eat. The servant said to him, "Eat, boy!"

But he replied, "Who can eat what a devil shits?"

· 16 ·   Reward Drives the Familiar Spirits Away

· THE NIGHTS from Christmas to Twelfth Day are called the "undernights" in Bohemia and in some parts of Austria. During this time the familiar spirits are especially busy. Not far from

Saaz there lived a middle-class family; the housewife changed the maidservant in the time of the "undernights" as usual. On the first day of her service, the maid got up very early in the morning in order to get through with her work as soon as possible. To her astonishment, the kitchen and the other rooms had already been swept, the furniture had been dusted; in short, everything was in good order. The maid, who thought the mistress of the house did it, was astonished that the mistress should have gotten up so early. She decided to get up even earlier the next day. When the mistress of the house got up, she was very pleased with the new servant, for she believed she had done everything and she decided to reward her.

The following day the maid got up even earlier, but she found everything as the day before. On the third day, she still had not learned what was happening. As the mistress of the house was very courteous and kind with her and praised her industry, she finally told her that it deeply grieved her to find her mistress doing everything herself. The woman asked her with surprise what she was talking about. Thus they agreed to stay awake in turns for several nights to find out who was the mysterious helper.

On the first night, between twelve and one o'clock, they saw two tiny familiar spirits in the shape of a boy and a girl entering. They both worked at such an amazing speed that in a short time everything was done. Astonished, they decided to watch the following night as well. They saw the same thing: the spirits came, worked busily, and left again. It struck them especially that the poor spirits were all naked. The charitable woman decided to do them a good turn and put down two full sets of clothes in the following night. When they came and saw the clothes, they started crying very loudly and the goblin said to his companion, "Now we are being paid here, too, and cannot go on working any more. Where shall we find another decent family?"

Lamenting, they took their presents, left without doing any work, and never returned again.

$\cdot$ *17* $\cdot$ The Thing on the Hedge

• A PEASANT from Lieblich went to the village of Heiden for some medicine. He quite often had to go there at night. When he neared the pastor's hedge, there was a black thing sitting on it. It cried, "I've got no head! I've got no head!"

The farmer heard it several times without saying anything himself.

The next evening it called again, "I've got no head! I've got no head!"

Now the farmer grew furious and cried, "Have you got a nose at least?"

At the same moment the thing came flip-flop and sat on his neck, and he had to carry it right to the hedge of the neighbor's house, where the pastor's land ended. When it happened again, he took another road. It always happened on his way back.

$\cdot$ *18* $\cdot$ The Frog with the Golden Key

• IN THE VALLEY of Fockenbach, beneath Vierscheid, there are the glassworks. A most beautiful girl is supposed to have been enchanted there. A man is said to have seen her. She said to him, "Come to a certain place tomorrow. A frog will be sitting there with a golden key in his mouth. If you draw the key out with your mouth, I shall be free."

The next day the man went there and tried to get the key, but he did not succeed. The frog uttered a loud cry, and the girl again stood before him and said, "On this mountain there is an oak tree; an acorn will fall down. Out of this a tree will grow. It will be cut into boards. A cradle will be made out of them. The child that will be rocked in it will deliver me. I have to remain here until then."

· *19* · *The Origin of the Lake of Vitte*

• ONCE THERE LIVED an enormous giant, who was very mischievous, on the Hell Mountains near Dörsenthin. One day he was in high spirits and wanted to drink the Baltic Sea. He lay down flat on the earth, so that his head and throat protruded beyond the beach. Then he started swallowing. However, he had overestimated his strength. Although he had taken many a deep draught, the water of the Baltic Sea had hardly diminished. At last his belly was swollen so much that he burst asunder. The water flew down into the lowland behind the beach, covered it completely, and thus formed the Lake of Vitte.

· *20* · *The Giant's Toy*

• ONCE A GIANT was plowing near the wood. A little man (of our kind) went toward him. The giant seized him and put him into his pocket. Then he got hungry and went home to eat his fill. The giant told his mother everything. His mother told him to set the little worm free where he had caught him. The giant went and put him on the ground, and then he went home where he asked his mother what this thing had been.

She told him, "After us there will come such people."

When he heard this, he went back to the place where he had released him and wanted to kill him, but the little man had left long ago.

Thus the giants have died out and we are living now. After us, even smaller people will come who will thrash in the oven.

· *21* · *The Duped Giant*

• A WILD GIANT tyrannized a country and devoured men. The people, therefore, deliberated how to get rid of him. They felled a big tree, split it, hollowed out the two halves, and then showed the giant the new bed, asking him to lie down in it and to see if it fitted him. The giant did so, and as he was comfortably lying inside, the people suddenly shut the lid and nailed it down. The giant choked painfully, and the people were relieved of their distress.

·22· *The Giant's Stone*

• IF YOU GO SOUTH from the village of Benzen about twenty minutes, you come into the pleasant valley of the Böhme, an affluent of the Aller that winds through gay, sap-green pastures. In the middle of this valley there rises, surrounded with cheerful green, a hill that people call Ohberg. On top of this hill an old knotted oak shields an enormous granite rock with its huge branches. What strikes you about this big stone is that several pieces, which obviously have been knocked off, are lying nearby. The following legend is connected with this stone:

Many hundreds of years ago two giants lived in Benzen and in the village of Hollige, which is situated half an hour away. They had a quarrel, and the giant from Hollige wanted to smash the other one's house. He took a big stone, tied a chain around it, and wanted to throw it toward the house of the giant from Benzen. Owing to the heavy swing, the chain broke and the stone landed in the Böhme Valley. Angry about his failure, the giant went to the stone and kicked it. Thus several pieces, which are still lying there today, were knocked off; they are estimated to amount to about five heavy cartloads.

Part III
Under the Spell of the Demon

•23• *The Enchanted Princess*

• THERE WAS a royal couple who wished to have children. They did not care how—even if it was to be with the devil's help! Finally they had a girl. But she was bewitched. When she was fourteen years old, she died and was laid out in a chapel. In the chapel she was guarded by soldiers. But at twelve o'clock in the night she always tore off the soldier's heads. The king was terribly afraid, because he had already lost many soldiers.

Now it was to be the turn of one of the youngest and best soldiers. But he was so terribly afraid that he asked the king for a leave from three to four o'clock in the afternoon, and this was granted to him. In his mortal dread, he ran into the forest and met an old man who was sitting by an old tree root. The old man approached and asked him what afflicted him so much. The soldier told him that he was to be on guard that night and that they all had had their heads torn off.

The old man said, "Don't worry, young man, all you have to do is to take this piece of blessed chalk and this of blessed clothes and to mark the place where you sit." (He was to make a circle round the place where he sat.) And then the old man told him not to be afraid from twelve to one o'clock. "When she jumps out of the coffin, she will call, 'I know that you are here, but I cannot see you!' She will be rumbling all night, but she cannot see you. The first night will go past like this."

The next morning the king wanted to see if anything had happened to him. He went there with his soldiers. He was glad to find him still alive and asked him to endure it for two more nights.

The next day the soldier asked again for leave. He went to the forest from three to four o'clock, and there he met the old man again. The old man gave him the advice to hide behind the organ during the coming night; but he told him again to mark the place with a circle, so that she could not approach. At twelve o'clock she again jumped out of the coffin. "I know that you are here, but I cannot see you!" She walked about like that from twelve to one o'clock; then she had to go back into her coffin.

The next morning the king went again to fetch the soldier, and he was glad to find him alive. And then he told him that if he would hold out for one more night, she would be alive like a human being. He would have saved her and might marry her.

On the third day the soldier took leave again and went to the old man. He asked him to help him the last night. The old man told him to hide behind the altar. She would then become most furious. She would run up and down and search all over. As soon as she ran about, he was immediately to lie down in the coffin. When she approached, she would ask him to get out of the coffin.[1] But he should not do so until she tried to pull him out. At this moment he should catch her forefinger and bite it vigorously.

And thus he saved her, and she was completely human again.

Full of joy, they both went to the altar. When her father came with his soldiers, he found the two kneeling by the altar. He was very glad and said to his son-in-law, "Now she will become your wife."

When they reached home, a great feast was given. They celebrated their wedding, and if they have not died since, they are alive to this very day.

•24• *The Tale of the Fäderäwisch*

• BÄRBELI WAS SITTING on a tiny chair and Marily had crawled to her mother's knee. The tale was finished, but the small listeners remained spellbound.

"Now then," said the mother, "we are going to bed!"

But Hans begged, "Still the tale of the Fäderäwisch!"

"You silly boy," said his mother, "then you will again be afraid at night."

But Hans would not give in, and finally the mother told them the tale.

In the deep forest there was once a house where a little man lived. Everything around belonged to him, and he was very

---

[1] The German text changes from indirect speech into direct narration here.

rich. One fine day he came to a peasant who lived on the border of the forest and who had three pretty daughters.

He said to the peasant, "Peasant, give me one of your daughters for a wife."

At first, the peasant did not want to. But when he considered that the little man was very rich, he gave him the eldest one. The little man took her to the forest.

The next year he came again and said, "Peasant, my wife has died."

The peasant gave him the second one.

But the year after this the little man came again and said, "Peasant, the second one has died, too."

Now the peasant gave him the youngest one.

The youngest one liked to stay with the little man. She had everything in abundance. The little man gave her a key to every room, but there was one room which she was not allowed to open. She was curious to know all about this room, and one day when the little man was gone, she opened the door. Terror-stricken, she nearly fell down. Her two sisters were hanging from the ceiling—long, stiff, and dead! In her fright she did not know what to do. The little man might be back any moment. At last she had an idea. She took off her clothes, rolled herself first in honey, and then in bed-feathers, and then ran out of the house. She had gone on for only a little while when she met the little man.

But he did not recognize her and said, "Whereto, wherefrom, you featherfoot?"

"I'm coming from the midget's house."

"What is my dear bride doing?"

"Stands by the hearth and makes pap."

The little man went on.

The girl, however, went to her father and told him everything. He went to the wood with other peasants, and they set the house on fire and hanged the little man on a tree. He is still hanging there today, unless he has fallen down in the meantime.

Again the small listeners were spellbound, again Hans pleaded for a while, "One more tale!"

But this time he had no success.

"That will do," said the mother, and that settled it. The children were put to bed, and soon the old ones, too, were lying under the high featherbeds.

·25· *The Girl Who Married the Devil*

· THERE WAS A LOVELY but finicky girl. No man in the whole region was good enough for her. She wanted to have an especially noble suitor.

Once there came a man with a pointed moustache and pomaded hair who looked particularly elegant and smart. He put up at the inn, spat out in a wide bow with the other fellows, and showed off. "I'll have this girl whom you are all running after!"

And he set to work. He went to the girl's house, and he was successful. The girl liked him.

She said to her mother, "Mother, there's somebody for me. This is just what I wanted! I like this man."

The mother was a little cleverer than the girl. She did not trust the windbag. She was afraid that he might deceive the girl.

The girl said, "Nonsense! What do you know, old woman! I shall always be as well off as you!"

The fellow urged her to marry him; he did not want to wait. The girl was given a dowry like no one else in the whole region. The bridegroom came on horseback; the coach followed to fetch the bride. Everybody was standing there open mouthed. The girls were not a little envious of her.

Her mother cried; she did not want to let her go with this fellow. When the girl was sitting in the coach, she gave her two little dogs. She said, "If anything happens to you, you may send me one of them." The dogs' names were Mulli and Jolli.

The bridegroom sat down beside the girl, and they left. And now a light dawned upon the girl. She said, "You smell as if you were burned! Why do you stink like this?"

He tucked away one of his feet under the seat. He said, "You will have to get used to my odor! If you come to my castle everything will smell like this!"

All of a sudden they saw the castle standing on a mountain. She had not expected it to be so fine. The doorkeeper ushered her in and led her to her rooms. The girl closed the door. She was cautious because her mother had warned her. She thought, there is something wrong! She sent one of the dogs, Mulli, home. "Hurry to mother and tell her to come and help me!" Well, the little dog left.

Meanwhile the bridegroom came up and called, "Are you ready at last?"

The girl called, "You will have to wait a moment!" She grew more and more anxious. She looked out of the window to see if Mulli was coming back with somebody.

Then the fellow came again and called, "If you don't get ready in short order, I will come in! I'll give you five minutes!" Then he left again. But now Jolli was talking to Mulli.

He called, "Mulli, where are you? Will you soon be here?"

Mulli replied, "Wait a moment. We are coming. The pastor, the mother, the mayor, and all his people are on the way to fetch her!" The girl cheered up.

But now the bridegroom came upstairs with an ax and called, "Are you ready?"

She answered, "Wait a minute! I'm getting ready and then I'll come!"

The devil called, "I've had enough of this!" He hit the door so hard with his ax that he did not hear Mulli and the people arrive.

When they heard the bangs from outside, they had an idea what was going on. They saw at once that they had to deal with the devil. The pastor, moreover, noticed the burned smell, and he knew right away what was the matter. From downstairs he made the sign of the cross upon the bridegroom, who had just struck the last blow on the door. When the devil saw the cross, he uttered a frightful curse and was gone.

The pastor took the girl's hand, and they quickly ran downstairs. As they went out of the house, a roaring and rolling sounded inside as if there were crowds of devils there.

The girl threw her arms round her mother's neck and said, "Mother, you were right! I will not be so exacting any more; I will take the first suitor from the region who comes—even if he be bowlegged!"

.26. *The Devil's Wife as Godmother*

• ONCE A MAN had a lot of children, and he did not know where to find godmothers. He therefore said to his wife, "I will go out in the street, and the first woman I meet must become a godmother." This is what he did.

In the street he met a miserable, ragged beggar. He took her home with him. At home his wife said, "What are you doing with this miserable beggar?" and sent her away. But outside the door she became a beautiful white lady, shining with marvelous splendor. They hurried out and wanted to bring her back, but she has disappeared; it had been the Holy Mother.

Now the man went out in the street again. He met a tall, beautiful woman. He asked her if she would not be a godmother. She said, "Oh yes, I will." He took her home with him.

As the child was baptized, the godmother said, "When the child is twelve years old, send her to me."

When the girl reached twelve years, she went to the godmother, who lived in a big, marvelous house. When she entered the door, three fiery men, who were cutting fiery wood, stood there. She went upstairs, and a fiery maid, who was washing fiery linen, stood there. She went up another stairs, and a fiery maid, who was holding a child in the chimney, stood there. Then she got to the room where her godmother lived. She rang, but the little bell spat fire at her. She repeated it three times, and each time it spat fire at her. She looked through the keyhole and saw her godmother with a horse's head on her shoulders.

She entered, and her godmother quickly threw the horse's head under the bed. Then she fetched a heap of food for her. But the child was terrified and could not eat. The godmother told her, "Eat and drink with relish!"

The child replied, "I cannot eat; I cannot drink with relish."
She said, "Why not?"

The girl said, "When I came in, fiery men, who were cutting fiery wood, stood there."

The godmother said, "Oh you silly child, they were our men; eat and drink with relish."

"I cannot eat, I cannot drink with relish."

"Why not?"

"When I came up the stairs, a fiery maid, who was washing fiery linen, stood there."

And her godmother said again, "Oh you silly child, it was but our maid who was washing; eat and drink with relish!"

"I cannot eat; I cannot drink with relish."

"Why not?"

"When I came up the second stairs, a fiery maid, who was holding a child in the chimney, stood there, and when I got to the door, the little bell spit fire at me."

The godmother said, "You stupid child, that was our maid. This is all nonsense."

But the child said, "When I came in here, you had a horse's head on your shoulders." At these words, the godmother went over and wrung the child's neck. The house was hell; the child's godmother was the devil's wife.

·27· *Mrizala and Her Bridegroom, Death*

· ONCE THERE LIVED a very respectable couple in a village. They had only one child, a daughter. As she became most beautiful, she grew very haughty. She had many suitors, but none seemed good enough for matrimony. One was too poor; the other one not handsome enough. This lasted for many years until the suitors stayed away by-and-by. She became an old spinster and did not get a husband. The younger girls laughed at her and mocked her; so she locked herself up in her room. One day she was crying bitterly. She was sick of life, and as her mother harassed her as

well, she uttered in her anger the following curse: "I wish
Death would come and marry me!"

No sooner had she pronounced this wish than her right
shoulder was touched by somebody from behind and she was
called by name. She started up in fright and thought, if this is
Death, then I am lost! He alone can know that my name is
Mrizala! She plucked up her courage, turned round, and found
a very pale but good-looking fellow standing there. He was
laughing all the while and telling her stories, and she almost
forgot having wished Death to become her husband. She wanted
to make sure that he really was Death. When he fell asleep in
his chair with fatigue, she secretly put a thread around his foot,
fixed it to a big ball of thread, and then she waited to see what
happened.

When the stranger woke up, he said goodbye and left. Mrizala
sneaked after him and saw that he went toward the church. She
followed him, for she wanted to know what he was doing there
at that time of the night. She could see him through the keyhole,
and she saw that he was roasting children with his comrades.
She was terribly frightened, ran home, and locked herself in her
room. Nobody could console her, for now she knew that Death
was her bridegroom. But she dared not tell her mother.

After a week there was a knocking at her window at midnight and a well-known voice called, "Mrizala, Mrizala, what
did you see from the church sill through the keyhole?"

"I saw nothing!" she replied trembling.

"If you don't tell me," Death went on, "your father will die
this very night."

Mrizala was taken aback, but as she knew that her father was
in good health, she answered, "If he dies, we shall have him
buried."

The next morning she got up very early and prepared the soup.
After a short while her mother came, too, and as they wanted to
let their father sleep a little longer, they ate alone. But when it
was nine o'clock and the father was still asleep, Mrizala said to
her mother, "Father is very late today. I will go and see if he is
really sleeping." When she came to his room, she found her
father still lying in bed and very ill looking. She approached and

shook him, but he did not stir; he slept forever. Mrizala started wailing and weeping, and when her mother heard her, she came, too.

She consoled Mrizala, "It is all right. Don't cry; sooner or later he had to die. Even if he has died very early, you must not cry. We shall have him buried." So Mrizala dried her tears, went to the priest, and had her father buried.

After another week Death again knocked at her window at midnight, "Mrizala, Mrizala, what did you see from the church sill through the keyhole?"

"Nothing. I have seen nothing," she answered again.

"If you don't tell me," replied Death, "your mother will have to die this very night."

But Mrizala remained silent this time as well and did not believe Death. However, what Death had foretold came about the same night. Her mother died. Mrizala wailed and lamented very much and thought she would be unable to live without her parents. After the burial she locked herself up in her room and cried so hard that the hardest stones would have melted.

After another week Death knocked again at her window at midnight and said in a soft voice, "Mrizala, Mrizala, my golden treasure, my bride, now tell me, what did you see from the church sill through the keyhole?" Mrizala remained silent and gave no answer. "Mrizala, my golden treasure, my bride, if you don't tell me today what you saw from the church sill, then I will lead you to your bridal bed this very night," said Death. But Mrizala remained silent. She died at midnight, and Death jubilantly fetched his bride.

When Mrizala, the bride of Death, had been buried for three days, a marvelous blood-red rose grew from her grave. It happened that a young prince came riding past with his servant and saw the marvelous blood-red rose on the grave. The prince ordered his servant to pick the rose. But the servant replied, "Sir, let this marvelous blood-red rose wither on the grave; it has been growing out of a maiden's heart. She might come and ask for your heart at midnight." But the prince insisted, and the servant had to carry out his order. However, he could not cut the rose, for she defended herself with her thorns. The prince dismounted, went to the rose, and lo! the thorns suddenly were gone. He could easily pick it. He put it on his hat, and they went on.

When the prince arrived at home, his parents were just eating their supper. He showed them the marvelous blood-red rose and put it with his hat on the table, where it emitted a lovely smell. He did not enjoy his supper, for he was looking at the rose and thinking of what his servant had said. His soup, his roast, and his wine remained untouched. Then he fell asleep in the middle of his thoughts and dreamed of a lovely maiden.

The next morning, when he got up, his throat was very dry; so he went immediately to the dining room to drink his wine. But the beaker was empty, and the soup and the roast were gone, too. He went to his father, who called all the servants and asked them if they had done it. Now the prince's servant stepped forth and said, "Your Majesty, the marvelous blood-red rose on the prince's hat did it at midnight. She will rob his heart." They all laughed at him. Only the prince was very serious; he could not stop thinking of this story.

After supper (the rose was still in her old place), the prince again left his soup, his roast, and his wine and hid in a corner, waiting for things to happen. When the keeper of the tower had called the twelfth hour, he heard music in the room and then a rustling noise on the table. The marvelous blood-red rose became a very beautiful girl. She washed her face, put on a fine white bridal gown, and then ate the soup and the roast and drank the wine. Afterward she became a rose again and was fixed on his hat.

Early in the morning he went to his father and told him everything. His father sent for his counselor, who opened an old book and read a page, "Death's bride can only be won by him who picks a blood-red rose from a grave, who receives her hospitably, and who holds her back in the twelfth hour." The prince knew enough. He again left his food and drink at supper and hid in a corner of the dining room.

At midnight the rose emitted an especially lovely fragrance. She again became a marvelous maiden, ate, and drank, but now the prince could not keep back. He embraced her suddenly and held her like this until one o'clock, and thus she could not transform herself into a rose any more.

There was great joy in the palace and a big wedding was soon celebrated. The prince forgot completely that he had married the bride of Death. Nine months went by in happiness. Then the young queen, who was nobody other than Mrizala, gave birth to a most beautiful child.

When she was nursing it at midnight, suddenly there was a knocking at her window and a well-known voice asked, "Mrizala, Mrizala, what have you done to me, your bridegroom? Now tell me at last, what you saw from the church sill through the keyhole on the night of our engagement?"

"Oh my bridegroom, I saw nothing, nothing at all in church," she replied.

"Mrizala, my bride, now your child has to go with me as well," he went on and strangled the young life.

In the morning she told her husband everything. Now he remembered his servant's words and trembled for his wife's life. He had all the windows and doors of the palace guarded, and before the bedroom of his wife, who was wailing over her lost child, a regiment of soldiers were placed on guard in order to save her from Death. But all this did not help, for not even a thousand regiments can get the better of Death.

And thus it happened that after a week she heard again the knocking at the window and a voice implored her, "Mrizala, my golden treasure, my bride, now tell me what did you see from the church sill through the keyhole in the night of our engagement. If you don't tell me, your husband will have to die tonight." Mrizala screamed with fear, "If my husband is saved, I will tell you, but you must never again call yourself my bridegroom. You were roasting children with your comrades!"

Now Death was standing before her. He took his ring off his finger and said, "Take this ring as a souvenir of our engagement, and remember that silence is not always opportune, even if cunning be used. Your parents and your child could still be alive, but now they will be my souvenir of our period of engagement.

But you live happily with your husband, who has redeemed you! We shall meet again."

They lived happily together for many years and were never afraid of Death. But their children lost the ring. Should you find it, bring it back to Death, and your reward—easy departure from this world—will not fail to come.

•28• *The Three Traveling Artisans*

• THREE TRAVELING ARTISANS went together into the world. They decided to work in the same town, and if this would not be possible, to move to another place. As they were going along, they met a man who asked them what they were up to. They told him that they were looking for work. He proposed that they go with him and work for him for a whole year. He promised them plenty to eat and to drink.

He led them to a room where there was a table with a red linen tablecloth and a coffeepot and a coffeecup on it. Then he told them that they would be free if they could guess what this was. If they did not find out, they would have to stay with him forever, for he was the devil. After this he left and was seen no more.

The three artisans led a happy life. They ate and drank to their heart's content and did not worry about anything. Soon the time they had been given to answer the question, one year and six weeks, was almost over. The shoemaker and the smith were soon asleep, and only the tailor was still awake. He thought, you had better leave. He set out and came to a fir tree in a forest. Lying underneath the fir tree, he suddenly heard a noise overhead. Well, thought the tailor, tomorrow the time will be over; this certainly is the devil who comes to fetch me!

However, on this fir tree all the devils happened to meet, and Lucifer asked the others about their achievements. At last it was the turn of the tailor's devil. He was a crooked fellow. He came forth and said, "I am sure to have three: a shoemaker, a smith, and a tailor." Then Lucifer asked the crooked devil what task he had given the three. He told him and said that they would certainly not be able to find out. Lucifer wanted to know all about it. The crooked devil explained everything, "The red linen tablecloth is the skin of a horse; the coffeepot is the horse's head; and the coffeecup is the horse's hips." When the tailor under the tree heard this, he rose immediately and went back to the others. When he reached them, the two had lost their senses. There was nothing to be done.

Then the devil came and asked them if they knew the answer. He saw that two of them were lying in the corner and did not move any more. He asked the tailor what was the matter with them. The tailor told him, "They are drunk. Leave them alone." The devil asked him whether they knew the answer. "Of course," answered the tailor, "they know it as well as I do. Just leave them where they are." Then the tailor went to the table, he sniffed and pulled at the red linen tablecloth, and there was a horse's skin lying in the room. Then he sniffed at the coffeecup and threw it down, and there were the horse's hips; then he sniffed at the coffeepot and threw it down, and there was the horse's head. When they saw this, the two jumped up.

So the devil had caught none of them. He proposed to the three fellows to stay for another year with him; they would have nothing to do but to travel through the world and to say, "Fill the glass for the money; that's all right."

Then the three fellows came to a large town and went to a big hotel. The first one said, "Fill the glass for the money; that's all right!" There was a rich merchant staying in this place. Now the innkeeper said to his wife, "This merchant has quite a lot of money with him, and the three fellows say nothing but 'Fill your glass for the money; that's all right'; we are going to kill the merchant, and it will be pinned on the three artisans."

In the morning everybody knew that the merchant had been killed. Everybody said that only the artisans could have done it. They were brought before the judge where they were to make a deposition. Now the first one stepped forth and said, "Fill the glass for the money; that's all right."

The judge said, "All right, that will do." He decided that the three artisans should be hanged, and they were brought to the gallows.

As the first one was placed on the scaffold, someone whizzed through the air, waving a white cloth and shouting, "Pardon! Pardon!" When he came near, he said that the three were innocent and that the merchant had been killed by the innkeeper and his wife. When the innkeeper heard this, he jumped with his wife into the watering trough.

Meanwhile, the year ended, and the three were free. The devil asked them to stay for another year. The tailor was quite willing, but the others did not want to stay any longer. So the devil paid them off, and the tailor entered his service once more. The devil told him that for a whole year he was to wear a sack, and that he would not be allowed to wash himself or to blow his nose. The tailor agreed and set out.

He came to a large town, and there was a king who had three daughters. It was known that any rich man who would come and pay the king's debts would get one of the daughters. The tailor said that he would be just the man; he would pay the whole debt if he was given one of the daughters. So the tailor went to the king, presented himself, and said that he wanted to have one of the daughters and that he was willing to pay the debts.

Now the tailor was presented to the first daughter, but she did not want him. When she saw the tailor in his sack, with his black face and dirty nose, she was disgusted. Then the second one came. When she saw him, she said, "Fie! I don't want him!"

Finally, the third one came along and said, "All right, if it has to be and if he is willing to pay the debts, I shall not mind." Meanwhile, the tailor's time was almost over. The tailor married the princess. And after a short while, the sack fell off and he could wash himself.

Then the tailor was cleaned and washed thoroughly. After he had been cleaned up, they saw what a handsome fellow he was. The two sisters were so jealous for not having got him that they jumped into the water and drowned themselves.

The Three Brothers

• ONCE THERE WERE three brothers who resembled each other so much that they could not be told apart. They went into the world together because they did not like to stay at home, their father and mother being dead. Each of them had a knapsack full of provisions, and for their protection, the eldest one had taken his father's bow and arrow and the second one his father's sword. Hans, the youngest one, whom they used to tease and whom they thought not very clever but strong, had taken an old big iron-bound stick. After they had been walking along for some time, they came to a big tree where three paths separated. The eldest one said to the others, "Brothers, now we have to part, for we cannot stay together all the time," and the others agreed. Since Hans had nothing left in his knapsack, he was given a little by his brothers, and before separating, they all put their knives into the tree and they decided that he who first came back to this place should look at the knives. If he found one of the knives particularly rusty, he would know that its owner was in difficulty, and he was to go along that one's way in order to help him if he was still alive. When this was settled, the oldest brother went to the right, the second one took the middle path, and Hans went to the left.

Now let us see what happened to the eldest son. The oldest one, who had gone to the right, went on and on in the forest, and as the way did not seem to end, he sat down, opened his knapsack, and started eating from his rich provisions. Suddenly he saw a little old man with an old greenish coat and hat come toward him, watch him eat, and behave as if he wanted to get something.

He threw a little piece of bread toward the little man, who took it quickly, approached, and said, "As you have given me a little bit, I will reward you a little," and with these words he touched his bow and arrow and said, "Whatever you want to shoot, your arrow will hit and never miss its aim." With this the little man disappeared behind the next tree.

The fellow took his knapsack and went on. Suddenly in the

middle of the forest, he saw a big, old-looking castle on a high
rock. Beneath the castle, two giants roasted a young ox on a stick
over a huge fire. A third giant was standing nearby, cutting a
piece out of the meat with his sword in order to taste if it was
thoroughly roasted. At first the hunter, the oldest brother, was
frightened, but then he took courage and said to himself that he
wanted to find out if the little man had lied to him. And he shot
the piece of meat that the giant wanted to eat right out of his
hand. The giants looked at each other and looked around to
find out where the arrow might have come from, but they saw
nothing. When the ox was roasted and the giants had divided it
up, he shot again, but this time the giant held his meat fast, and
therefore the arrow got stuck, and the giants saw where the
archer was.

One of them went right over and said, "You miserable
earthworm, you deserve death, but since you are such a good
archer, we will let you live; but you will have to serve us." He
took him and put him into his pocket, which was so big that the
hunter could hardly look out of it. The giant then went back
to his comrades.

When the evening came, they went closer to the castle and told
the archer that as soon as the sun set, a little dog would come out
of the castle and that he would have to shoot it before it started
barking; if he failed, he would be put to death. He was terribly
frightened, of course, for he had only one arrow left. And indeed,
as the sun was setting, the little dog came out, and he shot it.
There was a hole in the wall of the castle where the giants
wanted to get in, but they were not able to, because the hole was
too small. So they gave him a sword and told him to creep inside
and to try to sneak by the animals in the castle yard; in the
middle room he would find a sleeping princess, and in her right
golden slipper there would be a key which he should bring them.

Entering the castle, he went along many marvelous corridors
and rooms where he saw valuables, riches, and other objects
which fascinated him so much that he got to the princess only
after looking at them for rather a long time. He tried to take the
slipper off her foot, but she awoke and called, "Help me, deliver
me from the giants!" He therefore left the slipper on her foot,

unable to resist her request, for she was too beautiful. He went back to the hole in the wall where the giants stood waiting outside and told them to help him; he could not subdue the wild animals alone because the sword was too heavy for him. If he pulled from inside and the others pushed from outside, they would certainly manage to get in. Thus he persuaded the giants. As the first one was halfway inside, he cut his head off with the sword that he held ready, pulled him completely inside, and let him fall to the floor; he did the same with the second one; the third one, however, got stuck in the wall, as nobody pushed from outside, and he thrust the sword into his throat. Then he cut out their tongues, put them into his knapsack, and went back to the princess; but there everything had changed.

The princess was no longer alone. There were several male and female servants. Music was played and songs were sung. The princess was very kind. When the eldest son asked her what all this meant, she told him that a feast was going to be celebrated, because she would soon be delivered. She, her castle and everything inside had been enchanted by her father. He had to stay with her for seven days; he could not leave, since there was no exit to be found and he could not remove the giant from the hole in the wall. In the seventh night she offered him a ring as her bridegroom, and they slept together as husband and wife. When he woke up, everything had disappeared. Only the three dead giants were lying by his side.

Thus he went away through the wood. He was hungry; he had no provisions—no arrow to shoot with. Exhausted, he sat down. Again a little man with a greenish coat and hat came and asked what was the matter. "Hunger and fatigue prevent me from walking, and I cannot find the way out of the woods."

The little man replied, "I have nothing to eat; otherwise, I would give it to you, but I can show you the way to the inn nearby." He followed the little man out of the wood, where he saw a town.

The town was full of garlands and flowers. A great feast was being celebrated. He went to the next inn, where his second brother was sitting. He asked him how he had come there. "I came here yesterday. Tomorrow there is a feast in the king's castle, and I will stay here that long, for I want to get some of the roast." And then he related, "When we separated, I took the middle road and went through an endless forest; when I was having lunch, a little man turned up. He kept turning around. He seemed to be hungry, and so I threw him a little piece of bread; he thanked me, and in return, he made my sword victorious. With this, he vanished. I went on and soon got out of the wood and came to this town. Here everybody was in deep mourning, just as today everybody is full of mirth. A dragon and three giants haunted the place. The former devoured everybody within reach; the latter took by force what they needed, especially cattle. So I went out of the town to the fountain and cut off the dragon's seven heads and put the seven tongues into my knapsack. A royal servant saw the dead dragon and pretended to be the victor. In his honor the feast is arranged; if he kills the three giants, too, he gets the king's daughter."

Now the older one said, "I have killed the giants; here are the three tongues as a sign." Joyfully they ate and drank.

Early in the morning the second brother went to the king and proved by means of the tongues to be the dragon killer, and he announced that his brother had vanquished the giants.

There was a great fuss, and the servant was captured. The elder brother was ordered to come. Then there was a quarrel as to who was to marry the princess. The elder one renounced her, and the second one was to have her. A great feast was celebrated. They lived together for one year. The elder brother remained with them.

The queen asked them about the third brother, and they asked her about her brothers and sisters. She was said to have two sisters. Their father wanted to have the three of them married on one day. He had the two elder ones and their castles bewitched by a sorcerer. The youngest one, his favorite, was allowed to stay with him. The others would remain enchanted until a man delivered and married them.

They wanted to go hunting, but the queen warned them of the enchanted forest outside the town, "Many have gotten in, but none has come back." Nevertheless, they went deep into the wood and lost their way.

The oldest one said, "If only I had my arrows!"

The next oldest replied, "Had I but taken my sword!" It was getting dark. The forest was full of wild animals. At last they found a hollow tree for their night's rest. They lit a fire and sat down. There came an old woman and asked for permission to warm herself; they let her do so. Suddenly she took a stick from underneath her coat and hit the fire, which then went out. Though alive, the two were like stone, unable to move.

Meanwhile the youngest brother was going on endlessly through the wood. He sat down and ate the little that was left in his knapsack. He saw a little man and called him. He invited him to eat with him and gave him half of what he had.

"Since you have given me that much, you shall be luckier than the others." The little man took a little stick and said, "With this you knock on the earth if you are in trouble, and I shall help you." Then he vanished.

Hans went on and on. It was night again; he came to a mountain that was full of shrubs, and there he lay down to sleep. When morning came, he knocked on the earth in order to call the little man. The little man came out of a shrub, "This is an enchanted castle; do you wish to get in? But be careful and do not let the stick out of your hand." He showed him the way, and Hans followed. They reached the castle yard where they found men on horseback and animals not moving and as if they were made of stone. They went into the castle and entered the rooms.

In one of the rooms they found a cat lying on the bench, but it did not move. A woman was sitting by the spinning wheel like a rock with the spindle in her hand, but she did not spin. In the second room there was a clock on the wall, but it did not work; in the kitchen there was a fire, but it did not burn. The roast was in the oven, but it did not fry; pots were on the fire, but they did not boil. Then they came into the third room, which was full of precious things, and this was where the princess slept. But she did not breathe; she was neither dead nor alive.

Then the youngest brother wanted to get out of the castle again, but he could find no door. He looked in the kitchen for food, found some, and ate. Suddenly the clock struck eleven. The cat started mewing; the fire burned; the roast began to fry, the pots to boil. He thought, well, things are beginning to move in the castle. The woman spinned; the princess was awake. He talked to her and looked out of the window, where he saw a most beautiful garden. They went for a walk and came back at twelve o'clock, and everything was as before eleven o'clock. Again he could not get out. He had to wait until eleven o'clock. In the meantime he had something to eat.

At eleven o'clock everything was as the day before; everything was astir, they went for a walk again, and he told the princess that he would like to leave. "You cannot go away any more, even if you wish to." So he stayed for a whole year, and always from eleven to twelve o'clock everything was alive.

One day as they went again for a walk he struck the rosebush with his stick, and the little man came out of it. He told him, "I want to go away."

The little man said, "You cannot leave, but I will help you to redeem everything. Your brothers are enchanted, and a son has been born today to the second one. But follow me!" The little man lead him into the lower passage among the wild animals; he was to keep them back with his stick as they retreated. If he met fire, he was to strike it and walk right through it. At the end there was a snake which kept a green leaf in its mouth, and on the leaf there was a key. The little man told him to take it without fear; the snake would not do him any harm. He did as he was told and brought the key to the little man who was waiting. He went with him through the shrubs to a door he had never seen before. He opened it and was in the castle yard. All the stone figures were alive, and they led their horses to the stable as if they were coming back from hunting.

In the evening the little man went away. Hans went into the castle. Before leaving, the little man told him, "Your oldest brother's son is seven weeks old; the second brother's son is seven days old; yours is seven hours old." Full of joy, he ran upstairs. The spinning woman was rocking the child; the princess met him before the bedroom. At night he asked her about her two sisters, but she did not know anything. He told her what he knew about his brothers. While they were eating, two strangers, who were looking for a night's shelter were announced. They were the two brothers, who had been standing as stone figures underneath the castle and who had now been redeemed and had followed the light from the windows.

Looking out of the window in the morning, the older one saw his castle in the forest of the three giants. The second one saw the town. They both hastened to go to find their wives and children.

They saw each other from their castles; they met frequently and lived a pleasant life; and if they are not dead, they live on to this very day.

The servant was torn into four pieces by four horses, and the four parts were placed on the four corners of the market place as a sign for people never to lie.

· 30 ·   *The Girl Out of the Egg*

• A LAD did not like any of the girls in his village, and thus he went to look for one elsewhere. His mother told him, "All right, go and look for one. If hunger will not bring you back, thirst will." He went through the wood for a while and soon got thirsty. Suddenly he saw a nest with three eggs in a tree. He climbed the tree and put the three eggs in his pocket. Then he went down and broke one open. A girl jumped out of it.

She said to him, "Give me some water. Then I am yours and you are mine."

But he had no water, and thus the girl disappeared. He went on for some time. Then he opened another egg, for he was very thirsty.

Again a girl jumped out of the egg—a beautiful girl—who said, "Give me some water. Then I am yours and you are mine."

But he had no water, and thus she disappeared. Now he carefully took the third egg to a garden with a well. He had some water ready in a goblet when he opened the egg, and as the girl asked for some water and said that she would then belong to him and he to her, he gave her the water. Now the girl could not slip away any more.

He told her, "I will fetch a carriage, for I want to bring you home in a manner suitable for a bride." Then he left.

The girl, who was very beautiful, sat waiting by the well. There came an old witch with her daughter. She took the girl's fine clothes and gave them to her gypsy daughter. The girl jumped into the well and became a fish. When the fellow came back, the girl looked different; she was very ugly.

The witch had told her daughter, "When he comes back, you must tell him this: 'I have come out of the egg. The sun was shining on me, and therefore, I am all black. If I clean myself in my room, I shall be fair again!'"

When they reached home in the carriage, his mother said, "There, you bring a nice gypsy!"

The gypsy fell ill. "Go to the well; there is a fish. Catch it; I want to eat it. Then I will be as beautiful as before."

He emptied the well to catch the fish and to kill it. The gypsy ate it up. But she was as black as ever. When she threw the fish bones away, there came a duck from the next farm and ate them up. The duck grew beautiful golden feathers, for the girl had worn golden clothes. The woman from the next farm, where the duck came from, put the feathers into a pot when she plucked the duck. She used to go to church. When she came back, everything was gone. There was no food left on the table. When it happened again, she was on watch. She left, closed the door, and looked through the keyhole. Out of the pot with the feathers there came the girl from the egg. She sat down and ate up everything. The woman went in and caught the girl. She touched her, so that she could not withdraw. And thus the girl was delivered.

The woman went stripping quills every day in the house of the fellow who had found the girl in the egg. One day the girl said, "Let me go this time."

The old woman replied, "You cannot go there. The master of the house might see you and keep you there."

The girl said, "I shall put on ugly clothes. He will not look at me."

But he recognized her at once. As they were sitting by the table, stripping quills, he sat down with them, "Well, ladies, now you all tell a story. You certainly know a lot." So they all told a story. When it was the girl's turn, he said, "Now you tell your story."

"I know nothing, only a dream."

"All right, a dream will do as well."

She began her story: A young man did not like the girls of his village, so he set out to find one elsewhere. He found three eggs . . . and she told the whole story up to the moment where he went to fetch a carriage for her and left. "Then I woke up and I do not know what happened afterward." Thus he knew who she was and what had happened to her.

"Go on, my child, try to remember!" She went on.

The gypsy was walking up and down in her room, "Man, what are you doing with the girls? Why don't you go to sleep?"

But he paid no attention to her and listened to the story. Then he locked the gypsy up in her room, so that she could not leave. "I will ask my mother-in-law what kind of death a person deserves for such a scheme!" He went to his mother-in-law. "What kind of death does a person deserve who takes away a man's bride, throws her into the water, and gives him an ugly false toad instead?"

"She deserves to be put into a barrel with nails and to be rolled down from the highest mountain."

And this is what the man did. He had a barrel prepared with nails, put the witch and the gypsy inside, and let them roll down from the highest mountain. Then he married the girl who was his real bride.

I heard this story from my late mother.

Part IV
Tales of Bravery and Fidelity, Patience and Righteousness

· 31 ·   The Cruel Stepmother

· ONCE THERE WAS a man whose wife had died and had left him two children, a boy and a girl. He was so poor that he sent them begging in order to find their bread at the door of kindhearted people. One day they came to an unmarried woman who gave them something to eat and who charged them to tell their father to marry her. "When I am your mother," she said, "you will have pancakes every day." Now the children persuaded their father to marry this kind person, and he gave in and took her for a wife. On the first day the children were given the promised pancakes; on the second day they only got bread; and on the third, merely water.

The first night the woman said to the man, "Take these children out of the house. I can't bear them." So in the morning the father sadly took his children and led them into the woods. But the girl was more clever than her little brother. She took a handful of ash with her and spread it on their way. Having gone deep into the woods by different paths, the father ordered them to gather wood until he came back; he would go farther into the forest in order to fell trees. The sound of his ax would let them know where he was.

The children remained alone. But the father went and hung his stick on a tree. Then he went home. The stick kept knocking on the tree and, therefore, the children thought that their father was still near them. When it grew dark and their father still had not come back, they followed the sound, found the stick which knocked against the tree, but could not find their father. They were afraid and looked for the trace of ash which the girl had spread on the path, and thus they got back home. However, they dared not enter, but remained in the kitchen. Their parents were just having supper, and they heard the stepmother saying, "There is a lot of food left. If your children were here, they could eat it."

At this moment the children leaped forward and called, "Here we are!"

Their father cried with joy to have his children again. Only the stepmother was white with anger and fury, and she quarreled even more in the morning and threatened her husband, "If you don't get your dogs out of my sight, I shall kill them!"

So he sadly led his children for the second time into the woods. This time the girl took peas with her, which she spread on the way, in order to find their way back. When they were again in the middle of the woods, they did not want to stay alone until their father promised to take them back with him. He again put the stick on the tree and left without the children noticing it. When it got dark and the father still had not come back, the children went to the tree from which the sound was coming and as they did not find their father, they set out to go back and tried to follow the peas. But the peas had been eaten by the birds. So they did not find their way back and had to stay in the forest.

The next morning they tried to go back by choosing a direction at random, but they wandered farther and farther from home. After walking for a long time, they began to suffer from hunger and thirst. Finally they came to a spring. The boy wanted to drink, but the spring warned him and said, "Do not drink from me, or you'll become a black bear." The girl, too, asked him not to drink, for she would then be all alone and would not know what to do. The boy did not drink, and they went on until they came to another spring. The brother was terribly thirsty again, and the girl, therefore, asked the spring if they might drink.

The spring replied, "Yes, drink from me; you'll become a golden stag with a ribbon of silk." Thus the boy drank, and he became a golden stag and was led by the girl.

They came to a hollow beech tree and remained there, for inside they found a comfortable little room. The Holy Virgin came every day and brought them food. Nearby there was a castle. Once the lord dreamed that he was to go to the forest where he would find a girl and a golden stag in a hollow tree. He did as he was told, and when he was in the woods, he saw that his little dog ran barking around a tree. He approached and found the girl with the golden stag. The girl had in the meantime grown up and was marvelously beautiful. The lord of the castle wanted to marry her. She agreed on the condition that the little stag should eat what she ate, should stay where she stayed, and should never be separated from her. Her wish was granted.

After a while the young wife fell ill. Her nurse would have liked to become the mistress herself, and as she looked very much like her, she threw her out of the window at night, took her place in bed, and sent for her mother to nurse her. The lady of the castle, however, was caught by the Holy Virgin and hidden in her cloak.

The lord sent for the sick wife to ask what she wanted to eat. She asked for the golden stag's lung and liver. The little stag was therefore brought to the bridge that led over the castle moat where he could be slaughtered.

But when the butcher wanted to kill him, the little stag started talking and said,

> Sister mine, deep in the lake,
> You and I are forsaken,
> My lung and liver shall be taken.[1]

The sister's voice answered from the water,

> Brother dear, high on the bridge,
> You and I are forsaken,
> Your lung and liver shall be taken.[2]

In the presence of this miracle the little stag was brought back to the castle. But the sick woman was asking more anxiously than ever for the little stag's lung and liver.

Now the lord of the castle went down to the bridge himself, and there he saw his lawful wife in the water. He pulled her out and learned what had happened to her. She was brought to the castle, while the false wife was burned at the stake.

[1] O Schwesterl in dem tiefen See
Ich und Du sind vergessen,
Mein Lungerl und Leberl wird gegessen.

[2] Brüderl auf der hohen Bruck,
Ich und Du sind vergessen,
Dein Lungerl und Leberl wird gegessen.

The Six Brothers

• ONCE A MOTHER had six children—all boys. When she was baking bread, the children wanted to have some. "Children, don't make me angry, or you shall become birds!" She had no sooner said so than the children became birds and flew out of the window.

Later on the woman had a girl. When the girl was seven years old, she wanted to know if she had any brothers and sisters. Her mother replied, "My dear, you had six brothers; they were very handsome!"

"Dear mother, where have my brothers gone?"

"Dear child, they have flown away; they have become birds!"

When the girl was twelve years old, she went looking for her brothers. She traveled and traveled until she came to the Night. The Night cooked her a hen for supper and told her to pick up all the bones and not to throw them away. Then she asked the Night to tell her where her brothers were.

"You must go to the Sun. She will tell you where your brothers are."

She went there and stayed for the night. The Sun cooked a hen for her, and again she was told to keep the bones. She again asked where her brothers were. The Sun said, "Go to the Wind. The Wind is everywhere. He knows where your brothers are."

She also stayed overnight with the Wind, and he cooked a hen for her as well. She was to eat the hen and keep the bones. Then the Wind asked her if she had all the bones.

"Yes."

"If you travel for three more years, you will come to where your brothers are." Then the Wind took a sled, put the girl on it, and blew her over the mountain. "My dear child, if you come to the mountain, make yourself a stair with the bones and climb the mountain!"

As the bones were all used up, she had to cut off her little finger in order to make the last step, and then she could get on top of the mountain. There she saw a little hut where her brothers were living. On the table there were six plates, six spoons, six forks, and six knives. She prepared the lunch.

When the six brothers came home, everything was ready on their plates. One of them said, "All right. Let's eat!"

The next one answered, "Then let's eat all at once. Should we get poisoned, then let's die together." But the meal tasted very good.

After the meal they went to see who was in their house, and they found their sister standing in a corner. "Dear little sister, what are you doing here?"

"I want to deliver you."

"Dear little sister, you cannot deliver us; you cannot carry it through!"

"Dear brothers, I will carry it through!"

"Then you must go into a hollow fir and sit there for three years without speaking to anybody."

She had been staying in the fir for two years when a hunter went hunting. His dog started yelping near the fir. The hunter went near and said, "If you are something good, come out; if you are something bad, then I shoot!" But there was no answer. He said for the third time, "This is the last time. Then I will shoot!"

The fir was all covered with cobwebs. He took the cobwebs away and found the girl lying naked inside. But she would not say a word. She was a very beautiful person, and he took his coat and gave it to her. Then he took the girl home, and she became his wife.

But he had to go soldiering, and she gave birth to a boy while he was away. He was a handsome boy. The hunter's mother was a witch, and she took the boy and threw him into the water and brought a cat instead. Then she wrote to her son that his wife had given birth, not to a boy but to a cat. She asked, "Is she to be killed or not?"

He wrote, "No, do not kill her; wait till I am back."

When he returned to soldiering, she had another boy. The witch wrote again that his wife had borne not a child but a dog. And she again threw the boy to the fish. She asked if she were to be killed this time.

But her son wrote, "No, it is not allowed!"

He returned home on leave for the third time, and after awhile his wife had another boy. It was the third one, and again the witch threw him into the water and wrote to her son, "Is she to be killed or not? This time it is a hare." He answered, "No mother. I will soon be home. Let her live."

When he came home, the girl could not speak yet. His mother wanted him to burn her, for she was no good. He was very sorry for her. But he carried thirty meters of wood to a meadow and put the girl inside. They lit a fire in order to burn her, but the fire would not burn. It kept going out all the time. He went home to get some fire. Before he came back, the six brothers had pulled her out of the wood. The hunter lit the fire, but the girl was already out of the wood.

The fire burned for a night and a day. When it was extinct, he felt very sorry and he dispersed the ash with the manure. He hoped at least to find one bone of his young wife, but he did not find a single one. He started crying, and suddenly it became dark. He did not know where he was. He came to a high fir and climbed on top of it. From this tree he saw a light. He went down and walked toward the light. He stayed in a house overnight and asked for supper. After the meal, he went to bed. But he was very much afraid, and he only pretended to sleep and put his right hand out of the bed.

The woman of the house said to her son, "Put your false father's hand back!"

Then he put his right foot out of the bed. Now the mother said to the second son, "My dear son, put your false father's foot back into the bed!"

But the little boy was too weak to put the foot back.

So the father put his foot back himself, got up, and said, "Is it you, my dear wife?"

"Yes, it is I!"

In the morning when it became light, he went home, leaving his wife and three children and the six brothers there. He fetched a big carriage, and they all got into it. There were eleven persons in the carriage. They went home, and he prepared a meal for all of them.

When everything was eaten up, he called his mother, "Well, dear mother, what sort of death do you deserve? You wanted to kill my wife, and you were telling lies. Dear mother, look at the children—the handsome boys—are they cats, hares, or dogs?"

He called the police. The police wanted to burn the woman, and this is what they did. They set up eighteen meters of wood and they burned the old witch. Then they celebrated the hunter's wedding for two days and two nights.

· 33 · The Feathers from the Bird Venus

· ONCE UPON A TIME there was a king who had a pretty daughter. She fell in love with a soldier who often stood guard in the castle. The soldier had a strong feeling for her, too, and they would have liked to get married. The king noticed that his daughter loved the soldier, and he would have liked to let her marry him, for the king loved her very much. But as the fellow was only a poor soldier, it could not be done, and he thought that he would remove him secretly.

So one day he sent for him and said, "I know about my daughter's love for you. Therefore, if you want to marry her, you must go to the bird Venus and bring me three of his golden feathers." He thought that the bird would eat him up.

The soldier, however, set out to find the bird Venus. First of all he came to another kingdom. The king there asked him where he wanted to go.

"To the bird Venus," was the answer.

"Well, if you go there, you might as well ask him about my lime trees." (You must know that the king had three lime trees standing before his house. They had been green but had now dried up.)

The soldier promised to do so. He was received hospitably and took a few days' rest. The king promised to make him a rich man if he could find out about the lime trees, and then the soldier left.

Then he came into another kingdom. This king also asked him where he wanted to go.

"To the bird Venus," he was told.

"If you go there, you could do me a favor. If you can fulfill my wish, I shall reward you richly."

The soldier promised to do so, and the king told him to ask the bird Venus why he was losing all his battles, whereas before he had always been victorious. The soldier promised to find out. After a rest, he left with a good provision of food and drink.

He soon came to a river and called the ferryman, "Ferryman ahoy!"

The ferryman came, took him into his boat, and asked him where he was going.

"To the bird Venus."

"Well, if you go there, ask him how long I am to ferry before I am relieved."

Then he set him down on the bird's island. The soldier mounted the steps and met the housekeeper, who was hanging linen on a rope. She was frightened and said, "Where do you come from? You must go back at once, for if the bird Venus finds you here, he will eat you up!"

The soldier replied, "This will not be so easy! Nobody has done anything to me so far." And he told her that he needed three golden feathers for his king, that he had to know why the other king's lime trees were drying up, why the third king was losing his battles, and why the ferryman was not being relieved.

When the housekeeper heard this, she said, "You must be hungry; eat some of the pancakes I have just made, but hurry up, for if the bird Venus finds you here, he will eat you up." When he had eaten his fill, the housekeeper told him to hide under the bed, so that the bird Venus could not see him. "I will help you in finding out the answers; I sleep with him."

After a while the bird Venus came rushing through the air. "How it smells of human flesh!" he cried, entering the house. "Where is the human being? I want to eat him!"

But the housekeeper told him, "You are wrong. The human smell you perceive probably comes from me, for I am human, too."

The bird Venus believed her, ate his pancakes, and went to bed. The housekeeper crept into his bed also. As soon as the bird was asleep, she tore one of his golden feathers out and threw it under the bed to the soldier. But Venus woke up and asked what was the matter. The housekeeper said that she had dreamed of a king who had three lime trees that were drying up.

"Tell me. Why are they withering?"

"The king should have the corpses that are lying underneath burned, and then the lime trees would grow again." Then the bird Venus slept again.

After a little while the housekeeper tore another feather out and threw it under the bed. The bird became angry and asked what was the matter—why did she not let him sleep.

"I dreamed of a king who has won many battles and who is now losing all the time," said the housekeeper. "Why does that happen?"

"The king should appoint other generals. Then he would win again. The old ones should be killed." Venus fell asleep for the third time, and the housekeeper tore the third golden feather out and threw it to the soldier under the bed.

The bird jumped up and was furious. He was roaring with anger and asked why did she not let him sleep.

"Oh," she said, "I have been dreaming of our ferryman. Why does he always have to ferry over, and never be relieved?"

"It's his own fault. He only has to throw the oar at a person he is ferrying over, and then he will be relieved."

In the morning the bird Venus got up and smelled human flesh again. But the housekeeper calmed him down, telling him that she was human, too, and that it must be her smell. The bird was pacified, ate some pancakes, and flew roaring through the air. The housekeeper immediately called the soldier, gave him something to eat, and told him to leave at once. If the bird Venus came back, he would not get off so easily. Besides, he had the golden feathers and had heard what he wanted to know. The soldier thanked her and left.

He called the ferryman, who came with his boat. But he did not tell him what the bird had said. Only when he was quite far away did he call to the ferryman and tell him what he had heard from the bird Venus.

"Why don't you throw your oar at somebody you ferry over?

Then you would be relieved."

"Had I known that before, I would have done it with you!"

Then the soldier came to the king. "Well, what did the bird say?"

"Dismiss your generals and kill them; then you will win."

Now the king had some barrels prepared with nails. His generals were put in and rolled down the mountain. They were dead when they arrived at the bottom. Then he appointed some new generals and was victorious again. The king rewarded the soldier richly and gave him a horse and a carriage, so that he did not need to travel on foot any more.

After a long time he came to the other king. He was heartily welcomed, and the king asked him about the lime trees and what the bird Venus had advised.

"Well," said the soldier, "you must have the corpses that lie under the trees burned. Then the trees will soon be green again." The king was glad to hear this and gave him many presents. The soldier did not stay there long, for he was homesick.

When he arrived home, his king was frightened. He thought that the bird Venus had eaten him long ago. The soldier gave him the three golden feathers. When the king saw how rich he was, he gave him his daughter in marriage. When he died, the soldier became king.

· 34 · *The Gold-Rich King*

· ONCE THERE LIVED a gold-rich king. He had a queen, but they had no children. They were very sad. One day there came a beggarwoman. She saw that the king was very sad and asked for the reason. The king told her, "Why should I not be sad? We haven't any children!" She offered to give him some herbs, which he was to cook and give to his wife. First he should give some to the queen and then also to the cook. They would both have boys. He did as he was told and gave the potion to the two women. They both gave birth to a child. The children went to school together. They were learning fast, but the cook's son was doing better.

When they were a little older, the queen's son once said to his brother, "Let's go for a walk in the royal garden." The garden was badly kept.

"I am not going to the garden until my father has it improved," said the cook's son. He was very sad. His father asked him what was wrong with him. The boy told him that all the kings had beautiful gardens, whereas the garden of theirs was so shabby. The king sent for carpenters, locksmiths, and so on. When everything was ready, the brothers went to see it. It looked fine now. The queen's son saw a bust in the garden. It was the bust of a very beautiful king's daughter. He said to his brother, "Brother, there is the bust of a very beautiful princess in there. But I will never get her!"

His brother said, "I will go with you; come on." They set out to find her.

They went riding on and on. Once, when it was getting dark, they came to a castle that was all black. They entered. The queen's son fell asleep at once. The cook's son thought, there might be somebody coming at night—possibly witches.

At eleven o'clock three maidens came. They played cards together. When the clock started striking twelve, a gray man came. "Good evening, my daughters."

"Good evening, father."

"I have news," he said.

They asked, "What about?"

"The son of the gold-rich king has left on horseback. He wants to marry the king's daughter. But he will not succeed. He and his brother do not know that they cannot find her on their own horses. They can only get where she is on ours. And then there is a rod in the trough that they must take with them. Otherwise they will not get through the water."

He heard all this. When the clock had finished striking twelve times, they all had vanished.

In the morning the cook's son got up and fed the horses. He left their own horses there and saddled the others. Then they left. They came to a river that they could not cross. The cook's son struck the water with the rod, and it gave way. At last they reached the town where the king's daughter was living. (They let her sleep, for she was sleepy.[1])

The queen's son said, "How are we going to get her?"

"We shall manage," said his brother. They went to a goldsmith and had a golden stag made. It had a little wheel to wind it up. Inside there was a chiming clock and in the belly there was a little door where the queen's son crept in. His brother pulled the stag, and it looked fine.

The king's daughter was brought with six maidens in sedan chairs. She was carried to church. When she saw the golden stag, she fell in love with it. She and the maidens went to mass, and when they came out again, the fellow started turning the wheel and the chiming clock started playing. They looked with amazement. He had to play the whole day. When it got dark, he said that he could not pull the stag home and that he would like to leave it there overnight. The princess told him to carry it to her room. The brothers had agreed that at night he would come back and that they would ride away together. Left alone, the one in the stag still played for a while until the princess went to bed. Then he came out of the stag and told her that he was the son of the gold-rich king. He asked that she leave with him. When the cook's son came, they were ready to leave. The princess and the queen's son rode on one horse and the cook's son on the other one.

In the morning the musicians arrived who used to play to wake the princess up. They called at her window, but there was no answer. They went to the king and informed him. The king told them to let her sleep for another hour, for the day before she had been very much upset about the golden stag and was perhaps still sleepy. After an hour they called again at her window. There was no answer. Then the king went to see. He took the keys, for the door was locked. When they entered, the golden stag was there, but the princess was gone. The king called his soldiers at once and sent them after her.

Meanwhile, the brothers had come again to the river. They struck it with the rod, and the water closed behind them, so that the soldiers could not follow.

[1] In brackets in the German text.

They went riding on and on. They stopped again at the black castle. The princess and the queen's son fell asleep at once, but the cook's son did not sleep, for he thought that something might happen again. And at eleven o'clock, the three maidens came and played. When the clock started striking twelve, the gray man came.

"Good evening, my daughters."

"Good evening, father."

"Any news?"

"He has got hold of the princess, but she will never be his, for the stepmother will come with a glass of fresh water. The water is poisoned. If he drinks, he will die. If he does not drink, she will come with a horse. The horse is loaded with gunpowder. If he mounts it, she will light it and he will be blown up. If she cannot blow him up with the horse, she will come to their bedroom at night. She will spit fire at them and burn them. But if somebody is there and licks them with his tongue, then they will not be burned. If he tells his story, he will, after the last word, be turned into stone."

When the clock had finished striking twelve times, they had vanished. He had heard everything.

In the morning the cook's son fed the horses. He left the gray man's horses in the castle and the rod, too. They left on their own horses. After a short while the stepmother arrived with a glass of fresh water.

"Dear son, drink this glass of fresh water, so as not to be exhausted when you come to your father."

The cook's son said, "Do not drink. We have been suffering from fatigue up to now, but we can go on for a while."

Then she came with the horse.

"Dear son, mount this fresh horse, so as not to come to your father on an exhausted one."

The cook's son said, "Do not mount it! You have gone so far with an exhausted one, and you can go on like this."

At night he was standing by the bed with a drawn sword. The stepmother came and spat fire. He licked the two with his tongue and, therefore, the fire did not kill them. But his brother woke up and saw him standing there with his sword. He thought that he had come to kill him.

The cook's son was sentenced to be hanged. He thought that if he told them everything, he would be turned to stone, and that if he did not tell them, he would be hanged. He preferred to tell the truth.

As he stood under the gibbet, he said, "Pardon! I should like to tell you something."

His brother allowed him to do so. He told them the whole story.

"You see, brother, this is what happened. We came to the old castle. You were sleeping while I watched. When the clock started striking eleven, three maidens came. They played cards. When the clock started striking twelve, there came a hoary man. He said, 'Good evening, my daughters!' They answered, 'Good evening father.' Then he told them, 'The son of the gold-rich king has left on horseback, but he will not get the princess, for he and the cook's son do not know that they never can get there with their own horses but only with ours. And they do not know about the rod in the trough that they should take in order to get through the water.' When the clock had finished striking twelve times they had vanished.

"In the morning I fed the horses, and we left with the others. When we had the princess, we went back to the castle. You and your bride slept again, but I was awake. I was on guard. The maidens came again. When the clock started striking twelve, the hoary man came. He told them, 'The son of the gold-rich king has got hold of the princess, but she will never be his. The stepmother will come with a glass of fresh water. The water is poisoned. If he drinks, he will die; if he does not drink, she will come with a horse. The horse is loaded with powder. If he mounts it, she will light it and he will be blown up. If he does not mount it, she will come at night and will spit fire on them. If someone were there and licked them with his tongue, then they would not be burned!'" After the last word, the cook's son was turned into stone.

Now his brother knew what he had done for him. He thought, if you were on guard in the castle, I can do the same. He went there and watched. When the clock struck eleven, the maidens came. They sat down and played cards. When the clock started striking twelve, a hoary man came.

"Good evening, my daughters. Any news?"

"The words have been revealed, and he has already turned into stone. But if they knew that in our cellar there is a box with an ointment! Somebody would have to take the box and daub him with it to make him as alive as before. Our castle is bewitched, too. If somebody would daub everything here, then we should be delivered, too." With this the clock had finished striking twelve times, and they had vanished.

In the morning he got up and looked around until he found the box. He tried it with the stones in the courtyard. They turned into dogs and cats at once. Then he daubed the house, and everything was alive. Then he went home and daubed the stone. His brother was alive again.

"Oh, I have slept very well!" he said.

"You were turned into stone!" his brother told him. Then he gave him the kingdom where the castle was situated and helped him to find a beautiful wife.

I have been looking for a beautiful wife, too.

• 35 • The Tale of the Silver, Golden, and Diamond Prince

• THERE WAS ONCE a poor peasant who had three sons and a beautiful green meadow. When the hay harvest was over, a big haystack stood in the meadow. The three fellows had made it. But it happened that every night some of the hay was gone. Every night three marvelous horses came, and each of them ate a hole into the haystack. The peasant got angry and sent his eldest son out to the meadow at night in order to watch. His mother gave him cakes and beer.

In the meadow, the fellow lay down on the haystack. Then he ate his cakes, drank his beer, and fell asleep. The three horses came, as they did every night, and ate without the guard noticing it. When he came home, he said that he had seen no thieves.

The same thing happened to the second son. He too ate the

cakes and drank the beer. Then he fell asleep as well and did not notice that the horses tranquilly ate the hay. At home he said that there were no thieves to be seen.

Now it would have been the turn of the third son. But everybody thought him to be stupid. Whenever he wanted to do anything, they told him, "Go away, you simpleton. Not even we can do this. How could you?"

As the second son had not got hold of the thieves, the third one said, "Father, let me watch tonight. I am sure to catch the thieves!" The father did not want to listen to him, but finally he let him go. The mother, however, gave him only ash cakes and thin beer.

Thus the youngest one went to the haystack in the meadow. He did not eat; he did not drink; nor did he think of sleeping. He put a loop before each hole and kept the ends in his hand. Then he watched. At midnight three marvelous horses came to the haystack. Each of them put his head in one of the holes and started eating. Suddenly, the fellow drew back the loops and caught all of them. The poor animals were terrified and started praying, "Sir, a wicked hag has bewitched us. Free us, and we shall serve you whenever you wish. If you need us, go to the great wood. There is a young oak. Speak to it as follows:

> Little oak tree, open thee,
> Let the three fine horses free.

Then we shall come and help you." The boy let the horses go and went home. There he said that nothing had been stolen. He did not say a word about the horses.

The country in which the peasant and his sons were living belonged to a rich king. He had a beautiful daughter. The king had a high mountain of glass raised, on the top of which the princess stayed. He who was able to ride up the glass mountain and exchange a handkerchief with her would become her husband.

The peasant and his two elder sons went to the great feast at the royal court. Each of them had a good horse, but neither could reach the princess on the glass mountain.

As soon as the peasant and the two fellows had left the farm, the youngest one, the simpleton, went to the oak in the wood and said:

> Little oak tree, open thee,
> Let the three fine horses free.[1]

At once the three horses were there and asked what they could do for him. "Bring me a silver prince's dress and a silver riding habit!" ordered the fellow. One of the horses stood before him; the others fetched dress and boots, cover and saddle, spurs and rein—all of pure silver. The boy got ready and rode to the royal court. He could see from afar how the riders tried to reach the top of the mountain. He was no sooner there than he set spurs to the horse and reached the princess in no time. As soon as they had exchanged their handkerchiefs, he left again. He returned to the oak, put on his old ragged clothes and went home. There he sat down at his place by the stove and waited for his brothers to come. They told him about the bold silvery prince who was the only one to reach the top of the mountain.

Now the simpleton by the stove said:

> The silvery prince on his beautiful horse,
> Who took the royal castle in his course,
> Your brother it was, whom you have seen,
> His most courageous deed it's been.[2]

But his brothers laughed and mocked him.

Soon afterward the king arranged another great feast. Again the young men came on their horses to win the princess. The peasant and his two elder sons were there as well. They never thought of the simpleton. But he secretly went to the oak in the wood and said:

> Little oak tree, open thee,
> Let the three fine horses free.

And instantly, the three horses came out and asked what he wanted.

"Bring me a golden prince's dress and a golden riding habit," ordered the fellow. One of the horses stood before him; the others

---

[1] German text: "Oeffne dich du Eiche fein
    Und lass heraus drei Rösselein."
[2] German text: "Der silberne Prinz auf stolzem Ross,
    Der heut geritten zum Königsschloss,
    Euer Bruder war es, den ihr saht,
    Vollbracht hat er die kühne Tat."

fetched suit and boots, cover and saddle, spurs and rein—all of
pure gold. He made ready and went to the feast. Again he could
see from afar how the riders tried to reach the top of the mountain
and how they failed. He was no sooner there than he set spurs to
the horse and reached the princess in no time. The handkerchiefs
were soon exchanged, and off he went. Nobody knew who he was.
He returned to the oak, put on his old ragged clothes, and went
home. There he sat down by the stove and waited for his brothers
to come. They told him about the bold golden prince who was the
only one to reach the top of the mountain. The simpleton by the
stove said:

> The golden prince on his beautiful horse,
> Who took the royal castle in his course,
> Your brother it was, whom you have seen,
> His most courageous deed it's been.

But his brothers laughed and mocked him.

The king and the queen could not stop thinking of the mysterious rider and would have liked to know who he was. Therefore,
the king prepared a third feast, and the princess secretly thought
of a ruse. So the young men of the whole country met again at the
royal court. The peasant and his two eldest sons were there, too.
The simpleton, however, went to the oak in the wood and said:

> Little oak tree, open thee,
> Let the three fine horses free.

At once the horses were there and asked him what he wanted.

"Bring me a diamond prince's dress and diamond riding habit,"
ordered the fellow.

One of the horses stood before him; the others fetched dress and
boots, cover and saddle, spurs and rein—all made of diamonds. He
got ready and went to the feast. He could see from afar how the
riders tried in vain to reach the top of the mountain. He was no
sooner there than he set spurs to the horse and reached the princess
in no time. As soon as they had exchanged their handkerchiefs,
he left again. Yet the king's daughter shot after him and hit him
in the leg. But the fellow went riding on, although he was
suffering. When he returned to the oak he put on his old ragged

clothes, dressed his wound with the princess' handkerchief, and
went home. There he sat down by the stove and waited for his
brothers to come. They told him about the bold diamond prince
who was the only one to reach the top of the mountain and who
then had vanished. The simpleton by the stove said:

> The diamond prince on his beautiful horse,
> Who took the royal castle in his course,
> Your brother it was, whom you have seen,
> His most courageous deed it's been.

But his brothers laughed and mocked him.

When the feast was over and the mysterious rider had again
not been recognized, the king made known in the country that all
the young men, from prince to beggar, were to stay at home on a
certain day. On this day the king and the princess went from
village to village, from town to town. Thus they also came to the
peasant's farm. The two elder sons had to put on their best clothes,
and they were presented to the king and to the princess. "Don't
you have any more sons?" asked the princess.

"Yes," said the peasant, "I do have a third one, but he is very
stupid and sits by the stove all the time." But the princess wanted
by all means to see the simpleton. The peasant called him, and
since the fellow was limping, the princess looked more closely at
him. She recognized her handkerchief and she therefore knew
who had been the silver, the golden, and the diamond prince. He
had to get right into the coach and be brought to the royal castle.
When they came to the oak, the young man asked them to let
him go near the tree.

> Little oak tree, open thee,
> Let the three fine horses free!

he exclaimed once more. The three horses came galloping along
and brought him the silver, the golden, and the diamond riding
habits. Then the fellow got back into the coach, and they went
off. But the three horses escorted the coach right to the castle.

Soon afterward the wedding was celebrated. The horses asked
the prince to cut their heads off. But he did not want to do so,
because he was sorry for the poor animals. When they told him,

however, that this was the only way to deliver them, he did it. In an instant three princes were standing before him. They remained at the court, and the young man made them his counselors when he became king. And the three lived happily with the royal couple, and if they have not died since, they are alive to this very day.

· 36 ·   *The Girl without Hands*

• IN OLD TIMES, before there were any railways, there was a lonely inn on the highway where coachmen used to stay for the night. The innkeeper had a wife and a daughter. The mother died when the daughter was still going to school. The innkeeper did not want to get married again, but the coachmen advised him to do so in order to give the little girl a good mother. So he took a wife, and they lived rather happily together for several years. Then the man died. The girl was growing up, and now the people preferred to be served by the daughter; it was with her they talked things over, and this made the stepmother angry. She prepared a chest and an ax and sulfur and put them in the cellar.

One day when nobody was there, she closed the door and told the daughter to go the the cellar with her; she had to talk to her. The daughter said that she might tell her up there, for if somebody came to the inn, he would not be able to enter. But she was told that he could knock. Down in the cellar, the stepmother closed the door and told the girl to choose between two things—to be burned with sulfur or to have her arms and feet cut off (the arms right up to the elbows, the feet right up to the knees). The girl said that if it could not be helped, she would rather have her arms and feet cut off than to be burned. The stepmother did the deed. Then she rubbed the wounds with some ointment and brought her something to eat every day. But the guests started asking where the girl was. The stepmother told them that she had gone on a journey. But they insisted on knowing where and when and why, until she grew afraid that everything might become known.

One day when she was alone, there came an old customer, who

had been passing through for years. She went to the cellar and told the girl not to betray anything; otherwise, she would regret it. Then she nailed the chest down, dragged it up, and put it down by the entrance. When the coachman had eaten enough and was going to leave, he asked what he owed her and said that he wanted to pay his former debts as well. The woman told him that he need pay nothing if he would do one thing for her. He said he would if it could be done. Now she told him that in the hall there was a chest, which had been there since the days of war and which she wanted to get rid of. He was to take it with him, to carry it off the road, and to leave it there. He promised to do so, and took the chest with him.

Having put the chest down and going back to his carriage, he thought the matter over: Confound it! It's been there since the days of war. It can't be forbidden to have a look at it. He went back, took tools with him, approached, and opened the chest. He found the girl.

"Good gracious, what's this? Now I'll have to bring you back." But she implored him to leave her there, so that the wild animals might eat her up. He did not want to; he could not take it upon himself. He would bring her back to where he had got her from. He asked her how she had lost her arms and legs. She said that she did not know, but asked him again to leave her there, so that the wild animals might eat her. At last the coachman agreed and left.

Then she started hobbling through the woods until she finally came to a big garden. It was summer, and the apples were ripe. Some of them grew low enough for her to reach with her mouth. So she first of all ate enough and then she stayed in this part of the woods in order to feed on the apples.

The young king went for a walk in his garden and noticed that the lower apples were all gnawed off. He looked closely at them without finding out what had happened, for the bitings obviously came from human teeth, but the tracks could not be made out. So he placed guards there in the evening and in the morning. But they could not find out either, for she hopped there very early when it was hardly light. But as more and more gnawed-off apples were found, the king became angry and had sentries posted there all the time. They either had to bring him the wild animal or they would be punished. Thus they found her early in the morning. She asked the soldiers to let her go and promised never to return. But the soldiers told her they could not do so, but that they had to bring her to the king; otherwise, they would be killed. The king would probably let her go.

The king asked her where she came from and where she wanted to go, where she had lost her arms and feet, and how she had gotten into the woods. But she simply said that she knew nothing about it and asked him politely to let her go. She would not come back again. Hunger had brought her there. The king told her that he could not do this and that he did not want to. A room was given to her, where she was taken care of.

After a long time the king received a letter which he could not read; he grew angry and cursed. She heard him and asked him to give her the letter. He scolded even more and said, "What are you thinking of, if I cannot read it myself!"

But in his anger he threw the letter at her, and she promptly read it. Thus the king became attentive to her, and when he had another letter, he gave it to her, and in this manner he saw her quite often. The king often asked her where she came from, but she said nothing. He fell in love with her. He asked his mother if he could not marry this unknown person. His mother advised him not to do so and cried. Even if she were of high birth, he could not marry her. She could not give a party and could not attend one either; she simply was not suitable for him. But it was no use, he asked over and over again. He told his mother that he would not invite any people. And then he married her.

After they had been married for about a year, the king had to go to war. He left his wife, who was pregnant, in his mother's care. After some time his wife gave birth to two princes. The old queen immediately sent a messenger with the news to her son. The messenger had to go past the old inn and to stay there overnight. The innkeeper's wife got everything out of him—where he was going to and why, and what sort of a woman the queen was. She knew at once that it was her daughter. The man innocently told her everything. She gave him much to eat and to drink and made him a sleeping draught. At night she went and looked through his pockets, took the letter out, and replaced it with another one in which she wrote that his wife had given birth to two little poodles and that she was insane and asked what were they to do with her. Unsuspecting, the messenger brought this letter to the king. The king read it but did not believe anything. He wrote back that he did not believe it and that they should take good care of her and leave her in peace. On his way back the messenger went to the inn again. He got another sleeping draught. The innkeeper's wife changed the letters again and put a wicked one in the place of the king's kind one, saying that he did not want her anymore and that they should burn her.

The old woman could not explain to herself how her son could act like this, for he had thought very highly of his wife; she did not show the letter to the young wife, but wrote back telling him that she had given him a piece of her mind while it was time. For the second and third time letters were exchanged and they became worse and worse. He did not wish to see her again. They were to burn her together with her poodles. The old queen cried a great deal and at last showed the letters to the young woman. The young queen knew right away what was the matter. She sent for the messenger and asked him where he had rested, for she had recognized her stepmother's handwriting. But she said nothing; she declared that whatever her husband had decided was to be carried out. However, she did not want to be burned. They might light a big fire, so that everybody would think she had been burned. For she believed that her stepmother would lie in wait and that, seeing the fire, she would be satisfied. Meanwhile they might lead her over the big river and leave her in the forest, so that the wild animals might eat her up. She and the queen were crying a good deal. Finally they put a white sheet around her, placed one child at each breast, led her over the river, and left her in the forest. When she came to a small brook, she thought that the end was near, but first she would like to baptize her boys. As she was about to do so, a voice asked her what she was doing there. She was baptizing her boys. She could not do it by herself, answered the voice. Two men would be sent to her. And really, there came two men. One was called Peter, and one John. They acted as godfathers and gave the boys their names. They said that they could not give her a sponsor's christening gift but that she might utter three wishes; yet she should not forget the best thing.

Well, she wished to see her husband once again in her lifetime. It was agreed, but she should not forget the best thing. Then she wished to find a shelter and have enough to live on. That was granted, too, but she should not forget the best, one said again. Well, if it didn't matter, she would like to have her arms and feet back; and she gained them. The two men disappeared, and she saw a tiny hut; she went there and found a little furniture inside and some food.

The war that had lasted for several years now ended, and the king went raving mad when he heard from his mother that she had burned his wife according to his orders. He showed her the letters, and she told him she had never written them. Then she showed him his letters, which he had not written either. They sent for the messenger, but he had died in the meantime. Now his mother told him that she had not burned his wife, but had only sent her over the river and left her in the forest. He arranged a great hunt; in case he would find one bone of his wife and the children, he would say a prayer for them.

While they were hunting and searching, it started raining most frightfully and no shelter was to be had. When darkness fell and the rain had not stopped, one of the men climbed up a tree to look for a light. He told them that he could see a light somewhere. They went toward it. The place was so small that the king did not want to go in, but the owner told him to come in and to put on dry clothes. She had no vermin, and she would gladly give him her own dry clothes. She had recognized him at once, but he did not recognize her, because she had her arms and legs again.

The king sat down on a stool, but she did not give in and told him to go to the bed, which was small and simple, but clean. Finally he did so, but he did not feel safe. He lay at the edge of the bed. Then he dozed off, and one of his legs slid out. Now she said to Peter, "My son, go and put your father's leg back into the bed."

"What did you say, mother? We have no father but the one in heaven."

"Yes, he is our foster father, but this is your real father."

The king, who had not quite understood while dozing, let his arm glide out. Now she said to John, "Go, my son, and put your father's arm back into the bed."

"Mother, what are you telling me? We have no father but the one in heaven."

"That is our foster father, but this one is your real father." Now the king got up and asked if she was his wife.

"Yes," she said. But she had arms and legs! Yes, she was going to tell him later. He called his servants, ordered a coach, and had them brought to the ship. On their way she told him how she had lost her arms and legs and how she had regained them.

She was then hidden in the palace, and the king invited all the old widows for a meal, especially the innkeeper's wife. As he was drinking with all of them, he came to his mother-in-law, and he asked her what a person deserved who cut off other people's arms and legs.

"She deserves to be cooked in oil."

Now the queen came in from the next room and said, "Yes, you are the one! But this is much too good for you."

"Yes," said the king, "she must be torn into pieces by four oxen."

· 37 · *The Poor Brother's Treasure*

· THERE ONCE LIVED two brothers at Irksleben. One of them was a rich farmer; the other one had to earn his living as a jobber doing hard work at his brother's farm.

Being very hard up, the poor brother one day asked his rich brother for a bushel of rye. But the rich one hardheartedly sent him away. In the following nights there was a knocking to be heard at the poor brother's window, and he was asked to come and bring up a treasure. But he was afraid and did not go. Finally he told his brother, who asked him to call him if it should happen again. The following night the knocking sounded again. The poor man woke his brother, who went and found a dead horse. Furious about being duped like this, he cut off a leg and thought, may the poor wretch eat to his heart's content! He threw the leg through the window into his brother's room; however, he went there early the next morning to prevent his brother from eating too much at once. But looking through the window, he saw his brother counting a great heap of louis d'or. Now he was quite willing to offer him a bushel of rye, but his brother did not need it any more. Going back to the place where the horse had been lying, they found louis d'or all along the path where blood had dripped, but the horse was gone.

·*38*· *The Innkeeper of Moscow*

• IN THE TOWN OF MOSCOW there once lived a rich merchant. He was old and had a grown son. One day he said to him, "Son, you should look for a wife."

The son said, "Father, I have made my choice, but I am afraid you will not agree."

"All right, tell me all about it."

"I should like to marry the maidservant, whom we have had for seven years."

"Son, this is my very idea. Take her to church and marry her." The son did so.

They had been married for a year when he once went to a wine shop where he played cards and so on. It was nine o'clock, a quarter past nine, then he said, "I must go home, my wife will be waiting for me."

But the innkeeper broached another cask and said, "Don't be so kind to your wife; you will get home early enough. She is not as faithful as you believe."

"What are you talking about? I'll stake my whole fortune on my wife!"

"All right! You leave, and I shall sleep with your wife. But don't tell her about our bet." They wrote it all down, and the merchant went home.

In the morning he said to his wife, "Listen, I have to go away for six weeks, and you must keep everything in good order meanwhile." Then he left.

Whenever the wife needed wine for the shop, she sent the

maidservant to the wine shop to get some. One time the innkeeper said to the maidservant, "Look here, you could easily make 5,000 florins. You are poor; what do you think about it?"

"I should like to, if it is easy enough for me to do."

"Can you lead me into your mistress's bedroom?"

"It is possible while she is at the table." She left the door open, and while her mistress was eating, the innkeeper got in and hid under the bed. The wife went to her bedroom at ten o'clock, locked the door, took her ring and everything off, and went to bed. He saw that she had a birthmark under her breast. She said her prayers and after a short while she fell asleep. Now he sneaked out, took her wedding ring, and went off with it. Good! If the merchant comes, he has won the bet!

Forty-eight hours later the merchant came back. He went to the wine shop, laughing in advance. "Well, how far have we got? I am sure to have won the bet!"

The innkeeper showed him the ring and told him about the birthmark. But let us see how things went on for the merchant's wife.

She was awake early in the morning. She washed, dressed and wanted to wear her ring. It was gone! She thought, everything was locked, so the ring must have been stolen. She went to the goldsmith, had the same ring made again, and put it on her finger. When the merchant entered his shop, his first look went to his wife's hand. He saw that she had the ring. The real one was in his waistpocket.

Soon after this event he gave a dinner for the poor and said to his wife, "You put on your wedding dress, and I will put on my wedding suit. Then let us watch the poor." After the meal he took two pistols, and they went for a walk in the woods. He took her arm and they left. In the woods he called, "Stop!" He put his hand in the waistpocket, "Do you know this ring?" She grew white as a sheet. He said, "Well, I have made you rich, and you have deceived me terribly. Die!" He took his pistol out, cocked it, took aim at her, but when he wanted it to fire, it did not go off. He threw it away and took the second one, but the same thing happened again. Then he said, "Now we are both beggars. You may go where you choose, and I shall go where I choose!"

Meanwhile his old father was anxiously waiting at home, but nobody came. Early in the morning he went to the police, and they searched all over, but there was no trace of the couple to be found.

The wife had gone to the right and the husband had gone to the left. At that time it was possible to enlist in the army without being examined. So she bought men's clothes—she still had some money left—put them on, and enlisted. She joined the cavalry. She had a clever head and soon became colonel.

Later on, her husband enlisted in the same squadron. Riding past him, she recognized her husband at the first glance and took him as her officer's man. He was very meticulous and kept everything in good order; whenever there were women around, he left. Finally the colonel thought, you must find out why he behaves like this. He invited some handsome women, then he sent for his man and asked him to keep them company.

When he entered the room and saw the women, he went to the colonel and said, "Colonel, I feel sick and I am unable to keep them company. I must go to bed." He lay down and ruminated.

In the morning the colonel sent for him, "You were not ill. Why did you not stay with them?"

He answered, "Colonel, please don't reopen old sores. They have long ago healed up but started bleeding again now."

"What bothers you about women? Express yourself freely, or you will be shot."

He sat down and pondered, "Colonel, I'd rather be shot than tear open this wound again."

"Come on, I want to know all about it!" When the man saw that it was no use, he began his story. He had married a maid-servant, who had been in his house for seven years; she was poor but a real beauty. He had money and property. Once he left for six weeks, and meanwhile she behaved in a scandalous way with an innkeeper. "Here, I still keep the wedding ring. When I came back, my wife had a false ring, and I was a beggar, because I had lost my money in a bet."

The colonel had grown pale as death and shouted, "Four officers! Right on the spot! Tomorrow we must ride to town!" He chose four officers, and at six o'clock in the morning, they all came. The horses were brought from the stables; they mounted and rode to town at a trot.

They reached town at noon and went to the wine shop. They ate and drank. Then the colonel arose and said, "This is a fine shop over there."

"Yes," said the innkeeper, "I have gained it in one night. There was a merchant who trusted his wife. He left for six weeks, and I made a bet with him that I would sleep with his wife. And I won the bet."

The colonel said to the fellow, "What sort of maidservant did the wife have at that time?"

"A clever one. She owns the house over there."

"Go and fetch her. I must talk to her."

When she arrived, the colonel asked the innkeeper if he had a room, for the four officers wanted to talk to the girl. The innkeeper showed them a room without misgiving. When they had the maidservant in the room, the officers drew their sabers and asked her if she had served at the merchant's house.

"Why did you cheat the merchant? What have you done? Don't lie! I'll split your head with my saber!"

She went down to her knees, "The innkeeper bribed me with 5,000 florins, so I let him into the bedroom. He hid under the bed. The mistress used to undress at night and to take her ring off. At night he got up, took the ring, and saw the birthmark on her chest." (The day after this confession, one of the officers went to see her and said, "Here are another 1,000 florins for you, and I shall buy you another house.") When she had revealed everything, they went back to the main hall and called the innkeeper to account. At the beginning he tried to make denials, but the maidservant told him the whole story to his face. Now the innkeeper offered to return everything. "To return what? I am the wife!"

A woman had to come to examine her to see if she really was a woman. The innkeeper confessed everything and had to leave. They took his belongings and gave the rest to the poor.

She laid her saber down and received an enormous retirement pay—fancy her being a colonel of cavalry! She went back to the shop with her husband, and they lived happily. They had two children, a boy and a girl—real beauties they were. His father had long ago died from sorrow, and they erected a fine monument for him. And thus they lived in peace and harmony, and they are alive to this very day if they have not died since.

Part V
Magic Help and Gifts

· 39 · *The Three Spinners*

• THERE WAS A WIDOW with a daughter who was terribly lazy. When her mother told her to spin, she would not do so, but would just stand around all the time. Once the queen went past when the mother was beating her daughter. The queen sent her servant to ask why she had beaten her child. The mother told him, "She wants to spin all the time, and I have nothing to give her." The queen said that this was just the person she was looking for. She had a big room full of flax which the girl could spin. The girl would be well paid; she would even be married to her son, the prince.

The girl went with the queen to the castle. The first day, she had nothing to do. The second day, they went to another building, and there was a big, big room full of flax. She was given a golden spinning wheel and was told that after having spun the whole lot, she would never have to do any more work all her life long. Food would be sent to her.

Early next morning when coffee was served, she had done nothing but cry. She cried the whole day. In the evening she sat at the window and cried. Then she opened the window. Suddenly an elderly spinster came to the window and asked why she was crying. So she told her about the spinning and said that she could not spin at all. The spinster told her not to worry; she had two friends, and they would spin night and day for her. They did not want anything in return but to come to the wedding when the prince married her. Now the three brought their spinning wheels, and whenever somebody came, they hid and threw the thread out to her. When the queen came she said to the girl, "You see, homesickness is over and soon everything will be done." In the morning so much work had been done that she did not know how to explain it. As there was almost nothing left, the spinsters could only spin by night.

When everything was ready, the queen praised her. And the prince asked her if she had a wish. She said that she wished three old aunts of hers to be invited to the wedding.

One of them had a very thick thumb. In the evening as they

were sitting at table, the prince asked her what had happened. She answered, "It comes from picking." (Picking the flax.) The second one had a thick nose. When he asked her about it, she said that it came from the dust. And the third one had thick lips. He asked her, too, and she said that it came from licking. Now he called out, "My wife has been spinning so much! She must never do it again; I do not want her to get a thick thumb, thick lips, and a thick nose." So she was relieved.

· 40 · *The Magic Lamp*

· THERE LIVED in a town a tailor who had so many children that he did not know exactly how many. Once he was sitting at the table with his wife and said, "If only someone would take a few children, even if it be the mountain ghost!"

No sooner had he said this than a man with a green coat, who had one horse hoof and one human foot, came in and said, "Master, you have a son to hire out. You may settle it by choosing dice."

The lot fell upon Johann, the oldest one. He put his things together and went with the stranger. He cried and wailed, but it was no use. Necessity is an iron rod.

Getting out of town, the man in the green coat stopped. "You know, Johann, you are a bad walker; I shall put you on my shoulders and carry you for a while." As he said that, he lifted the boy to his shoulders and carried him through the air. On a green meadow he put him down again. In front of them three rods were sticking out of the ground. The ghost took one out and struck the earth with it. There was a rock before them.

The man asked, "Do you know, Johann, whom you are serving?"

Johann guessed the butcher, and so forth.

"No, you are serving the so-called mountain ghost. Now listen to what I tell you." There was a door leading into the rock, and it was open. The mountain ghost said, "You will go through nine iron doors. When you get to a small room, you will find a round table in the middle and on it there lies an old book. On this book there stands an old lamp. Bring these to me. You have a quarter of an hour's time. If you do not manage within this time, then you will die in there; there is no other way out."

Johann went in, got safely through the nine doors, came to the room, found the old black book with an old rusty lamp on top of it. He picked up both and was about to leave when he saw a marvelous garden with thousands of multicolored flowers and garlands. He thought, you could pick a few roses for your master so that he can see what fine plants are in the rock. No sooner had he cut three roses than he fell asleep.

After three years he awakened and wanted to leave. When he looked round, he found even more beautiful flowers in the garden. He broke four roses and slept for four more years. After this period he wanted to flee, but there was absolutely no way out. There were fruit trees and a bench where he sat down, and whenever he was hungry, he ate some fruit. This lasted for a while. Then one day he opened the old book. Three ghosts appeared before him and asked, "What does your majesty order?"

"Nothing." He closed the book and wondered if this might save him, but the three had disappeared.

He pondered by what means he might get home. He opened the book and put the lamp on top of it. At the same moment six air ghosts stood before him. They asked him, "What orders have you?"

"I should like to be at my father's house and go to sleep there." He closed the book and replaced the lamp, and everything happened according to his wishes. The ghosts did what he ordered; they laid him on a bench in his father's house. In the morning when he awoke, he was lying in a dark room. Ten years had gone past. During this time there had been a great plague. His father had died and so had all his brothers and sisters. Only his mother was alive, and she went begging from house to house.

Once she went to his room early in the morning and when she saw him lying there, she scolded him, "You rascal, you lout! Why did you not stay with your master? Now I have nothing, and you have nothing either!"

"Mother, be quiet. I have food and drink." He closed the door and opened the book and placed the lamp on it. Immediately six air ghosts stood before him and asked, "What orders have you?"

"Get food and drink fit for a king."

The ghosts said, "Close the book. Everything will be carried out." He did as he was told, and the ghosts went away. Three of them brought a table, two the tablecloth, and one food and drink. When everything was ready, he opened the door and cried, "Mother, come in. There is plenty to eat and to drink!"

"What are you telling me? You have no fire. Are you teasing your mother? You have not been cooking."

"Mother, once more, come and eat!"

She came in and saw that her son was already busy eating. She ate, too, and when they had finished, there were a lot of leftovers.

He said, "Mother, you keep what you cannot eat. There might be a time when you need it." So she put it away. In the back room there was her old beggar's basket. While his mother was sleeping, he opened the book. Three air ghosts appeared. "Take the beggar's basket and fill it with jewels and carbuncles." He closed the book and his order was carried out. In the morning when he woke up, he found himself lying in the heavenly splendor of the stones.

After breakfast he said, "Mother, not far from here there is a prince's castle and a part of the wall has collapsed. You carry your basket to the prince, so that he can build up his wall again. If he asks you who is sending this, you tell him 'The prince without land.'" She took the basket. It weighed ten hundredweights, but he sent air ghosts after her to help her. After a long journey, she came to the castle.

The first sentry called to her, "Stop. Where you are going?" She asked him to let her by, as she had to go to the prince. This was repeated with the second sentry. Then she went with her beggar's basket into a most beautiful room. In the middle there was a round table and on it there was a fine cloth with golden tassels. She went there and put the beggar's basket on the table and said, "How stupid my son is! What a stupid son I have!"

"What have you got here?"

"Your wall has collapsed, and my son has sent you these stones to mend it." The prince looked and saw that one stone was worth nine times his principality. He ordered his servants to carry the basket into the treasury. Then they had to fill it half full with ducats. The old woman put the basket on her neck; it was heavy, but the air ghosts helped her to carry it. Then she went home.

On her way she came to an inn where she had a mug of beer and a roll. When she had finished, she asked the innkeeper, "What do I owe you?"

"Forty hellers."

The woman took out seven ducats and put them on the table. Then she said, "If one is not enough, take all seven—then I need not carry them so far."

Before she left, the prince had told her, "When you get home, tell your son to come here."

But she had replied, "No! My son does not go to fine castles to be hanged."

In the evening she came home. Her son asked her what the prince had said, and she answered, "You shall go to the hall. But don't go; don't let them hang you there!"

He said, "Mother, in the house of a prince the wine room is called hall."

But she said, "No, don't go!" Then they had supper.

When his mother had gone to sleep, he opened the book and placed the lamp on it and six air ghosts came, "What orders have you?"

"Before the prince's castle there is a fine vast meadow; there build a castle of jewels and carbuncles and a bridge hanging on golden chains. And everything inside shall be fit for a prince."

"This can be done, and it will be carried out."

In the morning when he woke up, the new castle was standing there in marvelous splendor. It was made of carbuncles and jewels. Wherever the eye looked, everything that suited a prince was there. The prince went with his daughter over the bridge and into the castle. The prince gave his daughter to Johann, and they gladly celebrated their wedding and lived in peace and harmony.

Once Johann went hunting with the prince, and his wife was alone at home. The servant entered and announced, "There is a man outside who wants to buy old books and lamps for new ones."

The wife said, "We have only just gotten married; there are no old books and lamps." But the man sent a message for her to look under the bed where she would find them. If she would give them to him, he would give her new books and lamps instead. The woman let him come in. A tradesman entered, and the woman marveled at the new books and lamps. So she looked around and she found the old things in a trunk underneath the bed and exchanged them. Her eyes were dazzled when she saw the new things. While she was occupied like this, the mountain ghost opened the old book. The air ghosts appeared and asked, "What orders have you?"

"Carry the castle with its mistress to the seaside. When the sea is high, the castle will rise as well; when the sea is low, the castle will go down as well and the golden bridge will break into thousands and thousands of pieces, so that none of them will be bigger than the point of a pin."

"This can be done." They took the castle away and broke the chain.

The next day when the new master came back with his father-in-law, what did they see? The castle was gone! The father-in-law said, "You have made me lose my daughter and you have badly cheated me; therefore, you will have to languish in the dark dungeon." He then had him imprisoned with moldy bread and water.

Once, after almost a year, every prisoner was granted a wish, because it was the prince's name day. The jailer went to the son-in-law and asked him if he had a wish. Yes, he had one. He wanted his father-in-law to come to see him. The prince said, "Had I not sworn by scepter and crown, I should not go; but as I have done so, I must go to see him."

When the prince entered the jail, the son-in-law said, "Father-in-law, I have been granted a wish. Have a pair of shoes forged for me and put red-hot on my feet; I shall not rest before I have found my wife and the castle." The prince fulfilled his wish. He sent for a smith who put red-hot iron shoes on his feet. The son-in-law sat down on a heap by the street, took a pebble, knocked the shoes down, and set out on his journey.

He went on and on for a long time. At last he came to a big

forest. There a dead horse was lying on the ground. He stopped and thought, what has happened to you will happen to me as well. Then a dung beetle came and said, "Take a stone and knock the horse's brain open, so that I may find something to eat. In return I shall tell you where your wife is." Then he went inside and did not come out again.

He was hardly gone when an ant came and said, "Take a knife and cut the horse's belly open, so that I have something to eat. I shall tell you in return where you can find your wife." He did so. The ant went inside and was gone. He stood there for a while and thought, "Oh you stupid creatures, you have tricked me."

But then the dung beetle came out and said, "Tear my right wing off. Then you will be a dung beetle. You can get into every cleft and scratch. Your princess is at the sea. You fly toward the right window. It is broken, and you can get inside."

Then the ant came out and told him to tear off its right leg. Any time he put the leg in his mouth he would become an ant.

He flew to the seaside as a dung beetle, and there stood the castle. As a man, he first of all ate a piece of bread in a hurry and drank some sea water. Then he again put the dung beetle's wing in his mouth and flew toward the right window, which was broken. Then he put the ant's leg in his mouth; now he was an ant and crawled inside. The chief sorcerer and the princess were at the table. The sorcerer had just said, "We have just been here for a year now, and we have not celebrated our wedding yet. This will be the day."

He went into the wine cellar and brought two bottles of wine. One he would put on her side of the table and one on his. Then they would join hands and get married.

But before the sorcerer returned with the wine, Johann took the ant's foot out of his mouth and stood there.

"How on earth did you get here?"

"When the sorcerer comes, you take one of the bottles and put this sleeping draught in it. He will take your bottle and you, his. After drinking the wine, he will fall asleep." Then Johann put the ant's foot in his mouth again. The sorcerer brought the bottles. They joined hands and exchanged the bottles. Then they drank. After he had drunk, he fell asleep.

When the chief sorcerer was asleep, Johann went inside as an ant. There he took out the ant's foot, reached under the bed, and took the book and lamp out. Six air ghosts appeared, "What orders have you?"

Johann said, "Two have to hold the chap; two will go to the wood and bring a tree, which must have the bark removed. You tie him to the tree and put him near the sea. When the sea is high, he will rise as well; when the sea is low, he will go down as well, so the birds can eat him. Bring the castle back to its former place and make a bridge a thousand times more beautiful than the first one."

Then he shut the book and replaced the lamp, and everything happened as he had ordered. They brought the man to the seaside, and the ravens and birds ate him up. The castle went back with them to its former place. Then Johann told his wife what her father had done to him. When they arrived, the prince was standing at the bridge. His daughter spat at his feet and said, "We will not call each other father and daughter any more."

But the couple lived happily and peacefully for many years. Amen.

· 41 · *The Tale of Frost and His Neighbors*

· THERE WERE TWO NEIGHBORS living in the country on adjoining grounds, and not far off in a tiny house there lived a man whose name was Frost. One of the neighbors was a big landowner and the other one was a peasant.

One year, they both had sown rapeseed. The landowner's rapeseed was well developed in autumn because he had properly fertilized the soil. The peasant's rapeseed had remained very small. The winter was hard, and in the spring the landowner's rapeseed grew up quickly, whereas the peasant's rapeseed was still frozen in the earth.

When the peasant became aware of this in spring, he took a bundle of straw and went to the man whose name was Frost. When he arrived there, Frost asked him, "Where are you going?"

"Well," said the peasant, "you have frozen right in the ground all my rapeseed! Therefore I am going to set your house on fire."

Frost said, "What makes you think so? I haven't done anything."

"Well," said the peasant, "your name is Frost and you have frozen my rapeseed in the ground. You haven't frozen the landowner's seed, just mine!" He wanted to set the house on fire.

They quarreled for a long time. At last Frost said, "Leave my house alone. Come in. I will give you a wallet, and with its help all your wishes will be fulfilled. You just say, 'Three men out of the bag!' and everything you wish for will be there."

"All right," said the peasant, "then you better show me how this works. I cannot believe you." Frost took a small wallet and asked the peasant what he wanted to have. "Well," he replied, "first of all I should like to eat and to drink!"

Frost said, "Three men out of the bag! Lay the table; get food and drink!" No sooner had he said this than the table was set and there was plenty to eat and to drink.

"Well," said the peasant, "so far it looks all right. I hope it will be like this at home."

"Now then," said Frost, "if you want money, you shall have that as well." After the meal Frost said again, "Three men out of the bag. Money on the table!" Immediately there was a lot of money on the table. Then Frost said, "Now you go home and take your wallet, and whatever you wish will be yours." The peasant went home and showed the wallet to his wife, and whenever he wanted to have anything, he just said, "Three men out of the bag!" and there it was.

Now he had everything he wanted. The big landowner had noticed that he had grown rich, and once as he was walking along the border of his estate he asked him how he had managed to become so wealthy. The peasant said, "I have a small wallet, and I have but to say what I want to have, and there it is." Now the landowner asked him if he would not sell him the wallet; he offered him a lot of money, and the peasant sold it.

However, as the money was consumed, he was again very poor; he went back to Frost and complained to him. "Look here," said Frost, "you shouldn't have given away the wallet. You must try to get it back."

"Well yes," said the peasant, "But how? The landowner has it. How am I to get it?"

"Well," said Frost, "you must find out when he is leaving. I'll give you this wallet that looks exactly like the first one; you hang it in the place of the other one and take the first one with you. But you must not use this wallet at home, for if you say, 'Three men out of the bag!' the three men will give you a good thrashing." Now the peasant went home and watched. As soon as the landowner had left, he secretly went there, took the little wallet, and hung the other one in its place.

The landowner too had become very wealthy owing to the little wallet. When he came back from his journey, he invited a lot of friends and other landowners whom he wanted to surprise with the magic power of the wallet. The ladies and gentlemen were taking a walk in the park. It was almost noon, and eventually, one guest said to the other, "Well, it looks as if there will be no lunch here, for I cannot smell anything being roasted or cooked."

Toward twelve o'clock the landowner asked them to come to the table. They all went into the hall, but no table was laid, and they looked at each other, not knowing what to think of it. Now the landowner said, "Three men out of the bag, lay the table; get food and drink!" No sooner had he said this than three men came out of the bag and started beating the ladies and gentlemen with sticks, so that they fled through doors and windows. The landowner received his share as well. Outside, the guests kept shouting, "Hans! Josef! August! (These were the coachmen.) Get the carriage ready; let's get off!" The three men went on beating the landowner until it came to his mind to say, "Three men into the bag!" And everything was quiet again.

Having recovered a little, he considered how this might have happened, and he decided to try once more. But as soon as he said, "Three men out of the bag!" the three men set to work on him until his senses left him and he said, "Three men into the bag!"

Now he took the wallet and brought it back to the peasant and said, "I don't want to keep it any longer." And the peasant was glad and brought it back to Frost.

·42· *The Hare Herd*

• THERE WAS A KING who had only one daughter. She fell ill, and nobody could help her. It was made known that whoever was able to cure her should marry her, even if he were a poor fellow. First of all there came the kings, princes, baronets, and other people of high rank with their medicine. It was no use; she did not recover. Then the rich people were asked to come. But she still did not feel better. Finally it was proclaimed that anybody might come, no matter if he were a peasant or an artisan, if only he could help her.

There was a very poor man. He had three sons. His wife knew how to make all sorts of medicines. Their eldest son, who was a neat fellow, said, "Mother, make a medicine ready for me; everybody is allowed to go there." His mother prepared a medicine for him. She also gave him a loaf of white bread for the journey. Then he left.

On his way he met an old gray man who said, "Well, my child, where are you going? What are you carrying with you?"

"Why do you ask, you old cur?" he said. "Pig dirt!" He then walked off insolently, convinced that the princess would be his. When he got there, the guard searched him and asked him what he was carrying and why he had come. He really had pig dirt! They saw it at once and locked him up. Instead of being brought to the princess, he was imprisoned for three months. Afterward they sent him home. At home everybody thought that he would bring the princess, since he had been away for such a long time. They asked him what had happened to him. He said to his mother, "On the way I met an old man who asked me what I was carrying. I told him it was pig dirt. And when I got to the king, it really was pig dirt. Instead of leading me to the princess, they locked me up."

Now the second son said, "Mother, make a medicine ready for me. I will try, too." His mother prepared a medicine, and he left. On his way he met the old gray man, too. He asked again, "Well, my child, where are you going?"

He said, "Why do you ask, you old cur? Are you trying to do what you have done to my brother?"

"What have you got?"

"Pig dirt," he said. Before getting to the royal entrance door, he looked at it again. Well, I have still got my medicine, he thought. It is not pig dirt. I have been on my guard; the old chap dared not do it with me. When he entered, he was searched by the guard and now he had pig dirt, too. He was arrested, got a sound beating, and was locked up for six months because he was the second one to come with pig dirt. At home they thought that the medicine worked, since he did not come back. When he came home, his mother said, "Has it worked?"

He said, "Things have gone even worse with me than with my brother; I have been locked up for six months."

Now the youngest one, who was believed to be stupid, said, "Mother, make a medicine ready for me, too; now I am going to try."

The others said, "We have not succeeded, and you, fool, think you can cure her?" They laughed at him.

He said, "Mother, please! I want to try. Let me go." Now she made a medicine, but she only gave him a little loaf of brown bread for the journey. On his way he met the old man, too.

"Well, my child, where are you going and what are you carrying here?"

"Oh," he said, "where am I going? I am going very far. Let's sit down, I shall tell you. You see, the princess is ill, and he who can cure her will marry her. I want to try."

The other one said, "Where is your medicine? Let me see."

He said, "It's in this glass here. My mother has prepared it. I don't know whether it will be any good or not." The old man took the medicine and blessed it.

After this the fellow said, "I am hungry; you can eat with me." He took his loaf of brown bread, and they ate together. After the meal, he wanted to leave.

The old man said, "My child, here is a little flute. If you are in trouble, you blow it and you will be helped." He took the flute and went on. The old man left, too.

After a while he came across two ants who had a stick. One

pulled it to one side, the other one to the other side. He took the stick, broke it in two, and gave half to each of them. The two ants happened to be ant kings. After this he went on.

At last he came to the castle. The guards searched him. They declared the medicine to be good and led him inside. He went to the princess and gave her some of the medicine. She immediately felt better. She talked more than she had for a long time. When she took the medicine for the third time, she was all right again. She went for a walk in the garden.

When the king saw it, he felt sorry, for he did not want to give his daughter to this simpleton. He sent for his councilors and asked them what he should do. The fellow really was too stupid to be king. They told him that there was only one thing to be done. He should set another task for him. He should mix a quarter of poppy seeds with a quarter of ashes, and if the lad was not able to pick them out in one night, then he would not get the princess.

They put the poppy seeds and the ashes into a dark room, and he was told to pick the poppy seeds out in the dark.

My God, he thought, now I have cured her and shall not get her after all! How shall I do this work in the dark? I could not do it even in broad daylight. While he was sitting there and thinking it all over, with the moon looking into the room, the ant kings came, each with a crowd of ants. They started picking out the seeds, and the work was soon done.

In the morning the councilors came to see. They told the king, "It's neat work, as if the pigeons had done it. Excellent!" The king sent for the fellow and asked him how he had done it. He told the king not to worry about that, since the work was properly done. The king did not know what to do next. He sent for his councilors again and told them that he was at his wits' end. They told him to give the lad 300 woodland hares to tend. If he was not able to do so, he could not marry the princess.

It was proclaimed that the king would buy living woodland hares. Everybody caught hares, and within one day there were enough of them brought to the king. Now the fellow was told to tend the 300 hares. People gathered in the streets to watch the hares leaving their cages. There was a great fuss, but nobody could catch them again. The poor fellow stood there all alone. Then he plucked up his courage and went out of town, while everybody laughed at him. Walking along, he suddenly thought of the little flute that the gray old man had given him. When he was out of town, he started blowing it. The hares immediately came running along and remained by his side. The king had a big pasture, and he led them to it. There he drilled them; they were like soldiers.

Before an hour was over, the king knew all about it. "Well, he said, "what am I going to do with this fellow? I am afraid I shall have to give him my daughter."

Toward noon his daughter said, "Mother, give me the clothes of a servant. I am going to bring him his lunch." She brought him his lunch and ate with him. Then she told him to give her a hare for the king, for he would like to have one for supper. He said that he would gladly give her one, but that before he did she would have to go with him behind the bushes. He knew quite well that she was the princess. She thought that nobody would see her and that if he gave her a hare, he would never marry her. After playing around with her, he caught a hare and gave it to her.

She put it into her basket and thought, well, I have got the hare; so he will not bring them all back, and we shall not get married. She left. After a while he blew the flute, and the hare jumped out of the basket and came running back to the others. When the princess got home, her mother asked her, "Have you got a hare?"

"No," she said, "I haven't got any."

"Didn't he give you one?"

She said, "Yes he did, but when I had left, the hare jumped out of the basket and ran back."

The queen said, "Tomorrow I will go myself; I shall be more skillful and bring one home."

The next day the old queen dressed like a servant and brought him his lunch. She told him that His Majesty asked him to send a hare for his supper. "Why not?" he said. "I have got enough. But you will have to go behind the bushes with me." She looked round and thought, nobody can see me, and I shall not have to give him my daughter.

Afterward she took a thread and tied the hare's legs together. In this way it will not jump out, she thought. However, after a short while the hare tumbled out of the basket and rolled back, and the fellow untied it. So he had all his hares again. I have not been any more successful than my daughter, she thought.

When she came back, the king asked, "Have you got the hare?"

"Oh well," she said, "it overturned the basket and started tumbling back."

On the third day, they did not know what to do. Finally the king said, "Now I will bring him his lunch." He took a bag with him. When the fellow had eaten, the king told him, "The king sends you his respects and asks you to send him a hare, for he would like to eat one."

"With great pleasure. But behind this bush there is a dead ass. You must lick its arse three times. Then you can take a hare." The king did not like it at all. He looked around. Then he thought, Nobody can see me, so I will do it and then I will not have to give him my daughter. After having done it, he got a hare. He put it into his bag and tied it well. Then he put the bag on his shoulder and left. After a little while the hare started jumping up and down on his back until the bag fell down and the hare rolled back in the bag. The king remained there for a long while, but he was too ashamed to go back. When he reached home, he knew that now he had to give his daughter to the fellow. But perhaps there was still something to be done? He sent for his councilors again and told them, "Tonight he will come with the hares, for he has all of them. What am I to do? I do not want to give him my daughter!"

At night the fellow came with all his hares. What could be done about it? The councilors told the lad that he had to talk three bags full. They prepared a big scaffold, and he started talking. "Well," he said, "the first day when I was tending the hares, the princess brought me my lunch. After the meal she told me that His Majesty the king asked me to send him a hare. I said, 'Why not? But . . .'"

At this moment the princess cried, "Tie the bag up; it is full!"

He went on, "On the second day the old queen brought my lunch. After the meal she said that His Majesty the king would like me to send him a hare. 'Well,' I said, 'with pleasure.'"

At this moment the old queen cried, "Tie up; the bag is full!" She did not even let him go on as far as her daughter had.

He went on, "On the third day His Royal Majesty brought my lunch. After the meal he asked me to give him a hare."

The king cried, "Tie the bag up; it is full!" For he was afraid that everything would be made public.

Now there was nothing to be done about it. She had to marry him. They prepared the feast but with little pleasure. He became a very valorous king. He ruled the country so well that nobody else, not even a person of high birth, would have done better. Thus the simpleton was king, and his brothers became even poorer. If they have not died, they are alive to this very day.

·43· *The Peasant and His Three Sons*

• A PEASANT HAD three sons. He loved and respected the two older ones, because they were skillful and clever. But the third one often was beaten for his clumsiness and stupidity. One day the eldest son said to his father, "Father, I want to go traveling in order to make my fortune." He took his walking stick and left. He had not gone very far, when he met a well-dressed gentleman who asked him where he was going. "I want to make my fortune," said the fellow and wanted to go on.

"Wait a moment," said the gentleman, "you can make your fortune right here. Tell me what you want—gold, silver, or to learn an art?"

"Let me have gold," said the fellow.

"Well, if it is gold you want, here you are." He gave him a bag with gold. The fellow turned back and happily went home again. There he told them about his good luck, and his father loved him all the more for it.

Then one day, the second son said to his father, "Father, I want to make my fortune as well." No sooner said than done. He went along the same way as his elder brother. He, too, met the fine gentleman who asked him where he was going. "I want to make my fortune," said the fellow.

"Well, you can make it right now," replied the gentleman. "What do you want, gold, silver, or to learn an art?"

"I want silver," answered the fellow.

"Here it is—if this is what you want." The gentleman handed him a bag with pure silver. The next moment the gentleman had vanished. The fellow capered with joy and hurried home to his father.

The father was very content with his clever sons, and he despised the stupid son even more than before. One day as the third one had as usual been beaten by his brothers, he took his walking stick and went away. He had not gone very far when he met the fine gentleman who asked him why he was walking along so sadly. So he told him of his brothers' good luck and of his bad luck, and he wept bitterly. "Wait," said the gentleman, "you shall make your fortune as well. What do you want? Gold, silver, or do you want to learn an art?"

"I should like to learn an art!" said the fellow joyfully, and his sadness was suddenly gone.

"You shall be able to transform yourself into whatever you choose," said the gentleman. "If you want to be a golden pigeon, just spread your arms and move them as if you wanted to fly. If you want to be a golden fish, throw yourself into the water. And if you want to be a golden hare, run on all fours. If you do so, you will be able to surmount every obstacle!" After these words, the gentleman vanished.

The boy went on and he met a few men who recruited soldiers for their king, for a war had broken out not long before. As the fellow did not want to go home, he cheerfully went with them. When they approached the enemy, the king suddenly despaired, because he had left at home some important papers. "I'll give my daughter in marriage to the one who goes and fetches the papers within twenty-four hours; moreover, he will become my successor!" said the king.

"I shall do it," said the simpleton. No sooner had he said so than he was running over the fields like a golden hare. He came to a great forest. In order to cross it more quickly, he changed into a pigeon and flew over it. When he had gone a long distance like this, he saw a great water which he had to cross as well. He managed to get there, and just as he was about to throw himself into the water, he heard a woeful squeak, which came from a little mouse that was caught in a trap. "Let me free, and I shall help you as well!" called the little mouse.

"How could you help me!" said the fellow, getting ready to jump into the water.

"Help me," repeated the mouse, "and you will not regret it!"

"All right!" said the fellow and opened the trap. Then he jumped into the water and swam away. When he had crossed the lake and had come to the palace, he entered and wanted to talk to the queen. The queen received him most kindly and gave him the papers. "But how did you manage to get here in such a short time?" asked the queen. So the fellow told her of his good luck. And in order to prove his words, he transformed himself into a hare, into a pigeon, and into a fish before the queen. The queen wanted to keep a sign and tore out one of the hare's golden tufts of fur, one of the pigeon's golden feathers, and one of the fish's golden scales. The queen offered the fellow a handkerchief that was richly embroidered with gold. Then the fellow took the papers and set out to return.

After having swum through the lake, he was very tired, and as he had only been a few hours on his way, he wanted to take a rest. While he was asleep, a robber sneaked up to him and stole the papers, and as he woke up, the robber killed him. Then the robber took the papers and hurried to the king. The king was very pleased to have the notes, and when the war was successfully finished, he kept his promise and wanted to give the robber his daughter in marriage. The wedding was to take place the following day.

The little mouse that the fellow had set free happened to be near the lake again. Suddenly it found its savior dead on the shore. It quickly took a flute out of its wallet and began to play. The fellow opened his eyes, saw his little rescuer, and realized what had happened to him.

"Be quick and get ready," said the little mouse. "Tomorrow the wedding will be celebrated in the palace. If you hurry, you might be there in time. Here, take this fiddle. If you play it, everyone who hears it must dance."

The lad thanked his helper, jumped into the water, and hurried to the king's palace.

He first went to the kitchen and played the fiddle that the little mouse had given him. Immediately, the cook and all the maids started dancing. The fellow played on and wept bitterly. The queen came to the kitchen and recognized the handkerchief with which the fellow dried his tears. Meanwhile, the king had joined them, and the fellow told them about his bad luck. He related how he had obtained the papers and how a robber had then killed him as he lay asleep by the lake and how this robber was now trying to get his reward as well. The queen asked him to transform himself before them. Then they might believe him. So the fellow transformed himself into a hare and Lo! the tuft that the queen had torn out before fitted exactly, and so did the feather and the scale. Now the king and the queen saw that they had almost given their daughter to an impostor. The robber was captured and hanged, whereas the simpleton married the daughter and became the successor of the king. For many years his subjects lived happily under his government.

·44· *The Animal Languages*

• A PEASANT AND HIS WIFE (they were of course married) had an ox and an ass. They had the ass for driving across country and into town. Once the peasant told his plowboy to yoke the ox and to set the plow deeply, so that the ox would have to pull hard. When the boy came back with the ox at noon, the ox lay down instead of eating, for the boy had also beaten him thoroughly.

The ass asked him, "Hey, why don't you eat?"

The ox replied, "You are all right. You haven't done anything the whole morning, whereas I can kill myself pulling the plow, and on top of it the boy even beats me."

The ass said, "Then why do you do it? You have horns and legs!"

The boy came with a little pap, but the ox did not look at it.

The peasant was sitting in the courtyard with his wife, and he heard what the ass said to the ox. He said to the boy, "You yoke the ox again."

"He hasn't eaten anything!" said the boy.

"It doesn't matter!" said the peasant.

When the boy wanted to yoke him, the ox tossed him with his horns, and he flew against the wall and toppled over.

Now the boy went to his master and said, "Master, I cannot put the ox to. When I tried to do so, he tossed me with his horns, and I tumbled against the wall. Then he kicked me with his legs. Here! Look at my leg!"

The master said, "This afternoon you put the ass to; it is all his fault." The ass was not better off, and in the evening he did not eat either.

The peasant and his wife were again sitting at the door. This time the ox said to the ass, "Are you feeling sick?"

"Yes!" said the ass. "I was in the same situation as you. I had to pull until my eyes came out of their sockets; and moreover, the boy has beaten me heavily."

"You have given me good advice," said the ox. "Do as you told me!"

And when the boy came with the oats, the ass bit his arm and kicked him so that he flew out of the door.

The peasant heard everything and said to his wife, "I think we shall have to slaughter this ox. He is an obstinate ox."

"What do we do about the ass?" asked his wife. "The ass is still all right. We shall keep him."

Now the ass said to the ox, "Did you hear what the master said?"

"No."

"He wants to slaughter you!"

So the ox said, "Then I will pull. That's better than being slaughtered!"

The next morning the master said, "Try once more to put the ox to."

In the evening the ass asked the ox how it had been.

"As usual!" said the ox. "He has again beaten me, but I would rather pull and be beaten than be slaughtered."

Again the master was sitting at the door and heard everything, but he said nothing.

However, he could not help laughing, and his wife asked, "Why do you laugh?"

"Oh, about nothing," said the man.

"Do you have secrets?" said the wife. "We have been married for fifteen years, and you still have secrets!"

"I really cannot tell you," said the husband.

They were angry with each other. They went around like this for a week and even for a fortnight.

Then the maid said to the servant, "Things are going badly here. If it does not change, I shall leave."

The servant replied, "Then I shall do the same."

The watchdog noticed it as well. He roamed through the place with his tail between the legs. The cock on the dunghill crowed.

The dog said to him, "You seem to be quite merry. The mistress and the master are quarreling, and you crow all the while."

The cock replied, "I have a crowd of hens around. I am standing in the middle. They all obey. The master does not get along with his one wife. It must be the devil himself!" The man heard this. The cock still added, "If I were the husband, I should go to a bush and get a good stick and give the woman a sound thrashing."

And this is what the man did. He went to a bush and cut a stick. When he came back, he said to his wife, "Come along!"

"What do you want?"

He gave her a good beating. Now the wife no longer wanted to know why he had laughed, and from then on she was a good wife to him.

Part VI
Wise Men and Women

·45· *The Quarrel about the Woods*

• In 1496, the community of Langenau was given a parish woods. In the middle of the sixteenth century, the masters of Thüna-Lauenstein did not want to acknowledge this donation; on the contrary, they claimed the woods for themselves. Once the mayor went to Lauenstein in order to settle a question. In the antechamber of the house of the masters of Thüna he overheard a conversation of these gentlemen about the parish woods. Several points concerning the community of Langenau were discussed. Being caught, the listener had to take an oath never to tell a "person" anything about it.

At home, the mayor, persuaded of the importance of what he had heard, thought over for a long time how he might transmit the news to the people of Langenau in spite of the oath. One day as he was going to the field with his oxen, he said to several parishioners that he had to tell something to his ox and that anyone who would like to hear it should stay near him. When he arrived at his field, he shouted into the ears of his ox what he had heard and at the same time the parishioners could hear it. And thus they lodged a complaint about the parish woods.

Result: The parish woods remained the property of the community of Langenau.

·46· *The Swineherd Who Married a Princess*

• Once upon a time there was a king who had a very pretty daughter. No day passed without princes from far and near who wanted to marry her riding to court. The king was delighted about it, but he did not want to make it easy for the suitors. The princess had a peculiarity on her body. He who could divine it should become his son-in-law. Now this was serious! Of course, the princess was much more beautiful to look at than other girls, but anything special that was characteristic only of her could not be seen.

In the king's realm there lived a swineherd who was a very strange fellow. He had cut himself a flute and let his pigs dance to it. As he was not stupid at all, he thought: I think the princess will be mine! Thus on a fine day he drove his herd along to the castle. Not far from the princess's window he stopped his pigs, sat down in the grass, played the flute, and let the animals dance. After a short while the princess came to the window. She never had seen such a thing. And before the maidservants could ask where she was going, she was downstairs.

The swineherd let his pigs go on dancing tranquilly. But the princess did not look at this for a long time. "Listen, you, give me one of your pigs," she said, patting his shoulder.

"Why not? But as a gift? Lift your skirts to the knee, and you may choose one." The princess did not hesitate; she lifted her skirts to the knee and took a pig.

The swineherd had been watching carefully, but he had not seen anything peculiar. "Well, if it doesn't work this time, it will work the next time." He consoled himself and drove his herd away.

Who could have been happier than the princess? She had a flute cut, sat down in the middle of the castle yard, and wanted her pig to dance. But however hard she tried, the animal would not dance. Sadly, she went upstairs and went to bed. But at night she dreamed of the swineherd and of his dancing herd. Therefore she was delighted when, waking up, she heard him playing his flute again. She went to the window, and there he was. The pigs were merrily dancing! She quickly put on a skirt and threw a coat over her shoulders. Then she hurried downstairs.

Again the swineherd did not stop playing. "Hey, listen! The little pig of yesterday does not dance at all!" the princess complained.

"Look here. I might have told you right away. My pigs only dance in society," the rascal told her.

"Well, then give me another one!" the princess begged.

"A second one? Well, why not? Lift your skirt to your navel, and you may take one." The princess did not hesitate this time either. She lifted her skirt to her navel and took a little pig.

This time the swineherd seemed to be satisfied. He leaped with joy and drove his herd away. "This certainly is the peculiarity," he thought, "for there certainly is no other girl with three golden hairs on her belly."

At the royal court, however, there was a merry scene to be observed. The princess was leaning against a tree, playing her flute, and now the pigs danced. The king and the queen, the whole suite, and the suitors were laughing.

The next morning there was a good deal of movement at the royal court. It was crammed with princes. They were standing around all deep in their thoughts, for in the afternoon they were to divine again. "Well, what can there be peculiar about the princess?" one of the princes, who was standing alone, asked himself.

"What is peculiar about the princess?" somebody who was standing nearby asked.

"I am sure to know."

"You'd better go back to the wood with your pigs," the prince rebuffed the speaker, who was nobody else than the swineherd of whom I have told you before. "But wait! Here are one hundred talers if you tell me what you know," the prince corrected himself.

"With pleasure," replied the sly fellow. "She's got two golden hairs on her body." He took the money and went to town. He ate and drank in an inn, bought some chocolate, sweets, and marzipan. And when it was time, he went back to the royal castle.

And it was just the right moment. The swineherd was hardly in the hall when the doors were closed. The king was sitting on the throne and the princess was by his side. Then they started divining. One said a honey mouth. The next one eyes as shining as stars. The third one cheeks like pomegranates, and so on. But the king laughed and the princess shook her head. Then it was the prince's turn. When he mentioned the two golden hairs, the king stopped laughing and the princess did not shake her head any more.

Just wait, you will be even more surprised when I tell you what the princess has, the swineherd said to himself. And truly, the king and his daughter looked at each other not knowing what to say when the man in the shabby clothes talked of the three golden hairs.

"You have guessed it," the king finally announced, and beckoned the swineherd to the throne. "And you have counted wrong by one hair!" This was to the prince who went to the throne as well.

But who was to marry the princess? The king thought it over and over. Of course, he would have preferred the prince to the swineherd. But a king has to keep a promise, and thus he decided as a wise sovereign and as an impartial judge. "You two will sleep tonight beside my daughter, and her husband will be the man she is facing in the morning."

And so it was. The princess lay in the middle and to her right and left lay the swineherd and the prince. Being very tired, the princess soon fell asleep. She dreamed of the swineherd with the dancing pigs. The two suitors lay awake and could not sleep. What am I going to do to make the princess turn to my side? the swineherd asked himself and could find no rest. But while he was thinking it over, the prince grew fidgety. Suddenly he jumped up, ran to the corner of the room, and let his trousers down to relieve himself. "You want to be a prince and you shit in the king's room!" cried the swineherd. The prince, who was afraid the princess might wake up, pulled his trousers up in a hurry and lay down again. "I think luck is on my side," chuckled the swineherd. Then he took the sweets out of his pockets and ate chocolate, toffees, and marzipan.

Finally it grew light. And when the princess woke up, she perceived a frightful stench on her right side. She turned round, and there it smelled nicely like a marzipan shop. But the king was standing in the room. He had the stinking prince shut up in jail and prepared a great wedding for the swineherd and his daughter.

Where have I it all from? Well, the swineherd was my friend, and I was the king's coachman.

The Farmer's Clever Daughter

· A SMALL FARMER who had no luck with anything he did went into the woods in order to hang himself on a tree. As he was looking for a quiet and suitable place in the shrubbery, his neighbor, a very rich farmer, came to the woods carrying a pot and a shovel. Not knowing that he was being observed by the small farmer, the rich one dug a hole in the earth, put the pot in it, and placed dirt on top of it. Then he filled the hole up and uttered the following words: "Who wants to have the treasure must eat the dirt."

Then the rich farmer went away with his shovel. The poor farmer, however, did not hang himself after this event. He fetched a shovel and carried the pot with the money home. The first thing he did was to pay his debts to the rich farmer, who wondered why the poor fellow suddenly had such a lot of money. He thought of the hidden money, went to the woods, and found the hole empty. He knew that the small farmer had stolen his money! He was sure that it could only have been his poor neighbor. He hurried over to him and asked for his money, but the small farmer replied that he had fulfilled all the conditions and that, therefore, the treasure was his.

Thus the rich farmer could do nothing else than bring his case before the judge. The judge realized that the law was on the rich farmer's side, but also that the poor man was much more in need of the money than the rich man was, and therefore he left the decision up to God. He declared that he would ask the accused three questions. If he were able to answer them, then the money would be his; if not, he was to restore the money to the rich farmer. And these were the three questions:

What is the quickest thing? What is the sweetest? What is the fattest? He was given three days to think it over. The small farmer turned it over in his mind. He thought the quickest thing would be his drinking heifer; the sweetest would be sugar; and the fattest, his big sow in the stable. But he was not quite sure about it; so he told his daughter what had happened to him. She was not only curious but also very clever. And she told him that the quickest thing was the sun; the sweetest, sleep; and the fattest, the earth.

So when he came to the judge, he told him this and the judge, amazed to hear such clever answers, gave him the money from the judge's chair and then asked him who had told him the answers. Truthfully, the small farmer told him that it was his daughter, and the judge ordered him to send this clever girl before him.

But the girl replied, "If the judge wants to ask me any questions, he may come over himself; it is the same distance for him to come to me as for me to go to him." Now the judge sent her three hemp plants; with these she was to make a skirt, a sheet, and a towel.

She sent the judge three small wooden pegs with the notice that the judge might make a flax brake, a spinning wheel, and a weaving loom with these; then she would make the three objects he had asked for with the three hemp plants.

Now the judge declared that if she did not finally come, she would be brought before him by force. However, she should not come by day or by night, not with an empty stomach and not satiated, not on the road and not beside the road.

So she licked some salt and started in the small hours of the morning, riding on a goat. He was strongly impressed by all this, and as, moreover, she was very clean, he promised to marry her on the condition that she never interfere with his affairs; this would be cause for a divorce. Furthermore, she would be allowed to bring with her three of her dearest things.

She brought her father to the judge's house, because he was what she loved most at home. This was not quite to the judge's taste, but he could not object. He decided, however, to annoy the small farmer a little, so that he would be glad to leave again.

He sent him to a meadow where he was to tend fish. Naturally, the fish died without water. When the judge became aware of this and wanted to blame him, the old man replied as his daughter had told him, "They were all gentlemen fish; they could not understand my peasant language."

"Who told you this?" asked the judge. Truthfully, the old man told the judge, "My daughter, your wife."

The judge recognized that his wife had interfered with his

affairs, and this was cause for divorce. But he allowed her to take the three dearest things back to her farm.

As they were sitting at the farewell dinner, she put a soporific into her husband's wine, and when he was fast asleep, with her father's help she put him into a coach that stood waiting outside. Moreover she took a large purse with money and went with her father into the coach.

When the coach jolted over the uneven road, the judge awoke. Astonished and not knowing at first where he was, he asked, "Why are you still with me?"

"You have granted me the right to take with me the three dearest things. They are a purse with money, my father, and you."

After this they went back to the judge's house, for he realized that he had a faithful wife.

·48· *The Baron's Haughty Daughter*

• AT SCHWARZERSBERG there once lived a most beautiful baron's daughter. She was not only beautiful; she was also very haughty. A knight, who had heard about her, sent her a letter in which he asked for her in marriage. Her answer was that he was not worth the dust under her feet and even less so the dust on her shoes.

The knight became angry and considered how he could take revenge on her for this insult. At last he decided to disguise himself as a juggler and to play his tricks before her. As to the rest, he would see.

So he came to the castle and was allowed to show his tricks to the inhabitants. The lord of the castle liked the handsome man no less than his art, and he kept him at the castle for his pleasure. So the knight had plenty of time and opportunities to gain the young lady's love. They used to meet secretly, until she noticed to her dismay that her love would not remain without consequences. She told the juggler. He persuaded her to escape with him in order to avert disgrace and to save their lives. Her chambermaid, who knew of her secret love, helped them to escape. The young lady wanted to take her jewels with her, but the juggler did not let her. They left the castle at midnight and embarked on a small boat to cross the water. They reached the properties of the knightly juggler, who did not reveal who he was, and since he did not practice his art any longer, they became very poor.

When things were at their worst, he pretended that they could do nothing but go begging. So they went to another big castle which belonged to him. He had given an order that nobody should give anything to a female person who would wear such and such clothes and who would ask for charity. They should, on the contrary, send her away with hard words. The knight left the beautiful maid, pretending to look for help elsewhere, whereas she was, according to his orders, sent away from every door to which she came with hard and bitter words.

They met at the place agreed upon. The juggler had a provision of bread cut into small pieces, and he asked the maid what she had obtained. As she had nothing, he showed her his bread and scolded her for not even being able to beg at the doors. Then he gave her some of his bread, and they went on.

They came to his third castle. He let her wait outside and went in, pretending that he wanted to see if he could not find a job in the castle. He went in, told his father everything, and secured his approbation. Then he went back to the maid and brought her to a small mud hut. He went to see her every day, but nobody was allowed to tell her who he was. One day he arrived and gave her money to start a business; she was to keep a tavern. She obeyed with reluctance. The knight sent his warriors to her place. They drank, but they did not pay, and when she grew angry, they smashed everything to pieces and went away. The next day when the juggler came and heard what had happened, he scolded her again and told her that she was good for nothing.

Now he bought her some pottery, saying she should offer it for sale the next day on the market. She obeyed with tears at the threat that he would leave her. The next morning he rode over the market as a knight with his followers and right through the maid's pottery, so that there remained not one pot intact. The following day the juggler asked her whether she had sold her things and scolded her again. He proposed that she serve as a kitchen maid, as she was obviously unable to maintain a business of her own.

So she came to the kitchen of the castle. After a few days the juggler came to tell her that the next day there would be a feast and a great deal of food would be prepared, some of which she might put aside for him. As she said that she would not be able to do so, he told her to hang a pot between her legs. She would not have to walk and so the pot would not annoy her.

The wedding feast for the young knight was prepared. There was but the bride lacking. After the meal, the common people were to appear before the guests; the juggler went down to the kitchen and asked the maid for a dance. She refused, for the pot would have hindered her. But he dragged her along with him amid the dancing couples, and the more uneasy she became, the quicker he waltzed with her, until one piece of food after the other was rolling out of the pot. At last the pot itself rolled to the lord-of-the-castle's feet. Angrily he asked her who she was, and as she confessed to being the kitchen maid, he ordered her carried down to the prison.

This gave the juggler time enough to assume his normal form again. Then he went to see her, revealed himself to her, and asked her to marry him, for she had suffered enough for her haughtiness. He gave her magnificent clothes, led her back to the hall, and presented her as his bride. Everybody was there for the wedding, and everybody was happy, and later on the young knight succeeded to his father's and his father-in-law's properties.

· 49 · Prince Ferdinand

· IN HIS EARLY YEARS Prince Ferdinand was a rather riotous and godless boy. When he was grown, his father, the king, one time said to him, "Ferdinand, instead of playing your godless tricks, you should rather try to make the fair Helena, the beautiful princess, your wife." He did not need to tell him twice. Soon afterward Ferdinand set out for the country where Helena's father was king.

In the first forest he met an old man in rags, who offered to change clothes with him. This suited the prince perfectly, for he thus would not be recognized. He therefore agreed. When they parted, the old man said, "Here, Prince Ferdinand. I wish to give you something which can be quite useful for your journey. Here is a ring, an orchis root, and a fern. If you put the ring into your mouth, you will be invisible; if you hold the orchis root near a lock, it will burst open by itself; and if you carry the fern with you, you will be able to hear for miles around what people are talking about, even if they speak in a low voice."

Prince Ferdinand went on. Late in the evening he saw a light which was burning before a den far away in the woods. He went toward this light. Before the den an old woman was washing potatoes. When he asked her for a night's shelter, she gave him the good advice to go on in a hurry; the people living there were robbers, and they would soon come home, and then he would fare ill. "Well," said Ferdinand, "I am a robber, too." Thus he was allowed to lie down by the stove. When the robbers came home, they were pleased to find a companion, for they had not been together for very long and had not yet chosen a chief. They agreed that he who could steal the most on the following day should be their chief.

On the highway the next day Prince Ferdinand came across a Jew with a big herd of fat rams. He went past the Jew and on purpose dropped his golden sword. Having passed over the next hill, he hid in a bush. The Jew first drove his herd on for a while, and when he thought the owner of the sword to be far away, he drove his rams into the bushes and went back to fetch the sword. In the meantime, however, Prince Ferdinand drove the rams away.

Although none of the other robbers had brought back as much as Ferdinand, they did not make him their chief yet. They wanted to set out once more the next day. This time Prince Ferdinand had a Jew who was driving a fat ox walking before him. When he was ahead of him, the prince loosened a new shoe. The Jew was very much interested in the fine shoe, and as he believed the other to be lying farther back, he tied his ox to a tree and walked back. Ferdinand, however, went off with the ox.

The robbers still did not make him their chief, and they agreed that he who would bring the greatest amount of money on the following day should be their chief. "Well," said the prince, "that's a mere trifle, if you can give me a horse." They gave him one. The next day Ferdinand rode to the town where the fair Helena's father was king. He tied his horse to a tree outside the town, made himself invisible with the help of his ring, and penetrated the royal treasury. Since the king had a great amount of money and valuables, the treasury was a fireproof vault with the most ingenious doors and locks, and whoever would enter there would first have to go through heaven knows how many other rooms with complicated doors and locks. The prince had only to hold his orchis root to the doors, and all the locks burst open. He took as much money as he was able to carry and wrote in the treasury and on all the doors the word "breeches-flap" before leaving. By means of the orchis root the locks were all closed again. The prince wrote "breeches-flap" on the big drawbridge over which he had to go and on all the houses and street corners he passed; then he leaped into the saddle with his treasure and rode back to the robber's den. Now the robbers, of course, saw that he was their best man and wanted to make him their chief. But Prince Ferdinand was satisfied to have proved what he was able to do and he traveled on.

Prince Ferdinand went to the town where the fair Helena lived. He applied to a shoemaker as a journeyman. He told the shoemaker that he would not work but that he would bring him enough money to satisfy him. With the help of his charms he made his way again and again into the royal treasury, and each time he marked his path by writing "breeches-flap" everywhere. At last the king became enraged. He deliberated with his councilors about how to catch Breeches-flap. They decided to catch him with a ruse on his way to the castle. They would fix a trapdoor on the bridge he passed, which would cut the head from the body, so that the body would fall into the water, while the head would remain on the bridge.

With the help of his fern, Prince Ferdinand could hear what was being said for ten miles around; therefore, he knew all about the trap. He decided to outsmart them again. On the following night, he visited the treasury and took the shoemaker with him.

When they drew near the bridge, Prince Ferdinand told the old man to go on, since he wanted to relieve himself. So the old shoemaker was beheaded. Prince Ferdinand, however, went invisibly as usual into the treasury, wrote "breeches-flap" again everywhere (on the drawbridge, too), and took the head of his old master with him. He had to leave the body behind because he could not get it out of the moat. He told the shoemaker's wife that her husband had met with an accident. He consoled her and promised that if she did not tell anybody, she would be well provided for.

The next morning the king was beside himself when he saw that Breeches-flap had again played a trick on them and had escaped. In order to discover whose body it was they had found, the king ordered the carcass to be carried from one house to the other through the whole town. He expected the wife of the dead man to burst out crying at this sight. Prince Ferdinand told his master's wife what was going to happen and asked her not to betray him. She promised, but Ferdinand, who knew women, did not trust her. When they came with the corpse, he sat down by the stove and started cutting wood. Everything happened as he had expected. When the corpse was dragged past, the old woman went to the window and cried out at the sight, "Good Lord!"

Prince Ferdinand, however, who was in danger of being discovered, cut his hand at the same moment with the ax, so that he was bleeding. When the police entered, the woman had to say that she had shouted "Good Lord" because of her journeyman's wound. Accordingly, they went on with their corpse, and as nobody in the whole town recognized it, the king gave orders to hang it on the gibbet outside the town. For he thought that Breeches-flap, who had taken the head with him, might try to get the body, too. In order to catch him, he placed twelve hussars on guard near the gibbet.

Prince Ferdinand bought a horse and a cart. In the cart he put two wicker bottles of wine and a big pot of black paint. With this carriage he went past the gibbet at night, dressed as an old woman. The hussars had just lit a fire to warm themselves, for it was deucedly cold. Prince Ferdinand stopped and asked if he could warm himself a little. They allowed the old woman to do so. After a while, she asked if the gentlemen wanted to drink a drop of wine, for she would like to show her gratitude. They accepted with pleasure. She got out the first wicker bottle, and it was soon empty. The hussars, who liked the stuff, asked her if they could have some more, and finally the old woman got out the other basket and offered it to them. But Ferdinand had put a sleeping draught into this wine and, therefore, the twelve hussars fell fast asleep after a short while. This is what Ferdinand had been waiting for. He quickly got out his pot and painted the fellows all black. Then he took the corpse, wrote "breeches-flap" on the gibbet, and went away. He buried his master the same night.

The next day when the hussars woke up, they were enraged. They would have liked to run away, but they had to go to the king and tell him what had happened. The king said, "This really is too much!"

He tried to think of a way to get Breeches-flap. At last he decided to arrange a big feast for everybody. He expected Breeches-flap, who was turning up everywhere, to come, too.

Everything was prepared, and the feast was announced. A prince from a distant country, who was of course Ferdinand, asked the king by letter if he might come as well. The king invited him cordially, and the prince arrived with princely pomp in a coach with a coachman and two servants.

While they were at the table where different sorts of wine were served, Prince Ferdinand said that he had brought a barrel of wine from his country and that with the king's permission he would like them to taste it. And so they did. The sleeping draught which Prince Ferdinand had again put into it worked at once. After a quarter of an hour, the whole company was fast asleep. Then Prince Ferdinand wrote "breeches-flap" on the wall, painted everyone with green paint, which he had brought with him, and disappeared.

When the king and his guests woke up, Prince Ferdinand was invisible among them. The king entreated Breeches-flap through a servant to step forward: Nothing should happen to him. But Ferdinand remained invisible. Only when the king asked him for the third time, did he step forth. The king asked him why he had done all this. Ferdinand said that he did it in order to gain Helena, since his father told him to ask for her as his wife. The king agreed immediately, but told Ferdinand that he could have had her more easily.

·50· *The Lazy Woman*

· THERE ONCE LIVED a woman who never wanted to spin. Whenever her husband told her to spin, she said that she had no reel. Finally her husband said, "Then I will go to the woods tonight and fetch some wood to make you a reel." He went to the forest.

His wife followed far behind him and kept shouting into the forest, "Whoever cuts wood is going to be hanged. Whoever cuts wood is going to be hanged!" So the man went home again.

"But father," she said, "you do not bring me any wood?"

"Well," he said, "there is someone calling in the woods, 'Whoever cuts wood is going to be hanged!' So I have come back. You had better not spin any more, so that I will not be hanged." And so the woman never had to spin again.

·51· *The Peasant Pewit*

· ONCE UPON A TIME there was a peasant whose name was Pewit. He was plowing in the field with his oxen. When he was in the middle of his work, the pewits came flying over and cried, "Pewit." The peasant became angry, for he thought that the pewits were laughing at him. He took a big stone and threw it at the criers. However, he hit an ox on the head and it fell down dead. The peasant dragged the ox home, skinned it, went to town, and sold the skin to a Jew. He got five talers for it.

When the peasant reached home, he told his neighbors that he had gotten one hundred talers for the skin. Then the avaricious peasants killed all the oxen, skinned them, and brought their skins as well to the Jew. But they only received five talers apiece. They realized that Pewit had duped them. When they returned home, they wanted to kill him.

But Pewit had foreseen this and had persuaded his wife to

change clothes and occupations with him. So he stood in women's clothes by the fireplace preparing lunch, while his wife climbed into men's clothes and was mending the thatched roof. The angry peasants brought her down and killed her.

The next day the peasant Pewit went to town with his wife, placed her in a corner, and put a pound of butter in her hand. People soon came and asked for the price of the butter. Of course, she gave no answer. After a while a man slapped her in the face, so that she fell down. Pewit had only been waiting for this. He came along in a hurry and called, "You have killed my wife!"

The other one was terrified when the woman fell down and did not get up again.

He begged, "Dear man, please don't tell the police. I'll give you all my money! Here, take one hundred talers!" Pewit took the money, put his wife in the carriage, and drove home.

The peasants opened their eyes wide when Pewit, whom they had killed the day before, came back from town in high spirits. And how astonished were they when he showed them one hundred shining talers! Then he told them that he had exhibited his dead wife in the market and that he had gotten one hundred talers for her. Now the avaricious peasants wanted to be as rich. They all killed their wives, went to the market, and exhibited them. But nobody gave them a penny. On the contrary, the police came and wanted to lock them all up in jail. The peasants drove home in a hurry; Pewit had again duped them.

Now the peasants attacked him and locked him in a chest. They wanted to take it out to the sea and to drown the scoundrel. Since a boat was not available, they placed the chest on the shore and went to have their lunch. Meanwhile a shepherd came along with his flock. Pewit lured his dog, and soon the shepherd followed. Pewit was sitting in his chest, shaking his head, and murmuring, "I can't write, I can't read, and they want me to be mayor! I can't write, I can't read, and they want me to be mayor!"

"Well, why are you so sad? I'd rather like to be mayor," said the shepherd.

The peasant answered, "If you care so much for it, I'm quite willing to tend your sheep. May you become mayor!" And they changed.

Soon the peasants came back, carried the chest into the boat, went out to sea, and threw what they thought to be Pewit into the water; the poor shepherd was drowned. In the evening our Pewit was back again. He was driving a big herd of sheep into his yard. Curious, the peasants approached and asked where all those sheep came from. Pewit said, "I had filled all my pockets with field stones when you threw me into the water. Each stone immediately became a sheep. And I just drove the herd out of the reeds and came home." Immediately they did the same: they filled their pockets with stones, jumped into the sea, and were drowned. Now Pewit's luck was complete. He inherited all the dead peasants' lands, and the whole village belonged to him.

· 52 · *The Woman in the Chest*

· IN A VILLAGE there was a priest who lived with his mother, whom they called the old Oferl, and with a cook. And then there was a schoolteacher who was very poor, because he had too many children and his income was not big enough. He had once been in the priest's house.

One time when the priest had slaughtered two pigs and put the meat into the chimney, the schoolteacher, who knew it, turned over in his mind how he might steal the meat. He secretly remained in the priest's house at night and waited until they bolted the door. When everybody was asleep, he went into the kitchen, took the meat, and went home.

In the morning when the cook went to see if the meat did not drip too much, there was nothing left. She immediately called the priest and Oferl. "Who has done this?" they asked.

"Well," said the cook, "nobody has been here but the teacher. He must have stolen it."

"I cannot believe it," said the priest, "for the teacher is quite an honest man." But the cook insisted that it could only have been the teacher. The priest wondered what they could do to find out, for he did not wish to have the teacher's house searched.

"I have an idea," said Oferl. "We'll tell the teacher that the meat has been stolen. And then," she said to the priest, "you tell him that you have to go for a journey, and as you are afraid to leave your valuables in the house, which could be stolen like the meat, you propose to leave them at his place until you come back. Then take a big chest. I'll hide inside. Give me some bread, so that I have something to eat, and then bring the chest to the teacher's house, so that I can see and hear if they cook any pork. In the evening you come and fetch me, pretending that you have not been able to leave." The priest liked this idea. He took a chest, and Oferl climbed inside, taking about two pounds of bread with her.

Now the priest went to the teacher and asked him if he would not kindly keep his valuables in his house, as he had to go on a journey. The teacher agreed. He went with him and helped the cook carry the chest and place it in a corner of the room.

At lunchtime, the teacher's children cried, "Father, let me have some of the priest's meat."

"Me, too."

When Oferl heard this, she was unable to keep silent and cried out, "So you are the meat thief! But now I know it. You wait, you will go to jail."

The teacher and his family were frightened when they heard Oferl's voice. He went to the chest, opened the lid, and saw her. He quickly made up his mind. He strangled her, put a roll into her mouth, and closed the lid again.

In the evening, the priest came back and said that he came for the chest again, as he had not been able to leave. Again the teacher helped carry the chest, this time back to the priest's house, and then he went home. Now the priest opened the lid and saw that his mother was dead. He called the cook, "Look, God has punished us for having wronged the teacher. She has suffocated. But what on earth shall we do? People might even believe that we have killed her ourselves in order to get her money (for she had a lot of money). We must get rid of her. Go right over to the teacher; he might advise us what to do." The cook went. The teacher came. The priest told him all about it and asked him to take her away secretly. He gave him £200.

The teacher took the money and the dead Oferl with the mug she used to carry with her when she fetched beer. He carried her to the public house, and as there were several steps leading up to the door, he put her on top of them, leaning against the door, which was closed, with the mug in her arm. He then rang the bell and hid himself. It was Saturday, and the waitress was very busy. She came in a hurry, for she knew right away that it might be Oferl, took the mug swiftly from her, and hurried back to fill it. When she took the mug, Oferl fell down the steps. When the waitress came back, she saw Oferl lying on the street, and when she tried to help her up, she saw that she was dead. She told the innkeeper and asked him what to do. It was not her fault. She only had taken the mug from her in a hurry, and the old woman must have fallen down and broken her neck. "You run over to the teacher," said the innkeeper. "Tell him the whole story and ask him to come over and help us out of this trouble, because if we don't get out of this, we both go to jail. Tell him that I'll give him £300 if he is able to help us." The waitress went to the teacher and told him the whole story. The teacher came over, took the £300, and told the innkeeper not to worry. Everything would turn out all right if none of them said a word about it.

Now the teacher knew a farmer in the place whose cabbages had once been stolen from his field. The farmer was rather a rude fellow. The teacher took Oferl, carried her to the farmer's cabbage field, and put her in a bent position beside a basket. In the morning when the farmer got up, he first of all looked at his cabbage field and saw her in the middle of it. He took a big stick, slowly sneaked to her side, and when he was there, he hit her with all his force. She fell down at the first blow. He looked at her, recognized the priest's Oferl, and saw that she was dead. "For heaven's sake, what have I done?" he cried. "This is the priest's Oferl; she certainly did not want to steal my cabbage but only came to get some herbs for her rabbits. What shall I do now? If anyone finds out, I shall go to jail."

He went to the teacher, told him everything, and promised him £100 if he would remove her from his field so nobody would suspect him.

The teacher took the £100, put the old Oferl into a bag, and went to the woods at night. After he had gone along for some time in the wood, he heard somebody coming. It turned out to be three brothers who were robbers and who had just come back from a robbery. Each of them carried a bagful of smoked meat. The teacher hid behind a tree, and as they came near, he cried, "Stop, you pickpockets!" The robbers were frightened, dropped their bags, and ran away. The teacher took one of the meat bags, put the bag with the dead Oferl in its place, and went home with the meat. In possession of the meat and of £600, he led a comfortable life.

When the robbers had run away for some time without hearing a sound, they went back, found their bags, took them, and went home. At home their mother asked them if they had got anything. They said "Yes," they had. Then their mother emptied the bags and took the meat out, and when she came to the third one, she got hold of the old woman's hair. "Well, you have flax in this one," she said.

"No," they answered, "it is all meat." She emptied the bag, and to her astonishment, an old woman fell out of it. Then they put her in the earth in a hurry, so that nobody knew about it, and ate their meat with relish.

·53· *A Peasant Sells a Cow as a Goat*

• A PEASANT whose sight was bad led a cow to the market in order to sell it. Three merchants soon noticed that they could make a good bargain. "We shall persuade him that he has not a cow but a goat, and thus we shall make a good deal of money," they said to one another.

"How much do you want for your goat?" the first one asked him while the others kept away.

"I am not selling a goat, but a cow," replied the peasant.

"You fool, can't you distinguish a cow from a goat?" The merchant started again.

But no business was done. Ten marks were not enough for the peasant, and he did not believe he had brought a goat instead of a cow.

The same thing happened with the second merchant, but he was

no more successful. When the third one came and asked about the
goat, too, the peasant became uncertain. He could not trust his
eyes, and as he did not wish to wait any longer, he sold the cow as
a goat. He went home with ten marks in his pocket and told his
wife that he had led a goat to the market instead of a cow and that
he had got ten marks for it. "Oh you fool, you have been cheated
and have sold a cow as a goat," his wife scolded him.

"So I have really been duped!" the peasant cried angrily and
went back to town at once.

The three merchants were still there, pleased with the good
bargain. They were astonished when the peasant invited them for
a drink to celebrate his profit. And when he asked them to wait a
moment, as he had to run errands, they laughed about the silly
fellow.

Now the peasant's sight was bad, but he was not stupid, as we
shall see in a minute. He went to the next shop and bought a white
straw hat. Then he went to see three innkeepers and instructed
them as follows, "When I come here with three merchants, you
bring whatever I order. When I turn my hat and ask, 'Is everything paid for?' then you answer, 'Yes, everything is paid.' Afterward I will come and bring the money." The innkeepers, who
knew him, agreed.

"Well, come on! Let's have a drink," he repeated to the merchants. The innkeeper brought what the peasant ordered. After
drinking merrily for a while, he called the innkeeper, turned his
hat, and asked, "Is everything paid for?"

"Yes, everything is paid," replied the innkeeper.

The same thing happened in the second and the third inn. The
merchants were astonished at the marvelous hat. "I wish I had
such a hat, too," one of them said. "You drink as much as you
want, then you turn your hat, and everything is paid for. This hat
certainly is very expensive? Perhaps you would sell it?"

"I should find it difficult to part with. But if you give me a
hundred talers, you may have it." The merchant agreed. He gave
the peasant the hundred talers and proudly put the hat on his
head. The peasant quickly set out for home.

The three merchants were in high spirits. Now they could
drink to their hearts' content. They had but to turn the hat, and

everything would be paid for. In the first inn they started a boisterous revel. After each round of beer there followed a round of strong liquor. Then this grew boring and they felt like changing the place. "Let's go to the next pub," they said. "Is everything paid for?" asked the owner of the hat, turning it round and looking defiantly at the innkeeper.

"Paid? Which of you has paid?" the innkeeper replied angrily. And since he was a sturdy man and the merchants were none too steady on their legs, they preferred to pay.

"Give that hat to me, you fool! You don't know how to handle it," the second merchant shouted angrily. But he was not any luckier. In the second inn as well they had to pay for what they had drunk. When the third merchant put the hat on his head with no more success than his companions, they realized at last that the silly peasant had duped them. Furious, they inquired where he lived, and as it was not far from town, they all went there in order to give the rascal a good thrashing.

The peasant had just come home and told his wife how he had fooled the three merchants. This time his wife was satisfied. But the pleasure did not last long. They had only just sat down to eat, when the peasant suddenly jumped up. Through the window he saw the three merchants approaching. They were hurrying toward the house with sturdy sticks in their hands. "Listen wife. I'll pretend to be dead. You go to meet them crying and tell them that I have died."

The wife did as she was told. But her wailing and lamenting made no impression on them. "Then we shall punish your husband after his death for what he has done to us," they told the woman and they entered the room. The peasant was lying on the floor. But this did not keep them back. They beat him so hard that the poor peasant could do nothing else but run away and hide.

The duped merchants had taken revenge. Satisfied, they went away, because you do not succeed every day in raising a person from the dead.

· THERE LIVED ONCE a poor shoemaker who was very badly off, having many children and no work. He did not know what to do. He had a very beautiful wife whom the men liked to see. Once she passed by a butcher's shop. The butcher called from his door, "Come in. We have some fine meat today. Take some with you."

"No, I cannot take any. I have no money. We do not earn anything."

"Never mind, I'll lend it to you." The woman went in and took two pounds of meat. She kept saying that her husband had no work. The butcher gave her a pair of boots and a pair of shoes to sole. She took them home.

The next day she passed by a baker's shop. The baker offered her bread and rolls. No, she did not want to borrow. But he insisted and gave her two loaves of bread and some rolls, and she took them. Two days later the butcher and the baker came for a chat. The butcher asked, "Are my boots and shoes ready?" The baker just accompanied him. After a while they went home again.

She was getting on very well with men, but her husband was awfully stupid. He was not able to read or write, and everybody laughed at him because he knew nothing. So he asked the others where they had all the news from. They told him to go to town and to buy a book. He would find everything in there—enough to become all-knowing. "Yes," they told him, "you may still learn everything, shoemaker."

So he went and bought the book. The bookseller took part in the joke, "Yes, there is such a book. You can become all-knowing, even a doctor. You only have to have a sign made saying: Doctor Know-All."

He went home and fixed the signboard. Then he sat down at his table, opened the book, and looked into it. While he was turning over the pages, two men entered the room. "Hey!" said one of them, "if you really are all-knowing, tell us who has stolen our horse."

"Well, let's see!" He opened the book, looked into it, then he pointed with his hand. The two men thanked him and promised to give him a lot of money if they found the horse. The two went across the field and came to an inn. They asked if anybody with a horse had come. Yes, somebody had left a horse there. What did it look like? Well, it had only one eye and on the other one it had a blinker. "Yes, that's it!" They took it with them and went back to the shoemaker. They gave him some money and went on. "You see, wife, now everything will be all right!"

After a little while, the king, who had heard of him, asked him to come to town. His wedding ring had been stolen. He thought, I want to see if Know-All is able to find it. He sent him the following message: if he came, he had to come riding and yet walking, he had to bring a gift and yet he had to have nothing, and he had to come naked and yet to come dressed. The shoemaker turned over in his mind what there was to do. He thought it over and over, took his book, and stared into it, and suddenly he knew. He took a goat out of the stable and a mousetrap with a mouse. He put on a suit of tulle. As he approached the castle, he straddled the goat and walked, and it looked as if he were riding. As he entered the room, the king saw that he had a suit on, although from afar he had looked naked. Then he offered the king the mousetrap. The king opened the trap a little, and the mouse was gone. Now the king asked him if he really was all-knowing.

"Yes, I am."

The king said, "My wife's wedding ring has been stolen. Where is it?"

"I cannot tell you right away. I need a week, and my family has to come; otherwise, they will have nothing to eat."

"All right," said the king, "you may fetch them." He went home and fetched his family and the book. When they were all in the castle and seated at a table, he opened the book, put his nose in it, and turned the pages.

There were three waiters in the castle; he had met them already, whereas his wife had not. One of them was tall, the second one a little smaller, and the third one very small. At noon the tall one brought their meal. The shoemaker said to his wife, "Look here, wife, this is the first one." The waiter was frightened and wondered if Know-All really knew that they had the ring. The next day when the second one came, the shoemaker said, "Look here, wife, this is the second one." On the third day when the third one came, he said, "Look, wife, this is the third one." The three waiters wondered if Know-All did know that they had the ring, and they decided to go to him and to ask him not to tell anybody. They would give him a lot of money and the ring, which he might conjure up somehow. They came and told him everything. He agreed with their plan. When he had received the money and the ring, he was at a loss what to do next.

The next day a cake was prepared for the king. The batter was already in the cake mold as the shoemaker swiftly slipped the ring within it. When the cake was brought to the king, the shoemaker called suddenly, "I know where the ring is. It's in the cake! The king must cut it open and be careful not to eat it." The king did as he was told, and he found the ring.

Now the king gave him a lot of money, so the shoemaker had everything he needed. "You see, wife, now we are well off and need not work any more." Then he took his belongings and wanted to go home with his family.

But the king still wondered, is he really all-knowing? He quickly swept the dirt in the room together, put it into a paper bag, and called, "Come back once more, doctor. You have forgotten something!"

The shoemaker thought, if it is mine, then it won't be worth much!

He called back, "I don't need it. It is just some dirt!"

Then they went back to their little house. Many people came to see him, and he made a great deal of money. He and his family were very well off, and if they have not died in the meantime, they are living to this very day.

·55· *The Wrong Song*

• THERE ONCE WAS A BOY who had to tend geese every day. He was always cheerful and merry. He used to smack them with his whip and to sing joyfully.

One day he went to the pasture and sang,

> We have seven geese and an old one, too,
> The meat of the priest is hanging in the chimney, too.

(Several days before, the priest's meat had been stolen.)

One day the priest went to the pasture and heard the boy's song. He went to the boy, praised him for singing so nicely, and told him, "My boy, you could sing this song in church after my sermon."

The boy agreed and said he would do so. Then the priest went on.

In the evening the boy told his parents how he had met the priest and what the priest had told him. The father knew right away what was the matter and taught the boy different words, which he was to sing on Sunday.

The next Sunday the boy went to church. The priest preached his sermon and afterward he said, "There is a boy who is going to sing a song. Everybody may pay attention to it and take it to heart. Get up, my child."

The boy got up and sang,

> We have seven young geese and an old one, too.
> The priest sleeps with the cook and with the maiden, too.

Part VII
Saints and Sinners

·56· *The Poor and the Rich*

• ONCE Our Lord went through the country as a poor man, thinking that he would like to find out how people were minded. He knocked at a stately house and asked for a night's lodging. The rich man looked at him and slammed the door shut without saying a word. Then he went to a poor man who lived in a thatched cottage. The people there asked him to come in and made some coffee and prepared a bed of straw. In the morning they made coffee again. After drinking it, Our Lord told the man to utter a wish. The poor man said, "I am content with what I have." Our Lord asked him if he would not like to have a fine house.

"Well," said the man, "that would be all right, if I can live there in peace." Then Our Lord left, and after a little while a fine new house was standing there.

The rich man saw it from his window and said, "What's this? Where there was a cottage yesterday, there is now a stately house!" His wife ran over to find out what was going on. The people told her what had happened. She told her husband.

"I could slap myself. The fellow was here, too!"

His wife said, "Ride after him. Perhaps he is still willing to do something for you." He mounted his horse and caught up with Our Lord. He made a great fuss and said that he had wanted to keep him and that he had left too soon! He should not bear him a grudge, but should rather do something for him as well. Our Lord told him to ride home. He would grant him three wishes.

It was very hot. The rich man was thinking aloud what he might wish and while doing so he slapped his horse, which started jumping. He said, "I wish you would break your neck!" With this the horse fell down and its neck was broken. Being very thrifty, he did not want to leave the saddle behind. So he put it on his shoulder. He was sweating a lot and became so angry that he said, "Now my wife is sitting at home in a cool room. I wish she was sitting on this saddle and could not get off again." Immediately the saddle was gone. When he came home, his wife was sitting on the saddle in the middle of the room, and she was not able to get off. He told her what had happened and said that

she might stay where she was. He was going to wish all the
treasures the earth held. His wife said, "This won't help me any.
You have wished me up here, and you are going to wish me down
again!" He could do nothing; he had to do what his wife told
him. So all this good luck brought him nothing but anger and a
dead horse.

· 57 · *The Black Woodpecker*

· ONE DAY JESUS, accompanied by Peter, came to a house where
the woman was just going to bake cakes. Jesus asked her to make
one for him and his companion. The woman took a bit of dough
and made it ready, but it looked too big to her, and she started the
work again. This was repeated until the dough, owing to the
frequent remodeling, was gone.

Now Jesus became angry and said that, for having been so
avaricious and unkind, she was to be transformed into a black
woodpecker. The woman shot out of the chimney, and because
she was wearing a red hood, the black woodpecker has a red head,
too.

· 58 · *The Road to Hell*

· THERE WAS ONCE A POOR MAN who was doing very badly. He
went into the woods, hoping to find relief there. While he was
trudging along, he met a man with a cock's feather in his hat.
"Why do you have such a wretched look?" the man asked him. So
he told him about his misery. But the stranger only smiled and
said, "Go home right away; there you will find what you need."

"But what am I to give you?" the poor man replied.

"Oh well, just give me what you do not know about," answered
the one with the cock's feather. And then he opened the poor
man's artery a little bit with a pin, and with the blood he wrote on
a slip of paper that the poor man would give him what he did not
know about. Then he was gone.

What he did not know about!

When the peasant came home, he found an immense sum of money in his cupboard and all his misery came to an end. But his wife, who did not feel at ease seeing this, asked him why he suddenly had such a pile of money.

"Well," he replied, "I have met someone in the woods who gave me the money in return for what I do not know about."

His wife exclaimed, "You fool, don't you know that I'm pregnant?"

So several weeks went past, and they had all they wanted. The new child, a boy, was born and was given the name of Hiasl. His father bought him a beautiful cradle adorned with gold and bedclothes of satin and everything the child needed; the house was built up anew, and the peasant and his wife went about in beautiful clothes. Servants and maids did the work. All the man did was buy things, but his main work consisted in eating and sleeping.

But he never was really happy, and he sighed whenever he saw his son, Hiasl. Hiasl was growing up, and as he had for a long time noticed his father's sighing, he wanted to know the reason; and so he finally went to his father and insisted that he be told all about it. His father also told him about that slip of paper written in blood, by which he had acknowledged his debt.

Hiasl told his father that he wanted to go and look for that paper and that he would not come back until he had it. Then he left. He came to a hermit whom he asked to show him the road to Hell. But the hermit could not tell him and sent him to a second hermit, who was supposed to have traveled in far-off lands and to be much cleverer than the first one.

And so Hiasl set out on a long journey to find the second hermit, and he came to the deep, deep forest where the second hermit lived. He asked him for the road to Hell. "My dear friend," replied the hermit, "you will have to go to the next forest. There lives a robber chief. He has traveled through the whole world and has accomplished every possible task. He certainly will know the surest road to Hell."

And so he went to the next forest; but it was so thick and dark and impassable that he would have given up had he not been looking for the road to Hell. And there lived the robber's brother, who was as repulsive and wild as the forest itself, and he hardly dared to ask him. But thinking of the paper, he took courage and asked him where the road to Hell was, and explained his quest.

"I shall tell you," replied the horrible man, "but you will have to do me a favor in return. I shall go with you and ask for the paper with the signature, but you must inquire for whom they are setting up the great throne that they have been working on in Hell for seven years. If you do so, I shall be satisfied with you."

Thus they went down the forest to Hell, where they found the robber's godfather, the devil Lucifer. He bade them a cheerful good morning and asked the robber what he wanted. "Well," he said, "we were quarreling up above in the world whether there exists in Hell a contract written with blood. The peasant so-and-so is said to have signed it. Go and find out." The devil searched all the regiments of devils, but only in the third regiment did he find the devil who had the paper.

"Here you are," said Lucifer to Hiasl, "but you can only get it if you do not wash yourself or blow your nose or cut your fingernails for seven years."

"Oh well," replied Hiasl, "I think I'll manage. But tell me, for whom do they set up the great throne in Hell?"

"Oh that," said the devil, and he whispered into Hiasl's ear, "For the robber who stands by your side."

Now the two left Hell and went back to the terrible forest. "Now then, what did my godfather say about the throne?" the robber asked his companion.

"Oh, you will be greatly distressed," replied Hiasl. "The devil told me that it is for you."

"Oh Lord!" cried the robber and was frightened to death. For the time being, he remained in the forest—not as a robber though, but as a hermit—and later on he went to Rome with a penitent heart in order to ask for the Pope's forgiveness for all his heavy sins. The Pope listened kindly to him, but then he imposed the following penance on him: for seven years he was not allowed to speak or to cry or to laugh, and he was only to eat what he might recover from the dogs.

Meanwhile the boy lived in the robber's hut in the deep wild forest and did not comb or wash himself or blow his nose or cut his nails. When the robber came back from Rome, he silently and gravely gave Hiasl all his money. Then by means of gestures he signaled that he was going to buy a couple of dogs.

The two lived together for seven years, and they both carefully observed the conditions imposed on them. And when the time was over, the boy found the contract on his bed and the robber obtained forgiveness for his sins. They separated. The robber remained in his hut as a hermit, but Hiasl traveled through the world with his money.

The country was governed by a king who had so many debts that not one stone in all his country belonged to him any more. He had three very beautiful daughters. The hermit went to the king and told him that if one of his daughters would for three years clean and kiss and then marry the pilgrim who would soon come, the king would be rid of his debts. "Well, this would not be bad," replied the king. "The pilgrim will certainly not be dirtier than the pigs in the stable."

He sent his three daughters to the royal dairy farm where they had to look after the pigs. The two elder ones, however, were very haughty and they secretly paid other girls to clean the hog pen. Only the third one handled the dung fork herself, and in addition to this she cleaned one dirty pig with brush and soap every day.

When Hiasl, the pilgrim, came with his knapsack full of gold and diamonds, the king received him kindly, led him to the hog pen, and called his daughters. The oldest one came. When she saw Hiasl all dirty with his hair entangled and hanging over the face and with long and filthy fingernails, she haughtily turned away and said to the king, "I do not clean such a pig."

Then the second one came. She looked at Hiasl, and her fine nose told her also that the pilgrim smelled frightfully. And she turned away with disgust and said to the king, "I should like to do it, but it is too awful."

At last the third one came. She saw at once that Hiasl would be more trouble than a pig—but only the one time—and then it would be easier. And she said to the king, "Father, I will try. For often there is a good kernel in an ugly shell." And she had a bath prepared with soap and brush, with scissors and comb. She had clothes from the king's cupboard brought over and started her work. Of course, it took her longer to clean Hiasl than to clean a dirty pig, but when his hair was cut and combed, his fingernails cut, and when he left the bath with royal clothes on, he had become such a handsome man that people stopped in the streets and turned around to look at him. The two older sisters almost choked with envy and anger. They went far away from the royal palace, and the one is said to have hanged herself, the other one to have drowned herself.

But the youngest one married Hiasl, and they both reigned for many years over a kingdom that was free from debts.

·59· *A Story about Our Lord Jesus Christ*

• OUR LORD JESUS CHRIST and St. Peter received a night's lodging from a peasant whom they promised in return to help with the thrashing the next day.

They were to arise at three o'clock in the morning. They did not come. The peasant tried to rouse them, but they would not get up.

When he came for the second time, he gave the first one, the one who was lying right before him, a sound beating. It happened to be Peter. They still did not get up. The Holy Virgin arranged for Peter to take the place behind, so that if the peasant came again, Our Lord should not get the beating.

The peasant came for the third time, and now he thrashed the one behind and said, "I just gave it to the one in front, so the one behind is to get it now!" They still did not get up.

When he came for the fourth time, the peasant had a light. He looked at old Peter and beat him again, for he thought that the older one should be more reasonable.

At last they got up, and when Our Lord came to the thrashers, he asked them how much there was to be thrashed. The peasant showed him. He took a candle and set the ears on fire. Immediately, the grains fell out and the straw remained intact. Then they left.

Now the peasant wanted to do the same. He piled the corn in his barn and set the ears on fire. But they were consumed by the fire and so were the barn and the house.

·60· *The Tailor in Heaven*

• OLD RIEHLER FROM FISCHERBACH told the following story when his daughter got married:

There once was a tailor who died and went to heaven. He came to St. Peter. Peter told him that sitting on his golden chair he could see everything that was going on in the world. He bade the tailor sit down, and then he left, because he had to look around.

Sitting on the chair, the tailor could see every good or bad deed that was done in the world, and thus he could see his neighbor stealing a bale of cloth. He did not know what to do about it. He took the golden chair and threw it at her in order to disturb her.

When Peter came back, he asked where the golden chair was. The tailor said that his neighbor had stolen a bale of cloth and that he had taken the chair and thrown it at her. Peter told him, "I am afraid I should have thrown it at you many a time!"

·61· *The Hermit and the Devil*

• THERE ONCE LIVED near Admont a pious wood brother, as the people who live in the Ensthal[1] used to call the hermits. The devil once appeared to him in the clothes of a hermit and said, "Which do you think to be the greatest sin?" The hermit suggested this and that. Finally the devil said, "Drunkenness is the greatest vice, the greatest sin." The hermit did not believe it. So the devil took him to a pub. There he paid for the hermit and then he disappeared. On his way back, the drunk hermit met a girl to whom he made an indecent offer. At last he killed the girl, for he thought that the only witness of his sinning should be put out of the way. The girl had been nobody else but the devil in disguise.

Now the hermit had committed three heavy mortal sins in one

[1] Enns Valley in Styria, Austria.

day. He went to a pious priest in the neighborhood and confessed his three great sins: drunkenness, indecency, and infraction of the sixth commandment. The priest did not absolve the sinner, but sent him to the Pope in Rome. The Pope ordered the hermit to go back to his cell, to remain naked and barefooted, and not to say a word, whatever happened, before he was redeemed. He did as he was told.

One day, a count from the neighborhood of Admont was holding a battue in his vicinity. The hounds came near the hermit's hut and they scented something. Following the dogs, the men broke into the hut and found a creature that was half man and half animal. It was nobody but our hermit, who, living in the wilderness, was covered with hair (even over his face), had long nails, had a long head of hair and a long beard, and who did not speak one word and did not even utter a sound.

The count ordered his men to bring the "animal" to his castle. There it was brought to the deerpark and trained, and everybody was highly amused with the docile and intelligent behavior of the creature.

Years went by. One day, a shining white apparition came up the stairs of the castle toward brother Claudius and called, "Claudius, you are delivered."

Claudius (this was the hermit's name) was indeed delivered at once. The hair fell from his body, and having regained his agreeable human shape, he told the astonished master of the castle about his life. Then he went back to his cell and led a godly life to his end.

.62. *The Devil and Our Lord*

• IN FORMER DAYS the devil used to go for a walk with Our Lord. One day, as they were going through the country, the devil said to Our Lord, "Listen. It's very strange with these humans. Whenever you have done something, they say that I have done it. For everything I have done they answer, 'This has been done by Our Lord.'"

"Well, well," said Our Lord to the devil, "it cannot be quite like this."

"Yes," said the devil, "it is, and I am going to prove it."

After a while they came to a meadow where an ox was tethered. "Throw this ox into that peat pit," said the devil to Our Lord. God seized the ox and threw it into the pit.

"All right," said the devil, "now let's hide in the bush. We shall see what the peasant says when he sees what has happened."

And after a short while the peasant arrived and found his ox up to his throat in the pit. "I say," he uttered, "where has the devil dragged you to?" With these words he turned around and ran to the village to look for help.

"Well," said the devil to Our Lord, "now I will drag the ox out again, and then we shall hear what the peasant will say this time." And he pulled the ox out of the pit.

When the peasant came back with his neighbors, the ox was grazing in the meadow. "I do not need you any more," he said to his neighbors. "The Heavenly Father has helped already. The ox is out again."

"There you are," said the devil. "Will you now believe me that people always put it all wrong?"

·63· *The Man in the Moon*

• A MAN was carrying wood and his wife was spinning on Christmas Eve. God became very angry. In order to punish them, he decided that they should not live together any more. He let them choose whether one of them wanted to stay in heaven and the other in hell, or one in the moon and the other in the sun. They chose the latter. And thus the man is now standing in the moon with his bundle of wood, and the woman is sitting in the sun and spinning.

Part VIII
The Devil and
His Partners

·64· *How the Devil Fetched the Mayor*

• A MAN AND HIS WIFE sent their little son on an errand to town. The road led through a large forest. Having gone along for some time, the boy suddenly met a man who told him, "Come on, you can do me a favor!" And he made a sign for the boy to follow him and leave the road. The boy obeyed and followed. They stopped a little off the road, and the stranger pointed to the ground. The boy saw a book lying on the moss. "Pick up the book!" ordered the man. The boy did so; it was the Holy Book! But underneath there was an immense amount of money, gold and silver. This is what the stranger wanted. However, he was not able to get it, for he was nobody but the devil himself, and for this reason he was not able to pick up the Holy Book. But the boy, who picked it up, knew nothing of this.

Now the stranger bent down, took a few handfuls of gold, and filled the boy's pockets. "Here, this is for your help," he said. "And when you are in town," he went on, "you go to the mayor's house and ask for a night's lodging. And if once during your life you should want help, you need only cry 'Christoph!' I will then appear and help you." The boy promised to do so, thanked him, and went on.

In town he went to the mayor's house and asked for a night's lodging, and he was in fact given a place to sleep. Now the mayor had noticed the boy's bulging pockets. Curious to know what they might contain, at night he sneaked to the boy's bed, took his clothes away, searched them, and found the money.

There is something wrong, he thought. The boy's clothes look shabby. How has he got hold of all this money? I will take the money away, he concluded. Nobody will believe the boy if he says that the money has been stolen! He took the money and brought the boy's clothes back to where they had been lying.

In the morning the boy woke up, put his clothes on, and found the pockets empty. He ran out in the street and shouted, "I have been robbed. The mayor has stolen my money!"

But the mayor was an important man and was held in great esteem. It was monstrous to utter such an accusation. A person could be sent to jail right away for it or even be sentenced to death! And this is exactly what happened to the boy. He was arrested, put in jail, and the town council deliberated on his sentence. They decided to send him to the gallows.

Sadly the boy sat waiting for his last hour. Suddenly he remembered the man from the forest. "Chris . . ." He had pronounced barely the first part of the name when the man was standing right before him.

"What do you want?" he asked. The boy poured out his grief, and the stranger said, "Everyone who is sentenced to death is granted a last wish. You therefore tell the gentlemen that before dying you would like to see your brother Christoph, and you write him a letter. They will give you three days. When you are standing at the gallows, pronounce my name and I shall appear and set you free." With these words he vanished.

The boy followed his advice. He wrote the letter and was given three days. But when they were over, the executioner dragged him to the gallows. And a lot of people went along to watch him hanged. The mayor was there, too. At the place of execution the boy suddenly cried, "Christoph!"

A stately coach drove up, and a fine gentleman got out. He went directly to the gallows and said, "Where is my brother?"

"Are you Christoph, the condemned boy's brother?" they asked him in amazement on seeing the gentleman's rich clothes that contrasted so much with the boy's shabby garments. "Yes, I am his brother!" replied the stranger. "What has the boy done to be sentenced to death?"

The mayor stepped forward and said, "He has offended me, the head of the town, pretending that I have stolen his money! He is now going to be punished for it."

But the stranger replied, "If you are innocent, pronounce in a loud voice, 'If I have stolen the money, the devil may fetch me on the spot!' "

"If I have stolen the money, the devil may fetch me on the spot!" No sooner had the mayor uttered these words than the stranger took him by the collar, lifted him into the coach, and drove off with him through the air.

This is how the devil fetched the mayor.

·65· The Dead Creditor

• THERE WAS A FARMER in Warnow who had no luck and who had gotten into trouble. One day he went to Gresmählen in order to borrow some money. But he did not get any; nobody wanted to do anything for him. On his way back he was in despair.

Going through the woods on a footpath near Hornberg, he met a man who asked him what was wrong with him. At first the farmer told him that he could not help him anyway. But the other one said that he could not be sure of that and that he might as well tell him all about his trouble. Now the farmer told him everything, and the other one asked him to go with him. The farmer followed the man, who led him a good long way into the mountain. A lot of money was there. He told the farmer to fill a barrel with money and proposed to lend it to him on the condition that he bring it back after a certain time. He should come to the same place and call "Koop!" three times.

The farmer promised to do this and then he went home with his money. From this time on he was successful in everything and was getting on well. When the time was over, he took a barrel with as much money as he had borrowed, went to the same place, and called "Koop!" in a loud voice. But there was no answer. He called again, and nobody appeared. When he called for the third time, a voice answered, "Koop is dead; keep what you have got!"

·66· An Old Woman Sows Discord

• THERE WAS ONCE A couple, Herman and Lise, who lived rather peacefully. Opposite their house was a fountain where an old woman was washing one day.

Seeing a well-dressed man going past, she asked him to give her a little money for a pair of shoes. The man replied, "If you are able to sow discord between the peaceful couple over there, you may come back to this fountain and you shall have a pair of new shoes, as sure as I am the devil!"

The old woman waited for Herman to go across country. Then she went to Lise and told her insolent lies about her husband's fidelity. Learning on this occasion when Herman was expected to return, she met him on his way and made him suspicious of his wife.

When Herman came home before, his wife would meet him with cheerful words of welcome; this time she did not. This aggravated his bad temper, and for several days he hardly said a word to Lise.

Lise complained to the old woman about the rude and unkind manners of her husband. The old woman retorted, "I will tell you the means by which you can regain your husband's love. All you have to do is to cut a few hairs from underneath his chin when he is taking a nap." But she told the husband that his wife was fostering murderous intentions.

When Herman was sitting in his armchair for a nap after a meal, Lise came with the razor and started carrying out her project. The husband jumped up, seized a stick, and slew her.

As soon as this story was known, the old woman went to the fountain to get her reward. The same Mr. What's-his-name was waiting for her, holding the new shoes on a stick. He broke into shrill laughter and said, "You even beat people like us. Wherever the devil fails, he sends an old woman!"

Part IX
The Stupid Ogre

· LONG AGO there lived an old man. He had three sons. The first one was a hunter; the second one, a fisherman; and the youngest one helped his father at home. The youngest one was said to be stupid by his brothers, although he was not. The old man fell ill and then he died. Now the brothers divided their father's property. The oldest one took the little house, the second one the cow, and the third one was given a ball of home-spun thread that they had found in the attic. The youngest one took the ball and went into the world.

When he had gone along for several miles, he came to a big forest. He was afraid of losing his way; therefore, he tied one end of the thread to a fir tree and unrolled it as he went along. Suddenly the devil appeared, watched him for some time with amazement, and asked, "Man, what are you doing here?"

"Well," he said, "I have to fell the trees of this forest, and as it takes too long to cut one tree after the other, I've drawn this string around the woods and then I'll pull it all down at once." The devil opened his mouth, nose, and eyes in astonishment.

Then he asked him, "And do you think you will manage?"

"Why, do you doubt it? You watch!" Then he pretended to start pulling down the trees.

But the devil was frightened and begged, "Oh, please, don't!"

The fellow answered, "Then how shall I show you how strong I am?"

"If you want, we can run a race," proposed the devil, for he was very proud of his speed.

"All right," replied the fellow. "But I can tell you right now that you will lose. I am not even going to start myself; my little son will run instead. He will be three years old in the autumn; he certainly will defeat you. I need not bother myself."

"Well, I am curious," said the devil. "Where is he?"

"Do you see the hazel bush over there? He is just taking a nap.

Go over there and clap your hands. He then will wake up and start running."

The devil went to the bush and did as he was told. At this moment, a hare darted out and was out of reach in no time. The devil ran after him, but he soon came back and said, "This time you win, but the next time you will not. Now we shall see who climbs more quickly, or I will take you to Hell."

"Oh well," said the fellow, "you are most ridiculous. You try and race my little daughter; she is three days old, and I am sure that she will win, too."

The devil got angry and asked, "Where is she?"

"Look over there. She is playing under that big fir tree. Go over and knock on the trunk. Then you will see who climbs best."

No sooner said than done. The devil knocked, and a squirrel climbed up the fir tree like lightning and had reached the top before the devil had climbed up the trunk. The fellow was laughing at the devil, who grew all the more angry and said, "Now you will have to wrestle with me. I will show you who is stronger."

"I'd never dream of wrestling with a weakling like you! You first try with my great-grandfather; he will shake your bones so much that half of it will be too much for you."

"And where is he? I cannot see him anywhere."

"Just follow me. We shall look for him. He will be asleep in one of these shrubs."

After walking about for a while, the fellow found a bear in a thicket. He said to the devil, "Look, he is lying over there and snoring. Go and wake him."

Now the devil shouted, "Hello, old great-grandfather, get up. I want to wrestle with you." The bear raised his muzzle and growled angrily, but then he put his head back on his paws and wanted to go on sleeping.

The devil said to the fellow, "Your great-grandfather seems to be afraid because despite my challenge, he does not come."

"You know that old people don't like being disturbed when taking a rest. You better go over and thrust your foot vigorously in his side." The devil went over and kicked the bear's groin with his horse's hoof. This was too much—even for a bear. Furious, he rose up and caught the devil with his paws. The devil tried to fight, but the bear pressed his ribs together until all his bones cracked. He cried with pain, and his eyes bulged out of their sockets. Finally, he freed himself with great anguish. Scratched and bleeding, he came back to the fellow and said, "I never should have thought the old one capable of this!"

The fellow answered, "That's for thinking you are stronger than others and wishing to fight with everybody. I hope you will remember this lesson for some time."

The devil was contrite; he knew that he could do nothing against men; therefore, he said, "I have now seen that you must be stronger than I am. If your great-grandfather and your children are doing so well, then I had better leave you alone. But look! Over there is a little lake. Let's run around it three times!"

"Stop this nonsense! You are going to lose again, I can tell you right now."

The devil replied, "I have to deliver a message to my grandmother; therefore, I am now going to Hell. But I shall be back in a moment and bring a sack with one bushel of ducats. It's all yours if you win again this time."

"If you want to get rid of your money, by all means you are welcome." They agreed to meet after one hour. Then they parted and each went his own way.

When the devil came to Hell, his companions asked him, "Who has drubbed and scratched you like this?"

He replied, "Never during all my life has such a thing happened to me. I met a fellow on earth who tied a rope around a wood and wanted to pull down all the trees at once. As we have caught many a poor soul in that wood, I asked him to leave the trees in place. He did as I told him. However, I wanted to know if he really was so strong. I therefore invited him to race me climbing up a tree and to wrestle with me." And the devil told his companions what had happened to him. At the end he said, "I have promised the fellow a sack holding one bushel of ducats if he himself runs three times around the lake with me. We shall start in one hour. But this time I am sure to win."

They both arrived at the appointed time. The fellow asked the devil if he had brought the ducats. The devil pointed at the sack and wanted to start the race. But the fellow said, "There is no hurry. Before I start, I will put something very heavy between my legs, because if I race you like this, I shall not slow down for three days and that is too long. Come on, perhaps we can find the proper burden for me."

They came to a meadow where a horse was grazing. The devil had never seen a horse before and said, "How about taking this between your legs? I think it should be heavy enough."

"If you think that it will do, then I will do you the favor. But you start right away, as I shall soon catch you." The devil laughed maliciously and ran away at full speed. The fellow mounted the horse and after a short while he had moved ahead of the devil. And he stayed ahead for the three times around the lake. Then the devil threw the sack with the ducats at the fellow's feet and leaped into the lake, roaring like thunder.

When the devil came back to Hell, his companions asked him, "Well, how was the race?"

"In all my devil's life I have never seen such a thing. I ran until my tongue was hanging down to my knees. But this human rascal, even with a big animal between his legs, left me behind after a short while."

The fellow, therefore, took the bushel of ducats, went home, and bought a piece of land, had a new house built, and married the richest farmer's daughter. He was lucky in everything he did. Owing to his brothers' fraud he had become richer than they, and he is alive to this very day, if he has not died since.

·68· *The Devil Duped*

· A PEASANT, being very hard up, was most desperate. He met a stranger who asked him what was the matter with him and who promised him a stockingful of money if he would give him what he did not know to be at home. The peasant agreed on the condition that he filled the whole leg of a boot. The stranger brought the money and wanted to pour it from the hayloft down into the leg that the peasant was holding up from below. However, the

peasant had cut off the foot of the boot, for he had only been
talking of the leg.

The stranger kept pouring money into it, and the peasant kept
shouting, "The leg is not full yet." Of course the money was
running out from the bottom. When the money was all gone, the
leg was still empty.

The stranger said, "I have nothing left, but there is a spinner
who has three pennies. I will go and get them." But the leg did
not get full with these either. Thus he lost the bet and had to
leave abashed.

•69• *The Devil and the Man*

• THERE WAS ONCE A DEVIL who went for a walk with a young
devil. The young one said to the old one, "I should like to see a
man."

"Well," said the old devil, "then let's wait beside this street until
one comes."

After a while an old man came creeping along. "Is that a man?"
asked the young devil.

"No," said the old devil, "that's been one."

Then there came a small boy. "Is that a man?" asked the young
devil.

"No," said the old devil, "that's going to be one."

Suddenly there came a hunter. "This is a man," called the old
devil. "You can talk to him." Then the old devil was gone.

The young devil went toward the hunter and asked him what
sort of a thing he was carrying on his shoulder. "This is my
tobacco pipe," said the hunter. "Would you like to smoke a little?"
He took his gun from the shoulder. As the devil put the gun into
his mouth, the hunter discharged it, and the small shot went
rattling down the devil's gullet.

"Your tobacco is too sharp for me," cried the young devil. "I
will have nothing more to do with you!" And with these words
he disappeared. But the hunter fired another shot after him.

After this the young devil did not wish to talk to any human being again and remained in Hell.

·70· *A Peasant Tricks the Devil*

· Do YOU KNOW where the Hollow Ground is? Well, it all happened in the Hollow Ground, and I was twelve years old when the man who told me this story died.

Up there, in the Hollow Ground, a peasant once cleared land and built a farm. It is now all covered with wood again. The Waldsteins replanted it in the seventeenth century. The peasant, who had made the land arable, was an industrious man. He had a young wife. However, hard times came. The harvest was bad. He lost courage and decided to commit suicide.

He went out in the woods because everything proved a failure and all was lost. "I cannot bear staying at home any more." Suddenly he heard steps. Looking up, he saw a hunter coming toward him with his gun shouldered, a hunting knife at his side, and a green hat.

The hunter said, "Hansjörg, why do you have such a gloomy face?"

"Well," said Hansjörg, "how do you expect me not to make a sad face? Everything I do is a failure. Hail destroyed all my crops last year. Now I do not know what to do. If it goes on like this, I will hang myself."

The hunter said, "But you have a wife at home."

He said, "Well, she cannot help either."

"I know," replied the hunter, "that she is a very cunning person. Perhaps she can advise you."

"I am by no means going to ask her," replied Hansjörg.

The other said, "I'll tell you what. If you sell me your soul—but you have to sign with your blood—and if you have enough work for me to do all the time, then you will be free. After thirty years the contract will expire, and then either you or I will have won."

The peasant thought it over for a while, staring at the ground.

Well, I have a great tract of woods. There is plenty of work for him to do. It must be the devil, thought Hansjörg. Otherwise he would not promise such a thing. "All right," he said, "I will sign the contract." They scratched the skin of Hansjörg's arm. The hunter took a quill out of his pocket and gave it to Hansjörg, who signed the paper. Then the other went into a hut and was not seen again. His roars of laughter filled the woods, sounding as if one person had outwitted another.

When the peasant reached home, he said, "Old lady, now we will get started, you'll see!" Then he told her that in the evening the other one would come and that at nightfall he was to be given his work. He let him cut down the wood wherever he liked and gather all the big stones that were lying around. (This is where the name "Waldstein" comes from; they are uneven blocks.) So they gave him some work every night. And in the morning it was all done, spick and span.

In this manner all sorts of work was accomplished. Fields and meadows were fixed. Oxen and cattle were brought. A house was built and all sorts of things . . . (We children sat with eager attention when he told us about this, and our ears were growing beyond our caps.) This went on for some years. But then the peasant began to get uneasy, not knowing what there was left for the other one to do at night.

"Well, Hansjörg," said his wife, "when those stones are re-moved, we shall have no water left. In this dry summer, the water has stopped running because the trees have been cut down!"

He said, "We have to have water. I have an idea! If he comes tonight, I know what he can do. He must dig a fountain so that I will always have running water—a hole right into the mountain until it yields water." When this was done, he said to his wife in the evening after the meeting, "Good heavens, here we are again! Now you fetch some grainy sand. He shall build a wash house." There was no sand left. It had all been used. So he said, "Well, old lady, I am at my wit's end. What else can I do?" And then he said, "Can't you think of anything, Applon (Appolonia)?"

"Well," she said, "how is he to get the water out of the hole?"

"Oh yes! We must have a rope and a winch to get it up!"

Then she said, "Now you heat the oven and put sand inside

so that it gets very dry. Then you tell him to make a rope with it, but he is not allowed to take any water; he is to make the rope simply with sand."

When the other one came again at night he said, "What is the matter? What is the news? It is going to be serious now!" They told him that he was to make a rope with the dry sand but that he was not allowed to use any water. He shook his head and looked at the peasant, then he said, "Listen! This is woman's cunning. I don't want to have anything to do with it; it cannot be done."

But Hansjörg replied, "Well, and our contract, what about it?"

"Well," he said, "I don't want to deal with woman's cunning."

"All right," said Hansjörg, "I will have nothing further to do with you. You go your way and I go mine. Our contract has come to an end if you cannot do this." There was a great crash and a smell so frightful that Hansjörg had to run away. This time it was Hansjörg who laughed. He had tricked the fellow.

The peasant of the Hollow Ground told us this. His name was Ilg. This all happened to his grandfather. It was up at the mountain looking over the Hollow Ground. The Hollow Ground is down below in the valley.

Part X
Numskulls

The People from Schwarzenborn

a) *They Hide a Bell*

• THERE ARE MANY stories about the silly actions of the people from Schwarzenborn. Once, for instance, the people from Schwarzenborn wanted to put their bell in a safe place. There probably was a war, and bells were being gathered. They took the bell to a nearby lake and put it into a boat.

Then they deliberated, "Well, if we let the bell down, then nobody will know where it is. We must have a sign to go upon."

Suddenly one of them had a good idea, "We will make a notch in the boat in the place where we drop the bell!"

b) *They Sow Salt*

• THERE WAS A TIME when salt was scarce. The people from Schwarzenborn said, "We are going to sow salt. We have still a few pounds left. If we sow these, we will have our own salt."

This was what they did. The salt came up nicely, and they were very pleased. But it was all stinging nettles.

Once they decided to see how it was growing. They went with their bare feet into the field, and it stung so much that they cried, "Oh, our salt is sharp. It is going to be sharp!"

c) *They Protect Their Seed*

• ONE DAY a man came to the mayor of Schwarzenborn and said that there was a cow in a field and how were they to get it out again.

The mayor said, "Well, let us see what can be done about it. We must send someone to chase the cow away."

"Yes, but he will trample everything down."

"Well, in that case, two men will have to carry the one, and he must take the shovel and drive out that cow."

d) They Dig a Well

• THE PEOPLE FROM SCHWARZENBORN once wanted to dig a well, but they did not know what to do with the earth they brought to the surface. At last the town council took care of the matter and decided that they should dig another hole and put the earth in there. One of the town councilors who thought he was cleverer than the others asked what should be done with the earth from this new hole. The mayor said, "What a silly question! The new hole must, of course, be big enough to hold both heaps of earth."

e) They Measure the Depth of the Well

• WHEN THE WELL was finished, the people from Schwarzenborn wanted to know how deep it was. As they had no metric measure, they soon contrived a very ingenious means to fathom the pit. They placed a bar across the well, and one of them clung to it, grasping the bar with both hands and dangling his legs into the well. A second one clung to his legs, a third one to the second one's legs, and so on until it grew too heavy for the first one.

"Hold on. I have to spit on my hands!" he shouted to the others. He let go of the bar, and they all fell into the well.

•72• The Parish Bull Eats the Grass from the Wall

• WHEN THE OLD CHURCH with its steeple and wall was still standing, grass grew on the wall and the people from Kastenholz were sorry that this grass was going to waste. So they took the parish bull and led him to the wall. Because the wall was too high, they had to draw him up so that he could eat the grass.

While they were pulling, the bull stretched his tongue out, and they shouted, "Look, he is stretching his tongue toward the grass!"

However, they had strangled him, and that is why he stretched his tongue out.

·73· *Stretching the Bench*

• A MAN in Mutschingen had a bench, and on this bench six men used to sit, deliberating what they were going to do during the week. In winter when it was cold, they would wear their furs and thus there was only room for five of them. They thought the bench had shrunk.

They said, "Come on. Let's stretch the bench. It's shrunk!"

They seized it and pulled; in doing so they got so warm that they began to sweat. They took their coats off. Then they went on stretching for a while, and at length sat down quickly; now there was room for six again. After a while, however, they felt cold and put on their furs again. And again there was only room for five of them. So they had to stretch again, and they did this the whole day.

·74· *Moving the Church*

• THE CHURCH was not standing in the proper place. In the opinion of the city fathers, it had to be pushed back a little. So they started pushing. One of them became especially warm. He took his coat off and placed it behind the church, on the very spot to which the church was being moved. A traveling journeyman came along, took the coat, and disappeared. When the owner of the garment looked for it, he believed, and so did the other city fathers, that they had pushed the church over the coat. They were very pleased with the success of their effort.

Part XI
Stupid People

Part XI
Stupid People

*The Poor People Who Wanted
to Be Rich*

• IN A VILLAGE there once lived a very poor old man and his wife.
They occupied a little room, for which they had to work, in a
rich farmer's cottage.

One day they were sawing their master's wood in the courtyard.
And, as they often had done before, they were talking about their
poverty. "You see, we are now very old and we have still to work
so hard," said the old man.

"Well, yes, the rich are better off. Look how our master lives.
It's heaven on earth," replied the old woman.

The old couple did not know that the farmer had been standing
behind the woodpile and had heard everything.

"All right. If you wish, you shall lead the same life as me," he
offered them.

The old people were greatly astonished. And before they could
say a word, the farmer led them into his best room. The choicest
things from kitchen and cellar were served to them.

"Eat and drink and be merry. You shall live like this all the time
if you can obey. See this dish on the table. You are not allowed to
uncover it; otherwise, your good time is over." After these words
the farmer left the room.

The old people were alone. Now they had what they had always
longed for. In the beginning they hardly dared approach the table.
At last they sat down and ate and drank and felt very much at
ease. The old man especially was most happy. He would have liked
to lie down on the bench by the stove and take a nap. But the old
woman was restless.

What could there be in this dish? Why am I not allowed to have
a look? she thought over and over again.

The man noticed how restless his wife was. He knew that she
was tormented by curiosity.

"What do you think?" she said. "Let's find out what there is in
this dish!"

"Be quiet and stay where you are! Be glad that you are comfortable at last," the old man scolded her.

"Let me just open the lid a little bit," begged his wife.

And before the husband could prevent her, the wife was busy with the dish.

A cry and a crash—as if a plate was breaking!

In the dish there had been a mouse. When the woman opened the lid, it jumped out, and terror stricken, the old woman let the lid fall. It was broken.

The noise was heard by the farmer as well. With a horsewhip in hand he entered the room.

"Who has allowed you to look into the dish?" he asked in a loud voice.

"It wasn't I, sir," replied the old man anxiously. "It's all my wife's fault!"

"This is the way Adam and Eve sinned," were the farmer's last words. Then he took his horsewhip and drove the two—who would have liked so much to be rich—out of the house.

·76· *The Clever Elsie*

• THERE ONCE LIVED a peasant and his wife. They had only one daughter, whose name was Elsie. She was still unmarried but already rather old. One day a stranger came to her mother and said, "I have heard that your Elsie is very clever; I therefore should like to marry her. May I see her?" This happened at noon. He was led into the dining room and was asked to have lunch with them.

After a short while the mother sent Elsie to the cellar to fetch some beer. When Elsie went into the cellar, she saw a pickax sticking in the wall. She was frightened and thought, if I marry this stranger, if God gives us a child, and if I send it for beer, the pickax will fall down and kill it. And she started crying, sat down, and remained in the cellar.

The others were waiting for the beer. After a while the mother sent the maid to the cellar. When she found Elsie, she asked her, "What is the matter with you?" Elsie told her the story of the pickax. The maid sat down beside Elsie and said, "How clever you are!" and started crying, too.

As the maid did not come back either, the mother sent the farm servant, who did the same as the maid. Now the mother went herself, and then the father, and at last the stranger. He consoled Elsie and said, "Since you are so clever, I shall marry you!" He married her and they lived happily and merrily to their end.

· 77 ·   The Ox as Mayor

· THERE ONCE LIVED a peasant. He had an ox with which he used to work in the fields. When he was plowing, his wife brought him his lunch. They had no children. While the two ate their lunch together, the ox went on plowing tranquilly. It was a very clever animal. One day as they were having their meal, the peasant said to his wife, "Our ox is so clever that it would be a pity to let him go on working in the field. Let's send him to school so that he can learn something." His wife agreed.

The next morning the peasant went to town with his ox. On his way he met a group of young fellows who were wearing colored caps. They asked the peasant where he wanted to go with his ox. "Well," he said, "my ox is so clever that I want him to go to school to learn something." The fellows said that they were going to school, too, and that they would take the ox with them. But he would have to give them some money for the books and material the ox would need. The peasant gave them the money and was glad that everything went so smoothly.

The boys took the ox with them and sold it right away. But once in a while they wrote to the peasant that the ox needed more books, for he had read the old ones to pieces, and to send some money. And the peasant always sent the money. After some years the boys wrote that the ox had now finished his studies and that he had become mayor. He might come and call on him.

The peasant went to town. By chance the mayor's name was Ox. The peasant found his way by asking and was admitted to the

mayor's office. He had to go up some stairs. When he entered, the
mayor was sitting behind his table with a sullen face and big
glasses. "Well," thought the peasant, "he has changed a little. But
there is still some resemblance." The mayor addressed him gruffly
and asked what he wanted. The peasant said, "Well, now you
pretend not to know me any more. And in former days you used to
shit on my spring bar!"

Part XII
Stories about Parsons

·78· The Damned Boys

• MANY YEARS AGO in a village in the district of Stolp there lived a pastor who used to emphasize certain sentences of his sermon by banging his fist on the pulpit.

Now wicked boys fixed thin needles through the board of the pulpit from underneath. The tops of the needles stuck out a little. Then the boys placed the cloth over them, so that nothing could be seen.

The next Sunday the pastor told his devout parishioners of the wonders God has achieved.

"And who has created our world?"

With these words he banged his fist vigorously on the pulpit, and, feeling a sharp stinging pain from the needles, he added in haste, "That was those damned boys!"

·79· The Dream

• A CATTLE DEALER once fell ill and sent for the priest, for he wanted to partake of the Lord's Supper. The priest came and asked him when he had last been in church.

"I cannot remember."

"Then you are not prepared, and I cannot administer the sacrament."

The cattle dealer recovered, and once again the priest met him. "Are you all right again?" he asked him.

"Well, yes, only there is this bad dream I have."

"What bad dream?"

"Well, I did not get the sacrament, and now I dream that I am dead and come to Peter and want to go into heaven. 'That won't do,' says Peter, 'you haven't had the Lord's Supper.' 'Can't I make up for it?' I ask. 'There certainly are some priests here?' 'I will go and find out,' says Peter and leaves. But he soon is back and says, 'No, it isn't possible; there are no priests in heaven.'"

The priest was rather angry, but the bailiff laughed when he heard it. He sent for the cattle dealer and asked him if he had other dreams. "Yes."

"Then tell me one, too."

"All right. This belongs to the first dream. Leaving heaven, I go to hell. I am still quite a way off when I hear a big noise. Getting near, I find all the priests there and they are quarreling with their lawyers. As I am tired from the journey, I sit down on a chair that is vacant. But I hardly sit down when a devil comes hurrying along and shouts, 'Get off, this is where the bailiff is to sit!'"

·80· *The Pig in the Church*

· ONE SUNDAY people were going to church in a village. As the pastor walked toward the church, a big black sow came running along. She jumped right between his legs, so that he had to sit on her and go with her. In this fashion he appeared astride her in the middle of the church and shouted to the people, "People, stick to God; I have to leave with the devil!"

Part XIII
Tales of Lying

· 81 · Catching Hares in Winter

· "It's going to be a hard winter."

"Yes."

"Then we shall catch hares."

"Really?"

"Yes. It's quite easy."

"But there is too much snow."

"I set up a brick and place a cabbage leaf underneath and on top of the cabbage leaf I put some snuff. The hare sniffs, takes some snuff, and hits the stone with his muzzle. The stone falls down and kills him. I have caught a lot of hares that way," said I.

A lad who heard this told them at home and wanted to do the same.

· 82 · Helping to Lie

· THERE ONCE WAS A NOBLEMAN who liked to tell terrible lies, but sometimes he got stuck. Once he wanted to hire a new servant. When one came to offer his services, the nobleman asked him if he could lie. "Well," he said, "if it's got to be!"

"Yes," said the nobleman, "I sometimes get stuck telling lies. Then you will have to help me."

One day they were in an inn, and the nobleman was as usual telling lies: "Once I went hunting and I shot three hares in the air."

"This is not possible," said the others.

"Then you better fetch my coachman," he said, "to bear witness." They fetched him. "Johann, listen, I have just been telling these gentlemen about the three hares I shot in the air. Now you tell them how that was."

"Yes, sir. We were in the meadow, and a hare came jumping through the hedge, and while it was jumping out, you shot and it was dead. Afterward, when it was cut open, there were two young hares inside." Of course the others could say nothing to this. On their way home the nobleman said that it was well done. "Well, sir," said Johann, "the next time you tell lies, try to keep out of the air. On firm ground it will be easier for me to help you."

*Notes
to the Tales*

PART I

ANIMAL TALES

· *1* · *The Fox and the Hare in Winter*

This tale is a combination of Type 1*, *The Fox Steals the Basket,* and Type 2, *The Tail-Fisher.* ZA 631.

Recorded by the teacher Heinrich Hoffmann between 1914 and 1918 in Blens, Rhineland, from the storyteller Marx.

In his *Type-Index,* Thompson does not mention any German versions of 1*; six versions, however, are known to me.

Type 2, *The Tail-Fisher,* is one of the most popular German animal tales. Over ninety variants are recorded, the oldest of which is contained in the Latin *Ysengrimus* by Magister Nivardus, written probably about 1150 in Ghent. A variant is also found in No. 1 of *Folktales of Japan,* one of this series. The combination with Type 1, *Theft of Fish,* which is far more frequent and, according to its contents, more natural than the one with Type 1*, is given as early as the twelfth century in the French *Roman de Renard.*

In connection with the whole complex, see K. Krohn, "Bär (Wolf) und Fuchs," *Journ. de la Soc. Finno-Ougrienne,* Vol. VI (Helsinki, 1889) and BP, II, 116.

· *2* · *The Fox and the Wolf*

Type 9B, *In the Division of the Crop the Fox Takes the Corn.* ZA 10094.

Recorded by Heinrich Hoffmann in the Rhineland. Location and date of collection and informant are unknown.

The tale, which is not frequently heard, has until now been recorded only in Spain, Finland, Yugoslavia, and Germany, where three versions are recorded. See Dähnhardt, NS IV, 249.

· *3* · *The Little Hen and the Little Cock*

Type 15, *The Theft of Butter by Playing Godfather,* and Type 210, *Cock, Hen, Duck, Pin, and Needle on a Journey.* ZA 130271.

Recorded in 1927 by Otto Roderich in Stutthof near Elbing, East Prussia. The informant was Mrs. Schulz, the wife of the bailiff of the domain of Stutthof.

The combination of Types 15 and 210 is current in eastern Germany. BP also records a Brandenburg and two Pomeranian versions. The ZA contains, besides the combination given here, an East Prussian one, No. 130356.

In his study, "Bär und Fuchs," *Journ. de la Soc. Finno-Ougrienne,* VI, 74–81, Kaarle Krohn points out that Type 15 originates from northern Europe, whereas Liungman, III, 19 supports a European southwest-northeast migration. The tale is known throughout Europe, but to a certain extent also in west Asia, North Africa, Madagascar, and in both Americas. Fifty-six German versions are known to me.

Antti Aarne showed in his study on Types 130 and 210, *Die Tiere auf der Wanderschaft,* FFC 11 (Helsinki, 1913), how an Asiatic tale changes in Europe under the influence of the local animal tales into a story with unaltered basic features but with entirely different particulars. The Asiatic ecotype is widespread, especially in Japan, China, India, and Indochina. Variants of Type 210 are found in Nos. 5 and 6 of *Folktales of Japan* and in No. 63 of *Folktales of China,* both volumes in this series. The oldest European version, combined with Type 125, *The Wolf Flees from the Wolf-head,* is given in 1148 in the Latin epic poem *Ysengrimus* by Magister Niverdus from Ghent. It is, however, doubtful if the Aesopian fable of the lion and the ass (ed. Halm, No. 323–323b) can be considered as a previous form of our tale, as Liungman, III, 32 pretends. For further details concerning the European history of this tale, see BP, I, 75–78, 237–254. Thirty-seven German versions of Type 210 are recorded.

·4· *The Struggle between the Wolf and the Fox*

Type 41, *The Wolf Overeats in the Cellar;* Type 103, *The Wild Animals Hide from the Unfamiliar Animals;* Type 104, *The Cowardly Duelers;* Type 130, *The Animals in Night Quarters.* ZA 5628.

Recorded in 1910 in Soller, Rhineland, from the storyteller Bernhard Heinen. The manuscript—the author is unknown—was found in Heinrich Hoffmann's legacy (in connection with this collector, see No. 1 of this volume).

The four tale-types are widespread and frequently narrated in Germany. More than one hundred variants are recorded of Type 41, almost fifty of the struggle between the forest animals and domestic animals (Types 103 and 104), and more than fifty of Type 130. A variant of Type 130 is found in No. 63 of *Folktales of China,* one of this series.

Type 41 is partly contained in one of Aesop's fables (ed. Halm, No. 31): a fox, fat from eating, gets stuck in the narrow opening of a hollow oak that serves as a pantry to the herds; another fox (in Horace, *Epist.* 1, 7, 28, a weasel) advises him to wait until he grows thin again. See Wienert, p. 60; EB No. 226. The first complete version is given in the twelfth century by Odo from Ciringtonia, who narrates how the wolf, Ysingrinus, is led into a cellar full of meat by the fox, Renaldus, and how he has to squeeze out again, while being thrashed and skinned, through the narrow vent of the cellar (Hervieux, *Fabulistes latins,* IV, 324). The oldest records of Type 130 are given in the twelfth century in the Latin *Ysengrimus* by the Magister Nivardus from Ghent and in the French *Roman de Renard. See* BP, I, 255 and the monograph by A. Aarne, *Die Tiere auf der Wanderschaft,* FFC 11.

·5· The Mountain Hen and the Fox

Type 56A, *The Fox Threatens to Push Down the Tree,* and Type 6, *Animal Captor Persuaded to Talk.* ZA 170476.

Recorded in 1940 by Dr. Mai in Ridnaun, South Tyrol. The German-speaking informant was a Mrs. Anne Klotz.

The combination of the two types is frequent. The first one is given as early as the Arabian *Kalila and Dimna,* a translation of the Indian *Panchatantra* (see Chauvin, II, 212, No. 81) and in the second half of the thirteenth century in the *Directorium Humanae Vitae* by Johannes de Capua.

Type 6 is also found frequently in medieval fable literature; see BP, II, 207–8.

Our two animal tales have about the same dispersion: Europe, West Asia, Africa, French and Spanish America. In Germany, eleven versions of Type 6 and eighteen of Type 56A are recorded.

·6· The Tale of the Little Sausage and the Little Mouse

Type 85, *The Mouse, the Bird, and the Sausage.* ZA 130273.

Recorded in 1922 by Otto Roderich in Stutthof near Elbing, East Prussia, from the wife of the domain farmer Schulz.

The tale is known throughout Europe and appears sporadically in Asia and North America. In Germany sixteen versions are now recorded. Most of them contain only two characters, usually the sausage and the bird. See BP, I, 206. A Louisiana French variant may be found in Richard M. Dorson's *Buying the Wind* (University of Chicago Press, 1964), pp. 258–60.

The tale was first narrated by the German poet Hans Michael

Moscherosch in his *Gesichte Philanders von Sittewald,* Part 2 (Strasbourg, 1650), p. 927.

Our version passes into the cumulative tale used at the beginning of Type 2022, *The Death of the Little Hen.* This combination is very frequent here. Compare, e.g., *Neue Preuß. Provinzialblätter,* I (1846), 226; Strackerjan-Willoh, *Aberglaube und Sagen aus Oldenburg,* II (1909), 149; Wossidlo, *Aus dem Lande Fritz Reuters* (1910), p. 161; *Heimat* (Kiel, 1913), p. 210; Jungbauer, *Volk erzählt* (1943), p. 285; Benzel, *Sudetendeutsche Volkserzählungen* (1962), p. 67, No. 145.

·7· Bear, Fox, and Man

This tale is a combination of Type 157, *Learning to Fear Men,* and Type 104, *The Cowardly Duelers.* ZA 170493.

Recorded in 1940 by Dr. Mai in Greuth, South Tyrol, from the storyteller Schmoliner, who had heard the story from his grandfather.

In the fables of Aesop, Babrios, Avian, and their translators and epigones, we find most simple primal forms of Type 157: All the animals are afraid of the hunter; only the lion attacks him. The hunter hits him with an arrow and says, "This is my messenger."

The lion runs away and says to the fox who wants to stop him, "You won't fool me. If the hunter's messenger is so awful, how much more terrible is the hunter himself!" (see BP, II, 99 and Schwarzbaum in *Fabula,* VI, 192). But the first version which corresponds entirely to the modern tale is given only in a German poem of the fifteenth century, then in a meistergesang by Hans Sachs, in Rollenhagen's *Froschmeuseler,* etc.; see BP, II, 97.

Type 157 is very popular in Europe, in the Orient, among the neo-Latin population of North and South America as well as among the Negroes and Indians of North America. Fifteen Southern Negro variants are printed in R. M. Dorson, "King Beast of the Forest Meets Man," *Southern Folklore Quarterly,* XVIII (1954), 118–28. In Germany we list sixteen modern versions.

For Type 104, see the notes to No. 4.

·8· Why the Dogs Sniff at Each Other

Type 200A, *Dog Loses His Patent Right.* ZA 62646.

Recorded in 1937 by the teacher Gustav Friedrich Meyer in Kiel. Informant was the workman Julius Bargholt, born in 1877 in Plügge, Schleswig-Holstein, who had heard the tale from his fellow workmen.

This animal tale is found in several German meistersinger songs as early as the sixteenth century; see BP, III, 548. In recent times we have records of many versions of this tale from central Europe, and it appears sporadically in the United States. Eighteen German versions are known to me.

·9· The Skinned Goat

Type 212, *The Lying Goat.* ZA 145632.

Recorded before 1906 by Franz Wölfl in Langenlutsch in the German language enclave of the Schönhengster Land, Czechoslovakia. Printed in *Mitteilungen zur Volkskunde des Schönhengster Landes,* II (Mährisch-Trübau, 1906), 17.

Thompson classifies the second part of the tale of the skinned goat who hides in the foxhole and is driven away only by a bee or a hedgehog under Type 2015, *The Goat Who Would Not Go Home.* But as the two motifs form a complete unity in the predominant part of traditions, I do not agree with this separation, especially since Type 2015 refers to BP, II, 104, where quite differently structured genuine chain tales are recorded (closely related, for instance, is Type 2030, *The Old Woman and Her Pig*). Thirteen versions of Type 212 are recorded in the German-speaking area. Most of them end with the episode of the stubborn goat. A variant is found in No. 29 of *Folktales of Hungary,* one of this series.

·10· The Hedgehog and the Hare

Type 275A*, *Race between Hedgehog and Hare.* ZA 203161a.

Recorded about 1860 by Schönwerth in Spielberg, Upper Palatinate, Bavaria. The informant is unknown.

Tales about a race between a slow and a fast animal obviously belong to the oldest stock of human narration. Dähnhardt, NS, IV, 46–103 and BP, III, 339 55 point out that there exist three principal forms:

1. By its perseverance the slow animal beats the fast but careless one (that usually falls asleep during the race). This is Type 275A. The oldest redaction of this version is given in the Aesopian fables (ed. Halm, No. 420); it deals with the race between the tortoise and the hare.

2. The slow but cunning animal hangs onto the tail of the bigger and fast one, as in Type 275. The oldest literary record is probably again an antique proverb: *cancer leporem capit* (see BP, III, 350); we

find the first complete record in a German manuscript of the thirteenth century; it deals with a race between a fox and a crab. A variant is found in No. 10 of *Folktales of Japan,* one of this series, 3. The slow animal defeats the fast one with a trick: it places relatives who pretend to be the runner on the road and at the end, as in Types 275A* and 1074. The oldest version is found in a Latin poem of the thirteenth century in the Addit. ms. 11619 of the British Museum. A version is found in No. 9 of *Folktales of Japan.*

All the three redactions are widespread throughout the world. Twenty-six German versions of Type 275A * are recorded.

· *11* · *The Cock Who Went Traveling*

Type 715, *Demi-coq.* ZA 135097.

Recorded by the teacher Hermann Galbach in Gross Jerutten, East Prussia, in 1928 from the pupil E. Czekalla.

Of this tale, which is very popular in Europe, the Orient, and North Africa, as well as among the neo-Latin population of North and South America (seventy-two French variants, for instance, are reported), we have remarkably few records in Germany. Only five variants are known. One of them is from the extreme west (Lorraine); the others are from the eastern and southeastern border of the German-speaking area (East Prussia, Transylvania). See Ranke, SHM, III, 76.

First references to our tale are found, according to BP, I, 258–59 and Boggs, *The Halfchick Tale in Spain and France,* FFC III, in Ph.N. Destouche's play, *La fausse Agnès,* and in 1778 in the *Nouvel Abailard* by Rétif de la Bretonne.

· *12* · *Straw, Bean, and Coal*

Type 295, *The Bean, the Straw, and the Coal.* ZA 210601.

Recorded before 1938 by Elfriede Strzygowski in Hochwies. The informant was the small farmer Ludwig Mozbäuchel. The story was printed in 1959 in Peuckert's book, *Hochwies* (Göttingen, 1959), p. 188, No. 242, after being recorded in 1946 for the second time by Peuckert.

The first version of this tale, which is equally popular in northern, central, and eastern Europe and among the white, red, and black population of North America, is given in the *Esopus* of the German poet Burkard Waldis (1548). For the history and dispersion of the tale, see BP, I, 135–37. Eleven German versions are recorded.

PART II

SPIRITS, GHOSTS, AND GIANTS

· *13* · *The House Damsel*

Motifs F480, "House-spirits"; F406.2, "Food left out for spirits at night"; and F482.5.4, "Helpful deeds of brownie or other household-spirit." ZA 203546b.
Recorded by Schönwerth about 1860 in Wondreb, Upper Palatinate, Bavaria. The informant is unknown.
Stories of helpful house spirits rewarded with food are very popular in Germany as well as in north and central Europe. A variant of F480 may be found in No. 42 of *Folktales of China,* in this series.

· *14* · *The Household Spirit in Rötenbach*

Motifs F480–489. ZA 155648.
Recorded in 1926 by Erich Mönch in Rötenbach near Calw, Würtemberg. The informant is unknown.
Thompson has not paid enough attention to the variety of European household spirits, their appearance, their nature, and their actions. This tale is probably closest to F481.1, "Cobold avenges uncivil answer (or treatment)."

· *15* · *Household Spirit Brings Food*

ZA 45002.
Recorded in the second half of the last century in Magdeburg.
Balys has listed this type of legend as No. 4,372 in his *Index,* whereas Thompson has not quite correctly inserted it in Motif F480.3, "Thieving household-spirit." The story is well known in central Europe.

· *16* · *Reward Drives the Familiar Spirits Away*

In connection with this tale, see Motif F451.5.10.9, "Ausgelohnt. When dwarfs are paid in full for their work they cease helping mortals," and F381.3, "Fairy leaves when he is given clothes." ZA 141793.
Recorded by Virgil Grohmann about 1850 in Saaz, Bohemia. Informant unknown.

The extraordinary popularity of the "Ausgelohnt"—motif in northern, western, and central Europe diminishes toward the east and south. The oldest version is given in the *Epistolae,* II, (1751), 669 by Olaus Wormius (died 1654), who speaks of the familiar spirit of a baker in Leyden (Netherlands): "qui non reversus est, postquam nova tunica donatus fuit a pistore." See also BP, I, 364–66; Künzig, "Ausgelohnt" in HdM, I, 152–54.

·17· The Thing on the Hedge

Motif F472, "Huckauf." ZA 32109.

Recorded in 1930 by the teacher Heinrich Bügener in Heiden, Westphalia. The informant was the joiner Ferdinand Marx, who was born in 1878 in Heiden.

In his book, *Volkssagenforschung,* pp. 51–52, Friedrich Ranke has tried to interpret the almost numinous fear that has been transposed into the pictures of mythic imagination as the basic experience of the legend cycle surrounding the Huckauf. Stories of this kind are therefore old and widespread. The Greek *Ephialtes* shows features of the Huckauf motif. About 1200 Gervasius from Tilbury gives a first distinct legend from Catalonia. We have records of this motif in Germany since the fifteenth century.

The Huckauf legends are known in Europe as well as in Asia and in both Americas. As for literature, see "Aufhocker" in HdA, I, 675–77; Liebrecht, *Gervasius,* pp. 32–34, 137–40.

·18· The Frog with the Golden Key

ZA 2656.

Collected in 1923 by means of a questionnaire in Kurtscheid near Neuwied, Rhineland. The informant is unknown.

The story belongs to the old and widespread type of legends of the "Deliverer in the cradle" (Motif D791.1.3), which originates in the Descensus Christi ad Inferos of the apocryphal gospel according to Nicodemus and in the legend of the cross wood. See Friedrich Ranke, *Der Erlöser in der Wiege* (München, 1911), and Jacoby, "Kreuzbaum, Kreuzholz" in HdA, V, 487–99.

·19· The Origin of the Lake of Vitte

In connection with this legend, see Motif F531.3.4.2, "Giant drinks up river (lake, see)" and A928, "Giant drinks up ocean." ZA 110931.

Recorded by K. Rosenow in Vitte, Pomerania. Published in *Ostpommersche Heimat* (1937), No. 26.

The episode in this tale is also given in several tale types that contain the motif of the magic flight. Here, too, the ogre tries to drink up the ocean that was produced by magic and bursts asunder while doing so. See Types 313, 314, and 327.

·20· *The Giant's Toy*

Type 701, *The Giant's Toy,* ZA 147591.

Recorded by Professor Klatt in Wola Podleżna, Poland, from the German storyteller Leo Hein, whose ancestors came from the Warthebruch.

For questions about the age, the origin, and the dispersion of the legend, which is particularly popular around the Baltic Sea and in central Europe, see Valerie Höttges, *Die Sage vom Riesenspielzeug* (Jena, 1931). A version is to be found in No. 29 of *Folktales of England,* a companion volume in this series.

The motif of smaller people who will come after us after they have thrashed in the oven belongs to the sphere of dwarf legends. In the German translation of *Gargantua* (1582), the dwarfs are called "the little oven-thrashers"; see Grimm, *Mythologie,* III, 131; HdA, I, 783–84.

·21· *The Duped Giant*

ZA 185239.

Recorded in 1915 by Father Romuald Pramberger. The narrator, prelate Severin Kalcher from St. Blasen, Styria, heard the story from a wayfarer in Lessiach about 1860.

Motif G514.1, "Ogre trapped in box (cage)," usually constitutes the final episode in Type 328, *The Boy Steals the Giant's Treasure.*

·22· *The Giant's Stone*

Motif F531.3.2, "Giant throws a great rock." ZA 40008.

Recorded in 1906 by the elementary teacher Panning in Benzen, Lower Saxony. The informant is unknown.

This is one of the most popular etiological legends.

PART III

UNDER THE SPELL OF THE DEMON

· 23 · The Enchanted Princess

Type 307, *The Princess in the Shroud*. ZA 118015.

Recorded in 1935 by Hedwig Surmann in Rossberg, Silesia, from the storyteller Paschka.

Sixty German versions of this tale, which probably has its origin in east European vampirism, are known to me. See Ranke, SHM, I, 497; W. Kainz, *Volksdichtung aus dem Kainachtal* (1936), p. 141; G. Henssen, *Ungarndeutsche Volksüberlieferungen* (1959), p. 289 and Note, p. 363 (seven versions); Charlotte Oberfeld, *Volksmärchen aus Hessen* (1962), pp. 26–28, Nos. 15, 16, 17. Our tale undoubtedly has its peculiarities which distinguish it from other versions: the soldier does not hide, but makes himself invisible three times with the help of a magic circle, and the princess is delivered when he bites her finger.

· 24 · The Tale of the Fäderäwisch [1]

Type 311, *Rescue by the Sister*. ZA 150566.

Recorded in 1936 by the Assessor [2] Kohler in Friesenheim, Baden. The informant was his mother, Anna Maria Kohler, 50 years old.

This is one of the numerous redactions of the murderous bridegroom that we sometimes find in the form of prose fiction (first version in 1697 by the French poet Charles Perrault) or sometimes in the form of ballads, known since the middle of the sixteenth century (see the treatises by Ivar Kemppinen, *The Ballad of Lady Isabel and the False Knight* [Helsinki, 1954], and Holger Olof Nygard, *The Ballad of Heer Halewijn* [Knoxville, Tennessee, 1958]). Type 311 is known in Europe, in the Near East, and in both Americas. Fifty-three German versions are recorded. A variant is found in No. 79 of *Folktales of Norway*, one of this series.

· 25 · The Girl Who Married the Devil

Type 312, *The Giant-killer and his Dog* (*Bluebeard*). ZA 28477.

Recorded by Nikolaus Fox from Alfred Bidon in Franz near Weckingen, Lorraine.

Our tale differs slightly from the usual form of this type: the daugh-

---

[1] Featherbroom.

[2] One who has passed his second state examination (in law, etc.).

ter takes the dogs herself to the devil's house. Instead of the brother, her mother and the villagers rescue her. Fourteen German variants of this type are recorded.

·26· The Devil's Wife as Godmother

Type 334, *Household of the Witch.* ZA 203004.

Recorded about 1860 in Wondreb, Upper Palatinate, Bavaria. The manuscript belongs to the handwritten collections of Schönwerth. Collector and informant are unknown.

The story is known in eastern and central Europe only. In the eastern versions, the demoniac figure is death, who is always female here. In central Europe, where death is masculine, this female death-figure has been changed into a witch. From this peculiarity as well as from others we can draw the conclusion that the tale has migrated from east to west. Thirty-one German versions are recorded; see Ranke, SHM, I, 272. In some of them, which come mostly from western Germany, an attempt has been made to mitigate the old macabre features. This has, for instance, been the case in the version in the first and second edition of Grimm's KHM, No. 43, entitled "Die wunderliche Gasterei," in which the principal actors are a blood pudding and a liver sausage.

I am preparing a monograph on this tale that probably contains very old notions of the realm of the dead.

·27· Mrizala and Her Bridegroom, Death

Type 407B, *The Devil's (Dead Man's) Mistress.* ZA 143119.

Recorded in 1933 by the teacher Richard Zeisel in Schmiedshau, Slovakia, from the German countrywoman Genoveva Kußmann.

This tale is known in eastern Europe only; see BP, II, 126–27, where thirty-five versions are recorded (an additional thirty-six are quoted in AT). Our version undoubtedly belongs to the Slovak narrative tradition and so do the variants: ZA 142611; 142999; and 143001.

In his book, *Ungarndeutsche Volksüberlieferungen* (1959), p. 318, No. 97, G. Henssen published another German version from Hungary. He refers at the same place, p. 365, to a version recorded from the Koralpe in Styria, Austria (ZA 188237), which probably has its origin in the East as well. Over a hundred variants are known in Hungary. See Linda Dégh (ed.) *Folktales of Hungary,* a companion volume in this series, No. 4, "Pretty Maid Ibronka," for one of the best.

The permanent questions of the corpse-eating death bring Type 710, *Our Lady's Child,* to mind.

·28· *The Three Traveling Artisans*

Types 812, *The Devil's Riddle;* 360, *Bargain of the Three Brothers with the Devil;* and 361, *Bear-skin.* ZA 141141.

Recorded from his own memory by Wenzel Müller in Totzau, Bohemia.

The combination of the three tales is not unusual. We find it especially in Scandinavian versions (see BP, II, 432, 562; III, 14–15.) In the fundamental situation, one or several fellows who are having difficulties sign a contract with the devil by which they shall fall into the devil's hands, but this turns out in their favor.

The first tale, Type 812, is known throughout Europe. Twenty-nine German versions are recorded (see Ranke, SHM, III, 136). Type 360 is given in its simple form as early as the fourteenth century in the *Summa praedicatium* by the English Dominican Johannes from Bromyard (see BP, II, 563–64). It is spread throughout Europe as well. Twenty-two German versions are reported. Type 361 was narrated for the first time in 1670 by the German poet Grimmelshausen. This tale is also common to all the European peoples. We know forty-two German versions.

·29· *The Three Brothers*

The tale is a combination of Type 304, *The Hunter;* Type 300, *The Dragon-Slayer;* and Type 303, *The Twins or Blood-Brothers.* ZA 202 130.

Recorded by Schönwerth in Bavaria. Place and date of collection as well as informant are unknown.

Type 304 is widespread in central, northern, and especially in eastern Europe. With this oral dispersion may correspond the first appearance in the oriental collection of *A Thousand and One Nights* (see Chauvin, VI, 171, No. 329) as well as its very frequent occurrence in the Turkish narrative tradition (EB, No. 213 has twenty-four versions). Thirty-one German versions have been collected; see Ranke, SHM, I, 138–46.

Type 300 is one of the most frequently narrated tales and has almost global dispersion. In my *Zwei Brüder,* FFC 114, I have analyzed about 1,000 versions of this tale, which is found alone as well as in closest connection with Type 303. Today almost 2,100 versions are known to me, among which are over 200 German variants appearing either separately or in connection with Type 303 (see Ranke, SHM, I, 15–57,

111–38). A variant is found in No. 15 of *Folktales of Japan,* in this series.

Type 303 is also one of the most popular tales. In 1933 I knew and discussed sixty-five German versions; today I know ninety-nine. A version is found in No. 72 of *Folktales of Norway,* another volume in this series.

Our story ends in a very special way, differing considerably from the usual variants. The individuality of the east Bavarian storyteller seems to have had a transforming influence.

· 30 · *The Girl Out of the Egg*

Type 408, *The Three Oranges.* ZA 143008.

Recorded before the last war by Dr. Alfred Karasek-Langer in Münnichwies, Slovakia, from the German countrywoman Anna Brais, when she was 50 years old.

Walter Anderson, the great master of comparative folk-narrative research, was preparing a study on this tale when death took it out of his hands. According to his manuscript, the "egg-redaction" is especially popular in southeastern Europe.

The first record of the tale is found in Giambattista Basile's *Pentamerone,* V (about 1630), 9. However, Anderson points out in his manuscript that the Portuguese poet Fernão Rodrigues Lobo Soropita mentions the "tres cidras de amor" as early as 1600. Anderson has not found any variant prior to 1600. Seven German versions of *The Three Oranges* are recorded.

PART IV

TALES OF BRAVERY AND FIDELITY,

PATIENCE AND RIGHTEOUSNESS

· 31 · *The Cruel Stepmother*

Type 450, *Little Brother and Little Sister.* ZA 202984.

Recorded about 1860 by Schönwerth in the Upper Palatinate, Bavaria.

The story belongs to the old and widespread tale complex of the "Substituted Bride," which Arfert treats in *Das Motiv von der unterschobenen Braut in der internationalen Erzählungsliteratur* (Rostock, 1897). It is known throughout Europe as well as in western Asia,

Canada, and Latin America. There are twenty-one German versions
on record.

· 32 · The Six Brothers

Type 451, *The Maiden Who Seeks her Brothers.* ZA 145368.
Recorded about 1940 in Hedwig, Deutsch-Proben, Bohemia. Collector and informant are unknown.

We find the oldest versions of this very characteristic magic tale, although without the malediction at the beginning, as early as 1185 in
the *Dolopathos* by a Lothringian monk, Johannes de Alta Silva. A
mutilated version is furnished in 1634/36 by the Italian Giambattista
Basile. Three versions are given in Grimm's KHM.

The tale is known throughout Europe, in west Asia as well as among
the Latin and Negro populations of both Americas. Fifty-nine German
versions are known to me.

· 33 · The Feathers from the Bird Venus

Type 461, *Three Hairs from the Devil's Beard.* ZA 80307.
Recorded by the teacher Wiese in Warnkenhagen, Mecklenburg.
Date of collection and informant are unknown.

The tale is, as comparative folk-narrative research has proved, a late
European combination of two very old stories which probably have
their origin in the Orient or in India.

The first one is the tale of the child of fate. It is found in Indian
and Chinese literature at least as early as the third century after
Christ. Into this tale is inserted, as an episode, the story of the death-
letter (2 *Sam.* ii. 4, about David and Urias, in Homer about Proetos
and Bellerophontes), of which much older versions are known. The
second tale is the one of the poor man's journey to the other world;
on his way he is given questions for the powers in the yonder world.
It is first recorded in the Indian-Tibetan *Avadāna* collection (before
A.D. 1300) as well as in the Persian *Tutinameh,* which was termi-
nated about 1330.

We do not know when and where in Europe these two tales were
combined. Before 1800, no complete versions were recorded. The
wide dispersion—Europe, the Orient, Indonesia, China, North and
South America—is astonishing. From Germany alone forty-six printed
or handwritten versions are reported. A version from China is to be
found in No. 20 of *Folktales of China,* one of this series.

Detailed studies: Schick, *Das Glückskind mit dem Todesbrief*
(1912); Aarne, *Der reiche Mann und sein Schwiegersohn* (FFC 23);

Tille, "Das Märchen vom Schicksalskind," in *Zeitschrift für Volkskunde*, XXIX (1919), 22–40; and Liungman *Varifrån kommer våra sagor?* (1952), pp. 133–40.

· 34 · The Gold-rich King

Type 516, *Faithful John*. ZA 195238.

Recorded in 1935 by Anna Loschdorfer in Magyarpolány, Hungary, from a 76-year-old-German storyteller, Franz Mayer.

E. Rösch, *"Der getreue Johannes"* FFC 77 (Helsinki, 1928), as well as K. Krohn, Übersicht, pp. 82–89, believe the origin of the tale is in India and thus they share the opinion of Benfey, *Pantschatantra,* I, 416–17 and von der Leyen, *Indische Märchen* (Halle, 1898), p. 139. But if, as according to Rösch, a simpler oriental tale of the faithful servant or friend has been enriched in the twelfth century in Hungary by the European Amicus and Amelius legend with the motif of the sacrificed child, Krohn presumes the completely developed type to originate from India and to have migrated to western Europe.

This tale is very popular throughout Europe, in western Asia, and among the Spanish-speaking population of both Americas. Eighteen German versions are recorded.

· 35 · The Tale of the Silver, Golden, and Diamond Prince

Type 530, *The Princess on the Glass Mountain*. ZA 135014.

Recorded in 1928 by the teacher Hermann Galbach in Gross Jerutten, district of Ortelsburg, East Prussia.

This version of Type 530 may be considered to be representative of the Germanic type of this tale. The brothers' night watch, the ride to the glass mountain, and the discovery of the hero are complete and well narrated. The tale is found in the form ecotypical for eastern Europe (leap on a tower or a high building) that is found as early as 1350 B.C. in the Egyptian papyrus Harris 500 (see the latest publication of E. Brunner-Traut, *Altägyptische Märchen* [Düsseldorf, 1963], pp. 24–28).

In her studies "Prinsessen på Glasbjaerget," *Danske Studier* (1928), pp. 16–53 and "Glasbergritt," HdM, II, 627–30, Inger M. Boberg points out that the tale is of Indo-Germanic origin. She distinguishes three ecotypes: (1) an East European one, which begins with the funeral watch, and where the princess remains sitting in a high building; (2) a North European-Germanic one containing the watch on the field and a mountain, especially a glass mountain, as an obstacle which must be reached on horseback; and (3) a West European-Celtic Romance ecotype with a tournament as the principal motif.

The tale is very popular in Germany, where over sixty versions are recorded; see Ranke, SHM, II, 146–77.

· 36 · The Girl without Hands

Type 706, *The Maiden without Hands*. ZA 80443.

Recorded in 1897 by the teacher Schröder in Vellahn, Mecklenburg, from the postman Lunow. Printed in the dialect of Mecklenburg by G. Henssen in *Mecklenburger erzählen* (1957), p. 131, No. 80, and in High German translation in the same author's *Deutsche Volksmärchen* (1944).

This is one of the most popular folktales in Europe, and it is also frequently narrated in the Orient, West Asia, India, Japan, North Africa, and South and North America (in Japan, e.g., thirty-three versions are recorded; see Seki, *Folktales of Japan*, p. 99).

The distribution and popularity of the tale are connected with its literary history. BP, I, 298–311, Popović, *Die Erzählung vom Mädchen ohne Hände* (1905); Däumling, *Studien über den Typus des Mädchens ohne Hände* (1912); and others refer to more than twenty literary adaptations of the subject since the twelfth century. Moreover, the central motif of the innocently calumniated wife is one of the favorite themes of medieval and modern folk epics and literature; cf. the European popular books about Crescentia, Hildegardis, Florentia, Sibylla, Genofeva, Helena, Violetta, Hirlanda, Octovianus, etc.; also see Chauvin, VI, 167–70.

Under these circumstances, the oral and the literary productions have, of course, influenced each other. The motif of the innocently calumniated wife, therefore, also appears in numerous tales and noveltales, e.g., Types 451, 705, 706, 707, 709, 710, etc. It is not surprising that Germany possesses thirty-six versions of the tale of the girl without hands; see Ranke SHM, III, 53–54.

· 37 · The Poor Brother's Treasure

Type 834, *The Poor Brother's Treasure*. ZA 45035.

Recorded by Ph. Wegener in Irksleben near Magdeburg, central Germany. Printed in *Geschichtsblätter für Stadt und Land Magdeburg*, XV (1880), 63, No. 51.

In his review of Thompson's Type Index in *Zeitschrift für Volkskunde*, LIX (1963), 93, Anderson has overlooked (when enumerating the double-numbers) that Type 834 and Type 834A, *The Pot of Gold and the Pot of Scorpions,* are variants of the same type. The story is very popular, especially in central, eastern, and southern Europe. Eight versions are reported from India; see Thompson-Roberts, pp. 101–2. Seven are reported from China; see Eberhard, *Typen,* No. 176 and also No. 12 in *Folktales of China,* one of this series of volumes. Twenty are listed from Japan; see Seki, *Folktales of Japan,* No. 44. One comes from Korea; see Kučerjavenko, *Skazki utrennej svezesti* (1957), pp. 53–54. One also comes from Siberia; see Vasilenko, *Skazki . . . Omskojoblasti* (1955), p. 106, No. 19b. There is one from Texas in *Texas, Folk and Folklore* (1954), p. 46. Twenty-nine versions from Germany are so far known to me; see Ranke, SHM, III, 150–51.

As Eberhard notes a Chinese version from the fifth century after Christ, an Indian origin seems, considering the large modern dispersion in the Far East, quite possible, although we have not yet found any older literary version from this area.

· 38 · *The Innkeeper of Moscow*

Type 882, *The Wager on the Wife's Chastity.* ZA 14382.

Recorded in 1937 by the teacher Josef Stich in Neuhäusl, district of Rosshaupt, Czechoslovakia, from the German storyteller Franz Graf.

Twenty modern German versions are known of this novel-tale, which is very popular in Europe and which is sporadically reported from Asia, North Africa, and South and North America. We find a first complete version in Boccaccio's *Decameron* (ed. Wesselski, II, 9), from which Shakespeare probably took the subject for his *Cymbeline.* Older literary versions can be located in the *Patrañuelo* by the Spaniard Timoneda, in the Arabian collection *A Thousand and One Nights* (Chauvin, VI, 159, No. 323), etc. Two hundred years before Boccaccio there existed, however, a tale about a wager on the wife's chastity, which, instead of the episode concerning the secret knowledge of a physical peculiarity or concerning the theft of valuables belonging to the wife, introduces the old Brangäne-motif (the wife substitutes her maid in the love-night). We find the oldest variant of this version in the verse-tale *Von zwein koufmannen* (The Two Traders) by the German poet Ruprecht von Würzburg, who lived probably toward the end of the thirteenth century.

This tale was widespread in Europe in the form of a ballad. In his study, "Die Wette," in *Volkskundliche Gaben, Festschrift für J. Meier,* (1934), pp. 176–86, H. Schewe even tries to trace it back to the eleventh century. For further literature on this subject and its interesting history, see G. Paris, "Le cycle de la gageure," *Romania,*

XXXII (1903), 481ff. and P. P. Bourboulis, *Studies in the History of Modern Greek Story Motifs* (1953), pp. 53–104.

These three scholars agree that the subject has most probably come to Europe from the Orient through Byzantium.

PART V

MAGIC HELP AND GIFTS

· 39 · *The Three Spinners*

Type 501, *The Three Old Women Helpers.* ZA 153849.

Recorded in 1953 by Mr. Vollprecht in Ziegenhagen, Hesse, from a 94-year-old storyteller, Mrs. Degenhardt.

We find the tale of the three helpful fairies in a slightly changed form as early as 1634 in the *Pentamerone* by the Italian, G. Basile. See BP, IV, 235. Only thirty years later, the German poet J. Prätorius narrated the story in his *Abenteuerliche Glückstopf* in the manner generally known today. Thirty-two German versions are recorded; see Ranke SHM, II, 102–5. In Europe, the tale is known by almost all peoples. In his study, *Twå spinnsagor* (1909), C. W. von Sydow traces it to a German origin.

· 40 · *The Magic Lamp*

Type 561, *Aladdin.* ZA 143080.

Recorded in 1937 by the teacher Josef Stich in Neuhäusl, district of Rosshaupt, Czechoslovakia, from the Bohemia-German storyteller Josef Graf.

The tales *The Magic Ring* (Type 560), *Aladdin* (Type 561), and *The Spirit in the Blue Light* (Type 562) are related in their fundamental contents, but the arrangement of the episodes divide them into distinct narrative forms. The story of *Aladdin,* for instance, does not contain the helpful animals of *The Magic Ring;* the episode of the acquisition of the magic object closely connects it with the story of *The Spirit in the Blue Light,* but it takes a different development.

The tale of *Aladdin* has only become known through Galland's translation of *A Thousand and One Nights,* but it is not recorded in any manuscripts in this collection. The sixteen German records (see Ranke, SHM, II, 241f.) probably depend to a large extent on Galland's version.

One of the motifs common to Type 561 as well as to Type 562, and occasionally even to Type 560, the elopement of the beautiful princess by a ministering spirit (our version does not contain this motif), was known in Europe two hundred years before Galland. A German mastersinger song, printed about 1530, but probably older, reports this episode on the great philosopher and magician Albertus Magnus. See BP, III, 538.

· 41 · *The Tale of Frost and His Neighbors*

Type 563, *The Table, the Ass, and the Stick.* ZA 132984.

Recorded in 1928 by the typist Helene Lehwald in Elbing, East Prussia. The informant was the worker August Lehwald, who had heard the tale in his youth in Königsdorf, a district of Morungen, East Prussia.

The first version of this tale, which is well known in Europe, Asia, Africa, and both Americas, seems to be the one given in the Chinese *King lu yi* written in 516 A.D. Of course, tales of objects fulfilling wishes are as old as the human pleasure of inventing stories. The *Book of Kings* contains the story of the inexhaustible flour box and cruse of oil of the widow of Zarpath; Herodotus and Crates tell of a magic table; the *Panchatantra* has gold-producing animals. A medieval legend by the great magician, Albertus Magnus, deals with a sack out of which cudgelled servants are jumping. See Antti Aarne, "Die Zaubergaben," in *Journal de la Société Finno-Ougrienne,* XXVII (Helsinki, 1911), 1–96; Kaarle Krohn, *Übersicht über einige Resultate der Märchenforschung,* FFC 96 (Helsinki, 1931), pp. 48–53, and BP, I, 346–61.

Our version of this tale plainly shows its origin from the Baltic-White Russian area. Only here Frost is at the same time the one who wrongs and who rewards man. Our tale has not preserved the original sense; it has deprived the beginning of its mythic attributes, and it has made a human neighbor of Frost. The tale is very popular in Germany. Fifty-four versions are recorded from the last two centuries. A variant may be found in No. 21 of *Folktales of Israel,* one of this series.

· 42 · *The Hare Herd*

Type 570, *The Rabbit-herd.* ZA 195314.

Recorded in 1933 by Anna Loschdörfer in Veszprémfajsz/Bakonyerwald, Hungary, from the 38-year-old German storyteller Johanna Czizler.

The tale is widespread throughout Europe, in the Orient, and in

South and North America. In Germany fifty-three versions are recorded so far. It is striking that this extremely popular tale seems to be relatively young. According to BP, III, 268, the oldest version is given in the *Ammenmärchen*, I, 93, published anonymously in Weimar in 1791.

· 43 · The Peasant and His Three Sons

Type 665, *The Man Who Flew like a Bird and Swam like a Fish.* ZA 130374.

Recorded in 1932 by the teacher Hedwig Kopania in Dmussen near Skarzinnen, district of Johannisburg, East Prussia, from the storyteller Willy Raphael.

Of this tale fifteen variants are recorded from eastern, northern, and central Germany. It is unknown in southern and western Germany. This corresponds to the European distribution, which is especially dense in eastern Europe, with rather strong ramifications toward northern and central Europe. W. E. Peuckert believes this tale, therefore, confirms the opinion of the Swedish scholar C. W. von Sydow that the main borders of dispersion of a tale show its ethnical origin (*Deutsche Vierteljahrsschr. für Literaturwissensch. und Geistesgesch.*, XIV (1936), 279, Annotation 1. An East European origin of the tale is suggested, since the principal motif of the transformation into quick running, flying, and swimming animals is found there in other kinds of folktales, above all in the Russian byliny. See R. Trautmann, *Die Volksdichtung der Großrussen*, I (Heidelberg, 1935), 216, 220–23.

The remarkable fact that some tales remain within their primal ethnical area or hardly spread beyond its borders, whereas others are scattered throughout the world, is worth being closely examined from the psychological, philological, and ethnological points of view. See also Ranke, SHM, II, 388.

· 44 · The Animal Languages

Type 670, *The Animal Languages.* ZA 2423.

Recorded in 1936 by Dr. Dittmaier in Stieldorferhohn, district of the Sieg, Rhineland. The informant was the master mason Heinrich Knüttgen, born in 1853.

In his study, *Der tiersprachenkundige Mann und seine neugierige Frau*, FFC 15 (Helsinki, 1914), Antti Aarne traces the tale back to its Indian origin. And, in fact, it is given in practically every representative Oriental collection: for example, in the Indian *Rāmāyana*, the

Buddhist *Jātakas*, the Chinese *Tripitaka;* the Persian *Tutinameh,* and the Arabian *A Thousand and One Nights.* The first European version is found in the *Gesta Romanorum,* written about 1300. However, the example of the cock mastering ten wives is given as early as 1100 in Petrus Alphonsi's *Disciplina Clericalis.*

The tale is very popular in Europe, Asia, Africa, and in both Americas. Thirteen German versions are recorded now.

PART VI

WISE MEN AND WOMEN

·45· *The Quarrel about the Woods*

ZA 158097.

Recorded by Mr. Strauch in Langenau, Upper Franconia. Time of collection and informant are unknown.

In connection with this story, see Motif, H13.1, "Recognition by overheard conversation with animal." The episode is closely connected with the following related motifs, which are popular in legend and tale: H13.2.7, "Recognition by overheard conversation with stove" (see Types 301, *The Three Stolen Princesses,* and 533, *The Speaking Horsehead*); H13.2, "Recognition by overheard conversation with objects" (see Type 894, *The Ghoulish Schoolmaster and the Stone of Pity*); and D1316.5, "Magic-speaking reed (tree) betrays secret" (see Type 782, *Midas and the Ass's Ears.*

For variations of age and of dispersion, see BP, II, 275–77 and the complex Motif H13.

·46· *The Swineherd Who Married a Princess*

Type 850, *The Birthmarks of the Princess.* ZA 135048.

Recorded in 1928 by the teacher Hermann Galbach in Gross Jerutten, district of Ortelsburg, East Prussia.

Sixteen German versions are recorded of this novel-tale, which is narrated throughout Europe as well as in North and South America (see Ranke, SHM, III, 151–58).

In 1938, Mr. Schütt, a teacher in the Industrial School in Reinbeck, Schleswig-Holstein, sent me an extremely rude version of this novel-tale. In a letter he had added a remark that is most interesting for the teacher as well as for the folklorist concerning the impression such rude stories made on him when he was a child. "Sitting on the bench near the back door, we were delighted to listen to old Jule. Whenever she could not resist any longer our urgent demand: 'Jule, tell us a story,' she would open her toothless mouth and tell one story after the other. Later on I found many of these in other tale collections. But I still remember two of them that will probably never be printed anywhere, for the simple reason that they were told with such originality, in such a direct, rough manner, that a brain glossed with the polish of modern civilization would turn away with a shudder, exclaiming: 'How could you?' I cannot remember that we were shocked. But I still hear the monotonous voice of old Jule. We did not 'understand' the stories any better than we understood the two hundred biblical verses and the twenty psalms we had to learn by heart at school. But I think that we should not hesitate for reasons of popular psychology to record these kinds of popular stories and to classify them among 'Tales for Adults.' "

I did not have this tale from Schleswig-Holstein translated here, for it really is too rough. I give instead the "tamer" version from East Prussia, which might still be rather tough for a reader with delicate feelings.

·47· The Farmer's Clever Daughter

Type 875, *The Clever Peasant Girl*. ZA 188032.

Recorded in 1939 by father Romuald Pramberger in Frohnleiten, Styria, from the storyteller Johannes Zöhrer.

The different motifs of this old and widespread tale, rich in variations, go back to early times and to different ethnic spheres. The task, to come to the king neither naked nor dressed, which is imposed on the girl, the daughter of Brünhild and Sigurd, is found earlier in the old Icelandic *Saga of Aslaug*. The enigmatic question about the quickest, the sweetest, the fattest, etc., thing is answered by Amasis in Plutarch's *Symposium of the Seven Wise Men,* and the permission to carry away the most beloved thing is a favorite motif of old Talmudic stories. A similar motif involving the eating of excrement is found in the story entitled "The Two Brothers," printed in Richard M. Dorson's "Polish Wonder Tales of Joe Woods," *Western Folklore,* VII, 1 (January 1949), pp. 50–52. In connection with these questions, compare BP, II, 349–73; Jan de Vries, *Die Märchen von klugen Rätsellösern,* FFC 73 (Helsinki, 1928); and Albert Wesselski, *Der Knabenkönig und das kluge Mädchen* (Prague, 1929).

The tale is very popular in Germany, too. Sixty-four versions have been collected in the last two centuries alone.

· 48 · The Baron's Haughty Daughter

Type 900, *King Thrushbeard*. ZA 203008.

Recorded about 1860 by Schönwerth in Tiefenbach, Upper Palatinate, Bavaria. The informant is unknown.

According to Philippson's study, *König Drosselbart*, FFC 50 (Helsinki, 1923), the oldest literary variants, namely the verse-novel of the half pear, which was erroneously attributed to the Middle High German poet Konrad von Würzburg (d. 1287), and the *Clarussaga*, which was translated from French in the first half of the fourteenth century by the Icelandic bishop Jon Halldorsson, are stylistic transformations of the real folktale. It must thus have been known in the thirteenth century in its modern form. For Philippson, the origin of the tale is in Germany, whereas Krohn, *Übersicht über einige Resultate der Märchenforschung*, FFC 96 (Helsinki, 1931), pp. 144–49, is of the opinion that it has spread from Italy. It is known today throughout Europe, in Turkey, and it is occasionally reported in West Asia and in Africa and frequently in both Americas. Forty-three German versions are recorded. A version is to be found in No. 73 of *Folktales of Norway*, one of this series.

· 49 · Prince Ferdinand

Type 950, *Rhampsinitus*, beginning with Type 1525D, *Theft by Distracting Attention*. ZA 80008.

Recorded in 1892 by the headmaster Schnell-Mirow in Peetsch, Mecklenburg. The informant was an old peasant woman.

The first part of the Rhampsinitus tale was transmitted as early as the beginning of the fifth century B.C. by Eugammon from Cyrene in North Africa to two Greek architects of the mythic time, Agamedes and his son, Trophonios, who robbed the treasury of the king Augias in Elis. A little later, Herodotus (484–425) gives a complete version from Egypt. The tale has apparently migrated to Asia rather early, for the Chinese *Cheng King* translates an older Indian version, which, however, is lost as early as A.D. 266. As to the history of the tale, see BP, III, 395–406; Chauvin, VIII, 185–86; E. Brunner-Traut in *Saeculum*, X (1959), 182.

The tale is very popular in Europe, Asia, North Africa, and in both Americas. Twenty German versions of the last two centuries have been recorded. A version from Israel is to be found in No. 33 of *Folktales of Israel*, one of this series.

· 50 · The Lazy Woman

Type 1405, *The Lazy Spinning Woman*. ZA 75776.
Recorded in 1898 by the "Märchenprofessor," W. Wisser, from Mrs.
Schlör|in Wriebel, Schleswig-Holstein.

Seven German versions of this farce, which is widespread especially
in northern, central, and eastern Europe, are reported.

· 51 · The Peasant Pewit

Type 1535, *The Rich and the Poor Peasant*. ZA 130801.
Recorded in 1932 by Anneliese Braun in Alt Belitten, East Prussia.
Informant was the teacher Kordatzki in Alt Belitten.

The first version of this farce-tale was recorded in the eleventh century by a west European (probably a Lothringian or Flemish) clergy-
man. The next versions 'chronologically' are given about 1400 by the
Italian poet Giovanni Sercambi, about 1500 in the *Storia di Campri-
ano contadino*, 1550 by Giovan Francesco Straparola, and 1559 in the
Nachtbüchlein by the German poet Valentin Schumann.

Type 1535 is a farce of universal dispersion. It is well known
throughout Europe, in West and East Asia, in North and Central
Africa, as well as in both Americas. One hundred eighteen German
versions are recorded.

From the great number of well-known and popular motifs (see
Type 1535 and BP, II, 10), our version contains only the one of the
sold cowhide, of the killed woman, of the liberation from the chest,
and of the death of the envious peasants who want to get some cattle
out of the water.

· 52 · The Woman in the Chest

Type 1536A, *The Woman in the Chest*. ZA 203048.
Recorded about 1860 by Schönwerth in Neukirchen, Upper Palatinate, Bavaria. The informant is unknown.

This version of the joke is a variant, in its beginning, of the original
tale, *The Corpse Killed Five Times* (Type 1537), which probably came
from the Orient (see the monograph by Suchier, *Der Schwank von
der viermal getöteten Leiche* [1922]). Other variations are Type
1536B, *The Three Hunchback Brothers Drowned;* Type 1536C, *The
Murdered Lover,* etc. Type 1536A is popular throughout Europe, the
Near East, India, the Far East, North Africa, and South and North

America. Fourteen German versions are recorded. A variant is to be found in No. 9 of *Folktales of Hungary,* one of this series.

· 53 · A Peasant Sells a Cow as a Goat

Type 1551, *The Wager that Sheep are Hogs,* and Motif K111.2., "Alleged bill-paying hat sold" (see Type 1539). ZA 135004.

Recorded in 1928 by the teacher Herman Galbach in Gross Jerutten, East Prussia.

The combination of the two jokes is rather frequent. See BP, II, 8; compare Ó Suilleabháin, *Types of the Irish Folktale,* FFC 188, p. 276; Rael, *Cuentos Españoles de Colorado,* No. 360; Abu Naaman, *Baderech Leerez Haoscher,* No. 47 (see *Fabula,* IV, 187).

The first part (Type 1551) is old and widespread; for further details and its different variants, see Chauvin, II, 96, No. 51 (*Kalilah*); VII, 150, No. 430 (*A Thousand and One Nights*); Crane, *Exempla of Jacques de Vitry,* p. 141, No. 21; Oesterley, *Gesta Romanorum,* No. 132, etc.

Motif K111.2, "Alleged bill-paying hat sold," has only sporadically emanated out of Europe. The oldest records we know go back only to the seventeenth century (see BP, II, 9–10). Our combination cannot have taken place at an earlier date. Another tale in which this motif appears is No. 69 in *Folktales of England,* one of this series.

· 54 · Doctor Know-All

Type 1641, *Doctor Know-All.* ZA 143074.

Recorded in 1937 by the teacher Josef Stich in Neuhäusl, Bohemia, from the carpenter Franz Keim.

In his book, *Varifrån kommer våra sagor?* (Djursholm, 1952), pp. 384–86, W. Liungman points out western European and eastern Asiatic types of this farce. The eastern type is given in the story of the Brahmin *Hariśarman,* recorded by Gunādhya in the first or second century after Christ, whereas in Europe the motifs appear sporadically only about 1500 in, for instance, the discovery of the stolen money in the *Facetiae* of the German humanist Bebel, the divining of the cricket in the novels of the Italian Sercambi, and finally, the two combined in the seventeenth century in the French *Contes du Sieur d'Ouville.*

The farce is very popular in Europe and Asia and is found quite often in North Africa as well as in both Americas. Thirty-six German versions are known to me. A version is to be found in No. 11 of *Folktales of China,* in this series.

·55· *The Wrong Song*

Type 1735A, *The Bribed Boy Sings the Wrong Song.* ZA 210146.
Recorded by Professor Prettl in Szolatnek, County of Baranya, Hungary. The story had been handed down in his family.

The joke is told in Europe as well as in the United States. Six German versions are known. A text is printed in *Folktales of England,* a companion volume in this series, tale No. 62.

PART VII

SAINTS AND SINNERS

·56· *The Poor and the Rich*

Type 750A, *The Wishes.* ZA 5218.
Recorded in 1916 by the teacher Heinrich Hoffmann in Drove, Rhineland. The informant was a Mrs. Cahn.

This delightful legendary tale, which belongs to the widespread complex of stories dealing with the gods visiting earth, consists of two different types that Thompson has combined in Type 750A. In the first type, three wishes are granted for hospitality but they are lost through the couple's foolishness. In the second type, there are usually two partners, a modest one and a covetous one; each has been granted a wish by the god. (See Dähnhardt, NS, II, 140–53.) The one profits by it, the other one does not. In a new edition of Aarne-Thompson's *Type-Index,* these two tales will have to be given different numbers.

Our story belongs to the first variation and depends probably to a great extent on the Grimm version (KHM, No. 87). Stories of three wishes granted to a foolish couple are found in Europe with Marie de France (twelfth century), with the Middle High German poet Stricker (thirteenth century), the meistersinger Hans Sachs, etc. But we find similar tales in the Arabian narrative literature of the thirteenth and fourteenth century, for instance in Scheref Eddin, Damīri, and others. For further details concerning the very complicated history of this material, see BP, II, 210–29.

Our tale is very popular in Europe and Asia as well as among the European and colored population of both Americas. In Germany more than eighty versions of Type 750A have been recorded so far.

· 57 · The Black Woodpecker

Type 751A, *The Peasant Woman is Changed into a Woodpecker*. ZA 144018.

Recorded by Erwin Botha in Zöllnei, district of Senftenberg, Czechoslovakia. Date of collection and informant are unknown.

We have eleven German versions that have been recorded in eastern Germany in the former German language enclaves in eastern Europe. This agrees with the European distribution of this legendary tale, which is especially prominent in the east and north of the continent. It is, however, most remarkable that there exist Chinese parallels; see Eberhard, *Volksmärchen aus Südost-China*, FFC 128, p. 91, No. 49.

· 58 · The Road to Hell

The tale is a combination of Type 756B, *The Devil's Contract*, and Type 361, *Bear-skin*. ZA 185288.

Recorded by Father Pramberger in Ranten, Styria, Austria, from Johann Egger.

Both types are very popular in Germany. Seventy versions of the former and thirty-nine of the latter are recorded. N. P. Andrejev, the author of the monograph on Type 756B, "Die *Legende vom Räuber Madej,*" FFC 54 (Helsinki, 1924), is of the opinion that this tale was developed in the medieval sermon literature of western Europe. Nevertheless, today it is best known in eastern Europe.

The tale of *Bear-skin* was narrated for the first time in 1670 by the German poet Grimmelshausen. More often than with Type 756B, we find it combined with Type 475, *The Man as Heater of Hell's Kettle;* cf. BP, II, 423–26.

It is probable that the principal motif, not to wash, comb, shave, or to cut the nails for rather a long time, issues from an old rite of initiation or consecration; cf. HdM, I, 169–72. However, this custom is found as well in the funeral rites of different peoples and epochs (see K. Ranke, *Indogermanische Totenverehrung*, I [(Helsinki, 1951), 102–5]).

· 59 · A Story about Our Lord Jesus Christ

Type 791, *The Savior and Peter in Night-Lodgings,* and 752A, *Christ and Peter in the Barn*. ZA 202393.

Recorded by Schönwerth in Neustadt, Upper Palatinate, Bavaria.
Informant and date of record are unknown.

Both legendary jokes have already been combined in 1551 by the
German meistersinger Hans Sachs. See BP, III, 451–52. Type 791 had
been narrated even some decades before by Camerarius in his *Ap-
pendix fabularum Aesopicarum* (1539).

Both jokes are widespread in Europe. Forty-three German versions
are recorded of the first, one hundred six of the second, and thirty-
five are known in combination.

·60· *The Tailor in Heaven*

Type 800, *The Tailor in Heaven.* ZA 151530.

Recorded in 1948 by Hedwig Schlecht in Oberharmersbach-Zuwald,
Baden, from a 70-year-old trout farmer, Wilhelm Schwarz.

Of this fine legendary farce, twenty-five German versions from the
last two centuries are recorded. But the tale was narrated about 1500
by the German humanist Heinrich Bebel in his *Fabula cuiusdam sar-
cinatoris.* The stories in J. Frey's *Gartengesellschaft* (1556); H. W.
Kirchhof's *Wendunmut* (1563); and J. Wickram's *Rollwagenbüchlein*
(1558) are based on Bebel's variant. Grimm's version, which is No. 35
in the second edition of the KHM, is a combination of these three variants. The story of the *Tailor in Heaven* is known primarily in northern, central, and eastern Europe.

·61· *The Hermit and the Devil*

Type 839, *One Vice Carries Others with It.* ZA 188200.

Recorded in 1892 by Hans von der Sann in Styria, Austria, from the
storyteller Karl Reiterer.

The subject of this legend is given in the thirteenth century by
Etienne de Bourbon; in the fifteenth by John Bromyard; in the sixteenth by Johannes Pauli, Martin Montanus, and others. In Bromyard,
the *Vitae Patrum* are quoted as the source; see Wesselski, *Mönchslatein*
(1909), No. 81; J. Pauli, *Schimpf und Ernst* (ed., Bolte, No. 243);
A. Taylor in *Modern Philology*, XX (1922), 61–94. The legend has
never become very popular. There are only about thirty European
versions, of which four are from Germany.

·62· *The Devil and Our Lord*

Type 846, *Devil Always Blamed.* ZA 130276.

Recorded in 1932 by Emil Köhler, a student, in Schönmahr, East

Prussia, from the fieldhand Mrs. Radtke, who had heard the tale when she was a farmer's servant.

In Ranke, SHM, III, 125, I had given this legendary tale the number 792* because it belongs in the neighborhood of the stories dealing with the gods visiting earth. In my opinion, Thompson's No. 846 is wrong.

This fine tale about God's and the devil's common trip, which despite its farcical touch suggests an idea of the devil's eternal grief, is very popular in Germany, where twenty-four versions are recorded. In Europe, it is reported from the eastern and central parts of the continent especially.

·63· *The Man in the Moon*

Motif A751, "Man in the moon." ZA 45037.

Recorded about 1880 by Philipp Wegener in Magdeburg, province of Saxony.

Etiological legends about the origin of the lunar spots are narrated all around the world; see Thompson's *Motif Index*. In Europe it is usually a man who, on account of an outrage, is sent to the moon. This is also reported in Asia and in both Americas. There also exists in Europe, more frequently in India and East Asia, and almost exclusively in Mela- and Micronesia, the same story about a woman. There are also early stories about an animal (hare, rabbit, frog, etc.) in South and East Asia. The theriomorphous form is dominant in South Africa as well as among the Indians of both Americas. A variant using a similar motif (A751.1) can be found in No. 54, "The Man in the Moon," in *Folktales of China,* one of this series.

A careful examination of this subject would probably give important results not only for the theory of the polygenesis of etiologies but also with regard to the problem of early cultural migrations.

PART VIII

THE DEVIL AND HIS PARTNERS

·64· *How the Devil Fetched the Mayor*

Type 821A, *Thief Rescued by the Devil.*

Recorded from Hedwig Borowski in Lisken, East Prussia. Printed in *Unsere Heimat,* XI (1929), 172.

The tale of the devil as solicitor of the innocently calumniated was narrated in Germany as early as 1500 by the meistersinger Hans Folz from Nuremberg. A variant is given in Luther's table-talk. Although it was a favorite subject of literature until the nineteenth century (see examples given by BP, II, 566), the tale has never become really popular in Germany. Thus, other than this version from the Masuren,[1] we have no recent variants. The tale is, however, well known among the Scandinavians, the Finns, the Estonians, and the Slavs.

·65· The Dead Creditor

Type 822*, *The Devil Lends Money to the Man.* ZA 80508.

Recorded in 1897 by the teacher Sager in Wittenburg, Mecklenburg, from the maker of slippers Hinrichs.

So far the story has been reported only from eastern, northern, and central Europe. Forty-eight German variants are listed; see Ranke, SHM, III, 149–50. The oldest record known to me is given in Johann Prätorius's *Daemonologia Rubinzalii Silesii,* III, 38, which was first published in 1662.

·66· An Old Woman Sows Discord

Type 1353, *The Old Woman as Trouble Maker.* ZA 300009.

Recorded by Woeste before 1878 in Hemer, Westphalia. Informant unknown.

This story is popular throughout Europe as well as in India and in Arabian North Africa. The oldest version is given in the *Sēpher Scha'asiu'im* by Joseph ibn Sabara, written in Barcelona toward the end of the twelfth century (see BP, IV, 328–33). Since that time we find it in numerous European example-, sermon-, and jest-books; see Wesselski, *Märchen,* pp. 194–96. Its extraordinary popularity is proved by the numerous figurative representations. In his study of Type 1353, *Saga och Sed* (1941), pp. 1–93, Gjerdmann refers to eight Swedish churches with illustrations concerning this subject.

Whether the very early Indian tradition of the jackal who destroys the friendly relations between the lion and the bull by means of calumnies (*Panchatantra,* Book I) or the Arabian one in *Fāhiḳat al houlafa* by Ibn Arabschah (Chauvin, II, 195), where a deceitful slave takes the place of the European old woman, are lateral or original forms of our tale, as a number of scholars presume (Liebrecht, Köhler, Prato, Wesselski, etc.), will have to be examined more carefully.

Fifteen popular German versions of Type 1353 are reported.

[1] East Prussian lake district.

PART IX

THE STUPID OGRE

·67· *The Tale of the Youngest Brother and the
Stupid Devil*

Type 1045, *Pulling the Lake Together,* and Type 1072, *Race with
Little Son,* and Type 1073, *Climbing Contest,* and Type 1071 *Wrestling Contest (with Old Grandfather),* and Type 1082 *Carrying the
Horse.* ZA 134488.

Recorded in 1933 from his own memory by the carpenter's foreman Ernst Seroszinski from Elbing, East Prussia. He had heard the
tale in his youth from a shepherd in his native place near Memel.

Our tale is a combination of popular European farces about an imposition on the stupid devil or ogre. Most of these stories probably
originated in eastern Europe (see Oskar Hackman, "En finländsksvensk saga av osteuropeiskt ursprung," in *Bragens Årsskrift,* IV [Helsinki, 1910]). Type 1082 also has its chief distribution in the Slav and
Scandinavian area, whereas Type 1045 seems to be well known
throughout Europe.

In accordance with the northeastern cultural decline of these
stories, they are found in Germany as well as in the north and east.

·68· *The Devil Duped*

Type 1130, *Counting out Pay.* ZA 203270.

Recorded about 1800 by Schönwerth in Tirschenreuth, Upper Palatinate, Bavaria.

This joke probably originates in an old legend of St. Benedict, who
is said to have duped the devil in Speyer in a similar way with a bottomless boot. The motif had then been adapted by Hans Sachs in two
meistergesange in 1549 and 1563; see BP, III, 421–23.

Type 1130 is widespread in eastern and central Europe and to a
smaller degree in northern and western Europe. In Germany, twenty-three variants have been recorded so far.

·69· *The Devil and the Man*

Type 1157, *The Gun as Tobacco Pipe.* ZA 130849.

Noted in 1936 by the author Dr. Skowronnek from Schuiken, East

Prussia, who had heard the story sixty-five years before from his father.

This joke begins with the first part of Type 157, *Learning to Fear Man* (see also tale No. 7). Type 1157 is known in northern, central, and eastern Europe and in a few places in Abyssinia and the Near East. Baughman reports two English-American versions. A Finnish-American text from Michigan is given by Dorson, *Bloodstoppers and Bearwalkers* (1952), pp. 143–44. In Germany, eighteen versions are recorded.

·70· A Peasant Tricks the Devil

Type 1174, *Making a Rope of Sand*. ZA 151588.

Recorded in 1949 by Hedwig Schlecht in Kirnbach-Grün, Baden, from an 85-year-old master-mason, Bernhard Nock.

This tale is distributed mainly in eastern and northern Europe. Six German versions are recorded. A variant from Norway is found in No. 15 of *Folktales of Norway,* one of this series. The impossible task of making a rope of sand is found in the Assyrian *Achiqar-tale;* in the Latin proverb: ex arena funem nectere; in the Harbard-song of the Old Norse *Edda,* etc. See de Vries, *Rätsellöser,* FFC 73, 155, No. 1; BP, II, 513; III, 16; Liungman, p. 329 f.

PART X

NUMSKULLS

·71· The People from Schwarzenborn
a) They Hide a Bell

Type 1278, *Marking the Place on the Boat.* ZA 154227.

Recorded by Grüner in Ober-Werbe, Hesse, from a 74-year-old smith, Wilhelm Wittner.

This Gothamite story (Schildbürgergeschichte) is given in the Chinese *Tripitaka* (about A.D. 500). It is known in northern, central, and eastern Europe; in Asia; and in North America. Twelve German versions are reported.

b) They Sow Salt

Type 1200, *The Sowing of Salt.* ZA 154230.

For the origin, see *a.*

The first version is given in the German *Lalebuch* of 1598. There exist numerous variants of this joke motif: Eggs are sown to grow hens, cheese to grow calves, cow's tails to grow cows, horses' ears to grow horses, etc. See Wesselski, *Hodscha Nasreddin*, No. 423.

The joke is widespread in Eurasia. Fifteen German versions are known to me.

c) *They Protect Their Seed*

Type 1201, *The Plowing*.

For the origin, see *a*.

The German humanist Heinrich Bebel narrates the story for the first time in his *Facetiae* (1508). Today it is well known in northern, central, and eastern Europe. It is very popular in Germany as well (Twenty-one versions).

d) *They Dig a Well*

Type 1255, *A Hole to Throw the Earth in*.

Printed in Wilhelm Neuhaus, *Sagen und Schwänke aus dem Kreis Hersfeld und den angrenzenden Gebieten* (3d impression; Hersfeld, n.d.), p. 94.

Wesselski, *Hodscha Nasreddin*, II, 227 refers to Castiglione's *Cortegiano* for this joke. It is narrated throughout Europe. Eight German versions are known to me.

e) *They Measure the Depth of the Well*

Type 1250, *Bringing Water from the Well*.

For the origin, see *d*.

Like *b*, this joke was given in the German *Lalebuch* toward the end of the sixteenth century. Wesselski, *Hodscha Nasreddin*, I, 242 and Liungman, III, 337, point out that the motif of the living chain is given in other, very early combinations, as for instance in the Chinese *Tripituku*, where a chain of monkeys hanging on a branch try to get the moon out of the well and fall into it, or in the Indian *Kathāsaritsāgara*. Our story is very popular in Europe, in Asia, and in both Americas. Thirty German versions are reported.

·72· *The Parish Bull Eats the Grass from the Wall*

Type 1210, *The Cow is Taken to the Roof to Graze*. ZA 192598.

Recorded in 1938 by Dr. Misch Orend in Kastenholz, Transylvania, Rumania. The informant was Mrs. Anna Klöss, born in 1886.

This Gothamite story is given in the German *Lalebuch* of the sixteenth century.

It is known throughout Europe, western Asia, and both Americas. In Germany, thirty-six versions have been recorded.

·73· *Stretching the Bench*

Type 1244, *Trying to Stretch the Beam.* ZA 211245.

Recorded by Mrs. Grete Horak from a German informant in the Hungarian region called "Swabian Turkey."

This joke, which is known throughout Europe, undoubtedly has its origins in the old Jewish and early Christian legend of the stretched beam. See Günter, *Die christliche Legende des Abendlandes* (Heidelberg, 1910), pp. 99–100.

The story is most popular in Germany, where twenty-six versions are recorded.

·74· *Moving the Church*

Type 1326, *Moving the Church.* ZA 133294.

Narrated in 1929 by Mrs. Anna Maass in Bartenstein, East Prussia, from memory.

The farce is known throughout Europe. Baughman notes one American-English version. In Germany, twenty-six variants have been recorded.

PART XI

STUPID PEOPLE

·75· *The Poor People Who Wanted To Be Rich*

Type 1416, *The Mouse in the Silver Jug.* ZA 134993.

Recorded in 1938 by the teacher Hermann Galbach in Gross Jerutten, East Prussia.

The parabolic tale of the *Neue Eva* is scattered throughout Europe. Several versions are also reported from the Near East and from North and South America. The first reference is given in the *Exempla* of Jacques de Vitry, Bishop of Akkon, who lived from about 1165 to 1240; see Crane, *The Exempla of Jacques de Vitry* (1890), p. 13. For its further literary development in Europe, see Johannes Pauli,

Schimpf und Ernst, (ed. Bolte, II [1924], 349, No. 398). Eleven versions are reported in modern German narrative tradition.

·76· *The Clever Elsie*

Type 1450, *Clever Elsie.* ZA 133968.
Recorded in 1928 by the teacher Rimek in Gross-Schmückwalde, East Prussia. The informant was a 38-year-old coachman, Friedrich Schneider.

This delightful story involving a silly concern about remote possibilities is given for the first time in a poem by the German Heinrich Götting from Witzenhausen (see BP, I, 335–38). It is very popular in Europe, western Asia, and in both Americas. Sixteen German versions are recorded.

·77· *The Ox as Mayor*

Type 1675, *The Ox (Ass) as Mayor.* ZA 40256.
Recorded in 1958 by Eva Kautz in Ahausen, Hannover, from the storyteller Heinrich Intemann.

The first version of this joke is given in a satirical poem by Thomas Murner, printed in 1515 in Strasbourg (see Bolte in *Zeitschrift für Volkskunde,* VII [1897], 93–96). The story is widespread in Europe and is also found in the Arabian collection of *A Thousand and One Nights* (Chauvin, VII, 170, No. 445) as well as in the old jokes about the Turkish Eulenspiegel *Hodscha Nasreddin* (ed. Wesselski, No. 63, 385, 395). It is known today in the whole Orient, in India, in North Africa, and in Canada. Thirty-four German versions are reported. A version from Israel may be found in No. 66 of *Folktales of Israel,* one of this series.

PART XII

STORIES ABOUT PARSONS

·78· *The Damned Boys*

Type 1785B, *The Sexton Puts a Needle in the Sacramental Bread.* ZA 110625.
Recorded about 1933 in the district of Stolp, Pomerania. Printed in *Ostpommersche Heimat* (1933), No. 30. Collector and informant are unknown.

In the German versions, it is not the sexton who puts the needle in the sacramental bread, but boys who put needles on the edge of the pulpit. We know nine versions of this joke. It is usually reported from northern Europe, Germany, Flanders, and occasionally from eastern Europe.

·79· The Dream

Type 1738, *The Dream: All Parsons in Hell,* and Type 1860A, *Lawyers in Hell.* ZA 55, 382.

Recorded in 1927 by Frau G. Meyer in Horsdorf, Schleswig-Holstein, from the peasant Arend Ehlers, born in 1853, who had heard the story from his parents.

Both jokes are very popular in Germany, alone as well as in combination. Of the first story, fifty-one, and of the second one, thirty-six versions are recorded, most of them being combined in one story. Mock-stories like Type 1738 or 1860A have been current in the German joke literature for centuries. Walter von der Vogelweide (about 1170 to 1230) said about parsons. "They show us the way to God and descend into hell themselves." The Alsatian Franciscan friar Johannes Pauli reports in his book, *Schimpf und Ernst* (1522), that the pigs are driven into the water with the words: "You must as surely go in as the advocates go to hell" (ed. Bolte, No. 117). In a satire of the time of the Reformation, St. Francis is still waiting for the second Franciscan friar at the door to heaven (BP, III, 275, note 1). According to the *Antihypochondriakus* of 1764 (p. 117), heaven loses every lawsuit with hell, because all the advocates stay there, etc.

Type 1738 is reported from all over Europe, and sporadically from Canada and from American Negroes in Michigan. Type 1860A is dispersed in Europe and in North America. Variants may be found in Nos. 59 and 82 of *Folktales of England,* in this series.

·80· The Pig in the Church

Type 1838, *The Hog in Church.* ZA 154192.

Recorded in 1950 by the student Grüner in Nordenbeck, Hesse, from the shepherd Wilhelm Walker.

Sixteen German versions are known.

PART XIII

TALES OF LYING

· 81 · Catching Hares in Winter

Type 1891B*, Rabbits (Hares) Caught by Making them Sneeze. ZA
62986.
Recorded by G. F. Meyer in 1930 in Bramstedt, Schleswig-Holstein,
from the joiner Theodor Beuck, who had heard the story from col-
leagues.
Antti Aarne reports only three Finnish variants of this tale of lying. I can add the only German version.

· 82 · Helping to Lie

ZA 56383.
Recorded in 1928 by G. F. Meyer in Brackrade, Schleswig-Holstein,
from the storyteller Wihelmine Schröder, who was born in 1855. She
had heard this story from her parents.
The oldest version of this widespread tale of lying is given in the
Schāhnāme by the Persian poet Firdausi (935–1020). We find the
first European version in the Exempla of the Bishop of Akkon, Jacques
de Vitry (about 1165–1240). As to the further development, see Wesselski, Märchen des Mittelalters, pp. 226–27; Fischer und Bolte, Die
Reise der Söhne Giaffers (1895), pp. 203–5; and Müller-Fraureuth,
Die deutschen Lügendichtungen (1881), pp. 78–79, 139–40. The tale
is very popular in Europe (see Wesselski, loc. cit.). Six German versions are reported.
Thompson incorrectly classifies the material recorded by Wesselski
and Wisser, Plattdeutsche Volksmärchen, II, 186 in Type 1920D, The
Liar Reduces the Size of his Lie. This is an equally well known and
widespread tale of lying that is, however, completely different from
ours. In our tale, the helper does not prevent the narrator from keep-
ing up his lie but corroborates it with a new one. In a new edition of
the Type-Index, I would number the story 1920E* with the title, The
Servant Corroborates the Lies of His Master.

List of Abbreviations

Type = Aarne, Antti, and Thompson, Stith. *The Types of the Folk-tale.* (Folklore Fellows Communications, No. 184.) Helsinki, 1961.

BP = Bolte, Johannes, and Polívka, Georg. *Anmerkungen zu den Kinder- und Hausmärchen der Brüder Grimm.* 5 vols. Leipzig, 1913–32.

Chauvin = Chauvin, Victor. *Bibliographie des ouvrages arabes.* 12 vols. Liège, 1892–1922.

Dähnhardt, NS = Dähnhardt, Oskar. *Natursagen.* 4 vols. Leipzig and Berlin, 1907–12.

EB = Eberhard, Wolfram, and Boratav, Pertev Naili. *Typen türkischer Volksmärchen.* Wiesbaden, 1953.

FFC = *Folklore Fellows Communications.* Helsinki, 1910–

HdA = *Handwörterbuch des deutschen Aberglaubens.* 10 vols. Berlin and Leipzig, 1927–42.

HdM = *Handwörterbuch des deutschen Märchens.* 2 vols. Berlin, 1930–40.

KHM = *Kinder- und Hausmärchen. Gesammelt durch die Brüder Grimm.* 2 vols. 5th ed. Göttingen, 1843.

Liungman = Liungman, Waldemar. *Sveriges Samtliga Folksagor* 3 vols. Djursholm, 1950–1952.

Ranke, SHM = Ranke, Kurt. *Schleswig-Holsteinische Volksmärchen.* 3 vols. Kiel, 1955, 1958, 1962.

Motif = Thompson, Stith. *Motif-Index of Folk-Literature.* 6. vols. Copenhagen and Bloomington, Ind., 1955–58.

Wienert = Wienert, Walter. *Die Typen der griechisch-römischen Fabel.* (Folklore Fellows Communications, No. 56.) Helsinki, 1925.

ZA = Zentralarchiv für deutsche Volkserzählungen in Marburg/Lahn, Germany.

Bibliography

AARNE, ANTTI. "Die Zaubergaben," *Journal de la Société Finno-Ougrienne* XXVII (1909), 1–96.

——. *Die Tiere auf der Wanderschaft*. (Folklore Fellows Communications, No. 11.) Helsinki, 1913.

——. *Der tiersprachenkundige Mann und seine neugierige Frau.* (Folklore Fellows Communications, No. 11.) Helsinki, 1914.

——. *Der reiche Mann und sein Schwiegersohn*. (Folklore Fellows Communications, No. 23.) Helsinki, 1916.

ABU NAAMAN, M. *Baderech Leerez Haoscher*. Tel Aviv, 1954.

ANDREJEV, N. P. *Die Legende vom Räuber Madej*. (Folklore Fellows Communications, No. 69.) Helsinki, 1927.

ARFERT, PAUL. *Das Motiv von der unterschobenen Braut in der internationalen Erzählungsliteratur*. Rostock, 1897.

BALYS, JONAS. *Motif-Index of Lithuanian Narrative Folk-Lore*. Kaunas, 1936.

BENFEY, THEODOR. *Pantschatantra*. 2 vols. Leipzig, 1859.

BENZEL, ULRICH. *Sudetendeutsche Volkserzählungen*. Marburg, 1962.

BOBERG, INGER M. "Prinsessen på Glasbjaerget," in *Danske Studier* (1928), pp. 16–53.

BOGGS, RALPH S. *The Halfchick Tale in Spain and France*. (Folklore Fellows Communications, No. 111.) Helsinki, 1933.

BOURBOULIS, PHOTEINE P. *Studies in the History of Modern Greek Story Motifs*. Thessaloniki, 1953.

BRUNNER-TRAUT, EMMA. *Altägyptische Märchen*. Düsseldorf-Köln, 1963.

CRANE, T. F. *The Exempla of Jacques de Vitry*. London, 1890.

DÄUMLING, HEINRICH. *Studie über den Typus des Mädchens ohne Hände*. München, 1912.

EBERHARD, WOLFRAM. *Typen chinesischer Volksmärchen.* (Folklore Fellows Communications, No. 120.) Helsinki, 1937.

——. *Volksmärchen aus Südost-China.* (Folklore Fellows Communications, No. 128.) Helsinki, 1941.

FISCHER, HERMANN, and BOLTE, JOHANNES. *Die Reise der Söhne Giaffers.* Tübingen, 1895.

OESTERLEY, HERMANN. (ed.) *Gesta Romanorum.* Reprint. Hildesheim, 1963.

GJERDMAN, OLOF. "Hon som war värre än den onde," *Saga och Sed* (1941), pp. 1–93.

GRIMM, JAKOB. *Deutsche Mythologie.* 3 vols. 4th ed. Gütersloh, 1876.

GÜNTER, HEINRICH. *Die christliche Legende des Abendlandes.* Heidelberg, 1910.

HALM, K. VON. *Aisōpeiōn Mythōn Synagōgē.* Lipsiae, 1952.

HENSSEN, GOTTFRIED. *Deutsche Volksmärchen.* 4th ed. Stuttgart, 1944.

——. *Mecklenburger erzählen.* Berlin, 1957.

——. *Ungarndeutsche Volksüberlieferungen.* Marburg, 1959.

HERVIEUX, L. *Les fabulistes latins.* 5 vols. 2d ed. Paris, 1893–99.

HÖTTGES, VALERIE. *Die Sage vom Riesenspielzeug.* Jena, 1931.

JUNGBAUER, GUSTAV. *Das Volk erzählt. Sudetendeutsche Sagen, Märchen, und Schwänke.* Karlsbad and Leipzig, 1943.

KAINZ, WILHELM. *Volksdichtung aus dem Kainachtal.* Voitsberg, 1936.

KROHN, KAARLE. "Bär und Fuchs," *Journal de la Société Finno-Ougrienne.* Helsinki, 1889.

——. *Übersicht über einige Resultate der Märchenforschung.* (Folklore Fellows Communications, No. 96.) Helsinki, 1931. Also listed as FFC 96.

LEYEN, FRIEDRICH VON DER. *Indische Märchen.* Halle, 1898.

LIEBRECHT, FELIX. *Des Gervasius von Tilbury Otia Imperialia.* Hannover, 1856.

MÜLLER-FRAUREUTH, CARL. *Die deutschen Lügendichtungen.* Halle, 1881.

OBERFELD, CHARLOTTE. *Volksmärchen aus Hessen.* Marburg, 1962.

Ó'SÚILLEABHÁIN, SEÁN, and CHRISTIANSEN, REIDAR TH. *The*

Types of the Irish Folktale. (Folklore Fellows Communications, No. 188.) Helsinki, 1963.

PAULI, JOHANNES. *Schimpf und Ernst,* ed. JOHANNES BOLTE. 2 vols. Berlin, 1924.

PHILIPPSON, ERNST. *Der Märchentypus von König Drosselbart*. (Folklore Fellows Communications, No. 50.) Helsinki, 1923.

POPOVIĆ, PAVLE. *Die Erzählung vom Mädchen ohne Hände*. Belgrad, 1905.

RAEL, JUAN B. *Cuentos Españoles de Colorado y de Nuevo Méjico*. 2 vols. Stanford, California, n.d.

RANKE, FRIEDRICH. *Der Erlöser in der Wiege*. München, 1911.

———. *Volkssagenforschung*. Breslau, 1935.

RANKE, KURT. *Die zwei Brüder*. (Folklore Fellows Communications, No. 114.) Helsinki, 1934.

———. *Indogermanische Totenverehrung*. Vol. 1: *Der dreissigste und vierzigste Tag im Totenkult der Indogermanen*. (Folklore Fellows Communications, No. 140.) Helsinki, 1951.

RÖSCH, ERICH. *Der getreue Johannes*. (Folklore Fellows Communications, No. 77.) Helsinki, 1928.

SEKI, KEIGO. *Folktales of Japan*. Chicago, 1963.

STRACKERJAN, LUDWIG, and WILLOH, KARL. *Aberglaube und Sagen aus dem Herzogtum Oldenburg*. 2 vols. 2d. ed. Oldenburg, 1909.

SUCHIER, WALTHER. *Der Schwank von der viermal getöteten Leiche*. Halle, 1922.

SYDOW, CARL WILHELM VON. *Twå spinnsagor*. Lund, 1909.

VRIES, JAN DE. *Die Märchen von klugen Rätsellösern*. (Folklore Fellows Communications, No. 73.) Helsinki, 1928.

WESSELSKI, ALBERT. *Mönchslatein*. Leipzig, 1909.

———. *Der Hodscha Nasreddin*. 2 vols. Weimar, 1911.

———. *Märchen des Mittelalters*. Berlin, 1925.

———. *Der Knabenkönig und das kluge Mädchen*. Prague, 1929.

WISSER, WILHELM. *Plattdeutsche Volksmärchen*. 2 vols. Jena, 1914, 1927.

WOSSIDLO, RICHARD. *Aus dem Lande Fritz Reuters*. Leipzig, 1910.

Index of Motifs

(Motif numbers are from Stith Thompson, *Motif-Index of Folk-Literature* [6 vols.; Copenhagen and Bloomington, Ind., 1955–58].)

A. MYTHOLOGICAL MOTIFS

D. MAGIC

F. MARVELS

G. OGRES

H. TESTS

K. DECEPTIONS

Index of Tale Types

(Type numbers are from Antti Aarne and Stith Thompson, *The Types of the Folktale* [Helsinki, 1961].)

I. ANIMAL TALES (1–299)

II. ORDINARY FOLKTALES

A. Tales of Magic (300–749)

B. RELIGIOUS TALES (750–849)

C. Novelle (Romantic Tales 850–999)

D. Tales of the Stupid Ogre (1000–1199)

III. JOKES AND ANECDOTES (1200–1999)

IV. FORMULA TALES (2000–2399)

General Index

Wish: to marry death, 46; to see brother, 162

Wishes: granted, 87; wasted, 149–50

Wisser, Wilhelm (German folklorist,) xx, 220

Witch. punished by police, 71

Wives: dead, hanging from ceiling, 41; killed to be exhibited in marketplace, 135

Wolf: asks fox for advice, 9; attacks villages, 8; heads war party against fox, 10; meets fox, 8; runs aways, 14

Woman: in the sun, 157; not to be trusted, 131; outwits devil, 174; tormented by curiosity of, 183

Wormins, Olans, 204

Wossidlo, Richard (German folklorist), xx, 200

Wright, Thomas (English antiquary and folklorist), x, xiii

Ysengrimus, 197, 198, 199